DISPATCH TO DEATH
by Martha Miller

New Victoria Publishers

Published by New Victoria Publishers Inc., PO Box 27 Norwich, Vt. 05055, a feminist literary and cultural organization founded in 1976.

Cover Design Claudia McKay

Printed and bound in Canada
1   2   3   4   2006 2005 2004 2003

Library of Congress Cataloging-in-Publication Data

Miller, Martha, 1947-
  Dispatch to death : a mystery / by Martha Miller.
    p. cm.
  ISBN 1-892281-20-1
  1. Taxicab drivers Fiction. 2. Lesbians--Fiction. I. Title.
  PS3563.I4158D57 2003
  813'.54--dc21

                                2003008025

For Jackie Jackson—teacher, mentor, good friend.

Acknowledgements

Thank you to my writers groups and the writing classes at the University of Illinois who listened to and made suggestions for my first draft one chapter at a time. Thanks to those who read entire drafts and made suggestions: Jackie Jackson, Sandra Hayes, Jean Marcy, Carol Barry and my mom. Also thank you to Sam B. Davis, Richland Photography class, spring 2003. A special thanks to everyone who helped me and encouraged me to keep going: Jennifer Banning, Jean Hutchins, Marcy Jacobs, Jennifer Symons, Millicent Bliesener and Ann Steiner. And, finally, thank you to a gentle editor Barbara Guerra, my tougher editor ReBecca Beguin and to all the women who keep New Victoria publishing great books for lesbians.

PART ONE

Chapter One

The first time I met Anita Alvarez was October third, in the middle of an afternoon thunderstorm with the sky was so dark the streetlights came on. By the time I let two ladies from the high-rise off at the bank, rain was coming down in sheets, my windows were fogged, and I was getting ready to radio in and take a lunch break.

I had just hit the turn signal to pull back into traffic when a woman fighting a red umbrella that had turned itself inside out waved and ran toward the cab. It wasn't unusual to pick up a fare uptown. I didn't think much more about it until two weeks later when the police came to see me.

Her dark hair was wet and pasted to her head as she pulled the rear door open. She wore a black double-breasted suit, the skirt of which was short and snug and her matching shoes were sling-backed pumps. She tossed her briefcase across the back seat, pulled the strap of her leather purse from her shoulder, slid in and closed the door. The address she gave me was only four blocks away, one of those old hotels near the governor's mansion.

Rain beat on the hood of the cab and the wipers wouldn't go fast enough to keep the windshield clear. Usually when the weather is bad, some asshole decides he's in a hurry and cuts me off. That day was no different. I don't mind driving in a storm. Hell, my dad taught me to drive when I was an oversized (for a girl, anyway) twelve-year-old with braids and braces, and he told me that if you couldn't drive in rain or snow then you had no business on the road because in this part of the country we get weather. I could understand the idiots who learned to drive in Arizona. I actually knew one of them a few years ago. But not many folks move here from there.

I had to concentrate on driving and we were almost to Fourth Street when I checked the rearview mirror and caught her patting her forehead with a tissue and combing her short, dripping hair back from her face. She seemed the type who wasn't used to getting wet or taking a cab in the middle of the day. She was young, I figured mid-twenties, and pretty with a creamy complexion, like an expensive, hand-painted doll, though her nose was large—not enormous, but a flaw that made her seem more human. She looked into a compact and applied bright red lipstick as we pulled under the green canvas awning of the Manor View Hotel.

The fare was five dollars and forty-five cents. She gave me a ten and with a big cherry-red smile told me to keep the change. She wiggled her ass a little as she tugged her damp skirt into place and walked through the revolving doors into the lobby.

And that would have been that if I hadn't needed to use the can. I pulled the cab around the side, away from the circular drive that they reserve for guests, and went in to find the ladies' room. On the way out of the building, past the hotel café, the smell of hot coffee and food reminded me of my lunch break.

I circled the cab slowly behind the building and pulled onto Fourth Street. When I missed the light at Capitol, I used the opportunity to radio in to Betty. She asked if I would take a trip north on the way home. I was writing down the address when I glanced in the rearview mirror. The back window was foggy and raindrops thundered against it, but I know I saw the red umbrella behind me, crossing the street toward the gates of the mansion. I must of sat through the green too long because the limp-dick behind me hit the horn and after flipping him off, I went on with my day.

I didn't really wonder until later what business she had at the governor's mansion. I was thinking about the next fare, and my lunch, trying to remember if I'd finished the leftover chili the night before and, if not, how long the stuff had been in the refrigerator.

The trees along North Fourth Street were bright colors of red and gold. Intersections were flooded and traffic was slow. The brakes on Number Four were grabbing the way they did when they were wet. I picked up an old woman at the grocery store and took her to a high-rise on Eighth. That's how I remember it was the third—Social Security check day. When you drive a cab you can tell time by the people you haul and the places you haul them. Friday nights I pick up men too drunk to drive the family station wagon home from the bar. We pull up in front of a house and I know before I look that there will be a porch light on and a woman waiting. Those guys are the biggest tippers. It's like they think if they can buy my approval at least someone will be on their side. On Sundays you got church and on Thursdays you got bingo.

I've been working for the Red, White and Blue Cab Company since they bought out Yellow. I started at Yellow right out of high school as a dispatcher and part-time mechanic, worked in the office for a while then found out that the drivers made more money—the smart ones, anyway. See, there are a lot of fringes to driving a cab. I know where the illegal card games are. I know four or five working girls. And I can help a fare find anything but drugs. If they want drugs I just drive them by the projects and point.

7

No cabby with half a brain would go in there.

The streets were so clogged with rain and leaves that by the time I pulled into the trailer park I could barely tell where they were. I aimed the cab between the rows of trailers and hoped. The sky was clearing some, but the streetlamps were still on.

My trailer is the last one, next to the fence on the northeast end. I have a larger yard than the others because the owner can't fit another trailer in there. It's a little more to mow, but nice for the dog.

Alex is a border-collie-lab-mutt that Georgia brought home from the park a few years back. No tags. Hungry. An oversized puppy, really, with ribs sticking out. Some idiot probably dumped him, figuring he stood a better chance on his own than in the pound. That was a long time ago. Georgia's gone now, and Alex and me are growing old together. We're both set in our ways. Both creatures of habit. We're both a little past forty-seven, him in dog years, of course.

I drive six in the morning to six in the evening, sometimes later, except weekends when I work nights because the tips are better. I come home every day to let Alex out. It would be easier to eat fast food in town, but twelve hours is too long for a dog.

That's about all I remember about October third unless you want to hear about the chili that was left over but smelled bad, and how I ate a couple of peanut butter sandwiches and burped for the rest of my shift.

Anyway, two weeks later in the middle of the morning rush, Betty radioed for me to stop by the garage when I let my fare out. I wondered what I had done this time. Getting called in when you are busy usually meant that Ralph wants to chew you out. Forty-five minutes later I rolled onto the lot and parked Number Four next to a black and white. They were waiting for me at the door—two uniforms with Styrofoam cups of coffee in their hands. The older one was maybe my age, a black guy with a big belly. The smaller one was a woman, though it took me a minute to notice.

"You Trudy Thomas?" the black guy said.

"That's me."

"I'm Officer Wilson." He glanced at the woman. "My partner, Officer Matulis. We have some questions for you about a passenger you carried two weeks ago."

I motioned them toward the waiting room, which was really a wide area in the hallway with four black and chrome kitchen chairs, a table, six ashtrays and a cart with a Mr. Coffee. Cops are always coming to talk to cabdrivers on television, but this was my first time. In fact, the event was so rare that I could see some of the guys watching, trying to appear busy or nonchalant.

"They all run together," I told Wilson as I pulled out a chair. "I see so many people."

That's when he showed me the picture and I remembered her right away.

"What's she done?" It was a stupid question. I could see in their eyes I'd tipped my hand.

So Wilson said, "We just want to ask her some questions."

"Concerning?" I was trying to stall them so I could think. I don't really trust the police. I've always had a problem with authority figures.

"Ms. Thomas," Officer Matulis said. "Did you pick up this woman outside of Bank One on October third?"

"It could be the woman."

"Could be?" Wilson said.

"I did pick up a woman, right before lunch," I said. "Rain was pretty bad. How do you figure it was my cab?"

"A witness saw a lavender cab," said Wilson. "It didn't take us long to find out you drive the only one in the city."

"Oh." I studied the photo,

Wilson asked, "Where did you take her?"

I shrugged. "Betty would have the records. I don't remember." One thing I knew for sure, Betty would not have the records. She never writes down fares we catch for ourselves. I figure it's none of my business why.

"Think, Ms. Thomas," Officer Matulis urged. "It's important."

"What's happened?" I asked.

"There was a little trouble over at the governor's mansion," said Wilson.

I remembered the red umbrella crossing the street toward the mansion in the rain. That made me nervous and I started spilling my guts. "I took the woman to the Manor View, over that direction."

"And she went in?" said Wilson.

"I saw her go though the revolving doors. At the time I figured she was a guest."

Matulis was smart and she caught me on that. "At the time?" she said. "Did something happen to make you change your mind?"

Besides the fact that Anita was a twentyish nymph with dark hair and a nice backside, there was no reason for me to cover for her. I'm no hero— just a cab driver. I shrugged and said, "I might have seen her cross the street to the mansion after I let her out. I'm not sure."

"When was this?" Wilson demanded.

"A couple of minutes later." I was damned if I was going to tell them about the pit stop. Next they'd want to know whether it was number one or two.

"That was all?" asked Wilson. "Did she leave anything in the cab?"

"Look," I said. "If this is the woman, the trip lasted five minutes or so. She said nothing and left nothing. Now if you don't mind I need to get back to work. I don't get paid to sit here and talk."

Matulis pulled a card from her breast pocket and said, "Call us if you think of anything else. Or if you hear from her."

I shoved the card in my pocket. "There's no reason for her to contact me. She was just a fare in the middle of a busy day."

We stood and I hooked my thumbs in my jeans pockets. Wilson thanked me for my time, extended his hand and, after we shook, led the way outside.

Matulis held back. She tilted her head and said, "Do I know you from somewhere?"

I gave her a good look then. "I don't think so. I never had any problems with the police." None that I was going to tell her about, anyway.

"You look familiar."

"I'm a familiar looking person." I try to look different, but the effect always comes out like a middle-aged, dyke cabdriver.

"Maybe the Crone's Nest?"

That got me. I looked at her real careful then. "I go there sometimes."

She smiled and said, "I thought so."

"Wouldn't have spotted you as a patron."

She shrugged. "Well, I guess you can't always tell, can you?"

If I can see a woman walk about twelve steps, even if her hair is long and she is in heels and makeup, I usually can tell. Once I saw a movie where models walked out on the platform naked. One was a lesbian and even with her clothes off, I knew by the way she carried herself. But I had been so focused on the fact that I was talking to the police, so paranoid, that I forgot to watch Matulis walk. So I shrugged and said, "No, you never can."

She stepped closer to me then. I could see Betty at the phones over Matulis' shoulder, watching out of the corner of her eyes. It was unusually quiet. The room smelled of cigarette smoke, oil and exhaust fumes. "Really," said Officer Matulis, "if you see or hear anything else, if you remember anything, call me. It's very important."

"What'd she do?"

"Just call me, okay?"

I nodded in agreement, thinking the only reason she came out to me was to make it seem like we were on the same team and get my cooperation. The other drivers ribbed me later about how Matulis had hung back, and how she looked at me. I let them have their fun. If I got upset about that kind of thing, I'd be mad all the time. You know, we all have to live in an imperfect world, and some things simply aren't worth the energy.

That night when I turned the cab in, I cleaned it real good. I swept under the front seat and shoved my hand down the crease in the back. I found a half-eaten candy bar, gum wrappers, a broken filtered cigarette, the new purple Pilot pen I lost sometime last summer, three pennies, a baby's pacifier, a key and a used condom. The rest was just the usual dust and grime.

When I checked out that night I noticed all the other day drivers were gone. I shoved my roll of cash in my jeans pocket, zipped my bomber jacket all the way to my neck and pulled a stocking cap down over my ears. It would be dark by the time I got to the trailer court.

See, my other vehicle is a Harley. I keep it parked just inside the doors on the last bay. That evening the air was cold and crisp and the setting sun lighted up the western sky. I straddled the bike, pulled it upright, pushed back the kickstand and inserted the key.

A movement just inside the garage doors startled me. If a cabby's going to get robbed, right after checkout is the perfect time. I was imagining getting through the week without the money in my back pocket and hoping whoever it was didn't want the Harley, too, when Anita Alvarez stepped out of the shadows.

Chapter Two

From the beginning, the thing I found attractive about Anita Alvarez was her passion. It's hard to be so intense without seeming ridiculous. She was young, and that helped. She reminded me of my youth—seventies feminism, Roe versus Wade, stop the war, and the ERA. Back then I thought I'd die if things didn't change. And I saw that look in Anita's eyes that evening. She wore faded jeans and a yellow nylon windbreaker. Her hands were shoved deep in its pockets. I could see she was anxious.

"You probably don't remember me," she began.

I hit the Harley's kill switch, lowered the kickstand and threw my leg back over the bike, and said, "What can I do for you?"

"I rode in your cab," she said.

"I remember. Couple of weeks ago, right?"

She extended her hand. "My name is Anita Alvarez."

"Trudy Thomas," I said as we shook.

"I think I may have lost something that day." Her smile was for my benefit. I could read her eyes. She was worried. "Do you clean the cabs out very often?"

The answer was almost never, unless somebody pukes, or worse. I shook my head no.

"It was a key," she said. "May I check?"

I remembered the key I had pulled from under the back seat. It was in a baggie in my hip pocket along with the pacifier and my lavender pen. But I didn't tell her I'd already found it because I was curious why she wanted it so bad now when she hadn't needed the key for two weeks. "I'm on my way home. Talk to the dispatcher."

Outside on Eleventh Street a police car went by with the siren blaring. The city police sometimes set a speed trap near the cab stand around shift change. Cabbies are the worst drivers. Our livelihood depends on making our own rules. Three speeding tickets and we're off the road until we can go before a judge who will give us permission to earn a living. That only works a couple of times. More than one driver has lost his or her class C license in his own car.

I turned to Anita Alvarez, but she had stepped back into the darkness. I could barely see her. "It's all right," I said. "They're after a speeder."

"Can we talk?" she asked, coming toward me.

I shrugged. "Sure, but right now I have to get home. Someone is waiting."

"Please?"

I thought about Alex and the mess I'd have to contend with if I didn't get home. The dog had run my life for a long time, but I liked it that way. It was nice to have someone, even if it was a mutt dog, who met me at the door, who needed me. But I wanted to find out what was going on with the police and the governor's mansion. I wanted to spend some time talking to Anita. She didn't look dangerous to me, just nervous and a little scared.

"How about later?"

"Later?" She frowned.

"I have to get home. Check with the dispatcher inside. Maybe she'll let you take a look in the cab."

"No, I guess I can wait."

I shrugged and turned my back. The garage was cold. The wind was picking up outside.

"You'll come back tonight?" she asked.

I sighed. I didn't want to make another trip into town. By the time I took care of Alex and got my own supper it would be after nine. I have to get up at five to make it to work by six. But when I turned and met her eyes I knew I would not only come back into town, but I would probably give her the key and do any damn thing she wanted me to do. I mentally kicked myself for being such a pushover.

I stepped to the open bay door and pointed at the Alamo Tavern. "See that place over there?"

"Yes." She was close beside me.

"They make a good bowl of chili. How about we have dinner?" I looked at my watch, as if I didn't know that it was almost seven. "Say, nine o'clock."

"That would be wonderful." She flashed me a sexy smile.

A long time had passed since a woman had wanted my company for any reason. I thought of Officer Matulis coming out to me earlier. Now this fiery young thing stood before me. I counted myself on a roll. A stronger, more ethical dyke would have reached in her pocket and handed the woman her key. How many times in the weeks that followed did I wish I had done exactly that? But the most lively things in my life were the action adventure video rentals that I watched on nights I couldn't sleep. Just standing next to Anita Alvarez made me feel alive. I asked myself what Arnold

Swartzenegger would do, then kept the key in my pocket anyway.

When I unlocked the trailer door Alex was ready. He bounded out and down the steps barely smelling the air before he hiked his leg by the flower box. The air was cold and heavy with the scent of burning leaves. My neighbor Pinky was at it again. He refused to buy the paper lawn waste bags that the city ordinance against leaf burning mandated. He raked his leaves in small piles, then burned them in his Weber grill. I never understood why he bothered. We were in the old section of the park and the trees were fairly large. When he made progress on his own patch of lawn, the wind blew leaves from the neighbors—nature abhors a vacuum. I think he just liked breaking the law.

Pinky was my dad's best friend for as long as I could remember. He had seemed like an old man even when I was young. After my father died and I sold the house, Pinky helped me get the place next to his. I don't remember a time when I didn't know him. He worked at the same factory as Dad. When I was a little girl he had owned a red Indian that he rode in hill climbs. They stopped making those motorcycles a long time ago. Pinky was past seventy and still owned the black Harley 74 my father left to him. He kept it running himself—kept it looking like new, though he rode it less and less.

When I was a child, Pinky smoked large green cigars and gave me the rings when he unwrapped them. "Pretty girl should have fine jewelry," he said. I had been a tomboy, playing with green plastic soldiers in the dirt under the elm tree, but Pinky could always see the softer side of me.

I carried the mail in with Alex wagging his tail and circling my legs. When I tossed it on the kitchen table next to three days' worth of unopened, unsorted envelopes and added the rolled up newspaper to the stack, the whole thing cascaded to the floor. Startled, Alex crossed the room, sniffed an open magazine and looked at me reproachfully.

I scratched his ears as I knelt to scoop up the mess. "I know," I said, "you have to live here too."

He licked my ear and leaned on me.

"I have a date tonight," I told him. "Sort of."

I fed the dog, showered quickly and changed clothes. By the time I finished, Alex was sitting next to the door campaigning for his walk. He wasn't going to like it when I went back out without him.

In the summer it's easy; we have daylight until nine o'clock. Now that it is fall, it had been fully dark for over an hour. I thought a short walk around the neighborhood might soften the blow. The vet told me once that

Alex didn't know the difference between a big treat or a small one, a long walk or a short one. Big and small simply weren't dog concepts, but I always knew when I shortchanged him even if he didn't. His leash was curled up on the counter. When I reached for it, he did a little dance.

Outside the air was cold and wind was blowing. I pulled my stocking cap down over my ears and shoved my hands in my pockets, kicking leaves that covered the street as I walked. The lights in the neighbors' trailers looked warm.

Michael, the drag queen, lived in the nicest place on our row. His Toyota truck was not in the drive. His trailer was dark. It was his condoms night. Michael cruised the gay bars, the parks, and the streets where the hustlers worked giving away condoms and information about free AIDS testing. It was a volunteer thing. On Sunday nights he still did shows. These days he lived on disability, tips, and a multi-pill cocktail.

As we turned the corner Alex pulled at the leash. Had it been earlier little Wendy, the kid who lived in the corner trailer, would have been at the window waving. In the summer her mom let her offer Alex dog treats. The corner trailer was a regular stop. Tonight the lights were on and the front window fogged with cooking moisture, or maybe this late it was steam from the dishwasher. Wendy would be dressed for bed by now.

We went around the block. The park was quiet. The only sounds came from rustling leaves and tied-up dogs that barked as we passed. When that happened, Alex moved closer to my left leg, sometimes emitting a soft "Woof."

Back at home I washed up, changed my shirt and tried to comb my hair. At eight-thirty I pulled on my bomber jacket, gave Alex a new rawhide strip, and headed out.

On the bike, the cold wind came through the legs of my jeans. My fingers felt icy inside my leather gloves. The sky had grown dark and clouds covered the moon and stars. I parked the bike under the port at the cab stand, in case it started raining during dinner, and crossed the street to the Alamo. I was early. The place smelled of stale cigarette smoke and sour draft beer. A couple of old ladies at the bar were watching Larry King. Anita wasn't there.

I ordered a cup of coffee and chose the booth with the most privacy. I couldn't hear the TV. In the back a couple of young guys who probably should have been home with their wives and kids were playing a slow game of pool. Antonio came with my coffee.

"So what you doing out so late, Trudy?" he asked.

"Thought I'd get some supper," I told him.

Antonio smiled. "You need a menu?"

"I'm waiting for someone," I said. "When she comes in, bring a couple of menus."

His eyes lit up. "This a date?"

I could feel my neck turning red. I laughed nervously and said, "I have to take the fifth on that one."

"Ah, you joke with me," said Antonio. He hesitated, then added, "Where I come from, criminals have no rights."

"When you're right, you're right."

He shook his head and walked away. Antonio was from El Salvador. He sent money to his wife and five children back there. He once told me that one of his his country's greatest natural resources was husbands, brothers and sons who come to the United States to work. Antonio was the lover of Rosa, the Mexican woman who owned the bar. He might have been in his late twenties; she was closer to my age than his, but the arrangement seemed to work for all concerned.

By twenty after nine my guts were telling me that I'd been stood up. Anita had wanted this little talk. I was the one with things to do—like fall asleep in front of *X-Files* reruns and get up early and come to work. I could hear rain blowing against the Alamo's front tinted windows, flecks of ice striking the glass. My Harley would be dry under the carport. I could have been on the sofa, warm and full of a hot dinner with Alex curled up next to me. As it was, I was sitting in a bar alone, hungry, and facing a cold, wet and slippery ride home.

At nine forty-five I ordered a bowl of chili and a cheeseburger with onions. I'd had four cups of coffee by then and would probably be up half the night.

When I crossed the street toward the cab stand, I could see the Harley waiting for me under the front light. My hiking boots were sliding on the street pavement. I decided to ask the dispatcher if I could take Number Four home and pick up the bike tomorrow. The cab had front wheel drive and would be easier to handle.

The office lights were on. I called Lotty Walter's name as I came through the door. The place seemed empty. I walked around the half wall that separates the waiting area from the office. The first thing I noticed was a stack of invoices scattered on the floor and two of the desk drawers opened. The ashtray that Lotty filled with lipstick-smeared Lucky Strike cigarettes night after night was upside down beneath the desk. I wondered who shoved the stuff on the floor and who was going to clean it up. Then I noticed six Snickers bars lined up next to the phone. Lotty wouldn't be too far from them; I knew that much. Lotty was the wife of Freddy Walter, one of the night drivers. She was a bleached blonde, three-hundred-pound baby doll. For a big woman she wore the cutest clothes: faded bluejeans, sheer blouses in pastel colors. Her makeup was always perfect. I heard once that Lotty and Freddy spent all their time off on a king-sized bed, eating, drinking, fucking and sleeping. I don't know why that thought came to me as I walked toward the ladies' room in the back, calling her name. Most of the time I try to put it out of my mind.

Lotty didn't answer but the door was shut.

I waited, then knocked. "Hey, Lotty. You in there? It's me, Trudy."

Behind me the phone started ringing. That should get her attention, wherever she was. I watched the light flash on line one and was just about to go back and pick it up when the answering machine kicked on with the message, "You have reached the Red, White and Blue Cab Company. Our dispatcher is on another call. Please leave your name, phone number, address and destination, and we will dispatch a cab immediately." That was followed by a series of beeps and then silence. The caller had hung up.

I walked back toward the dark garage a little more uncomfortably and flipped on the lights. Everything looked normal. There were two cabs in the work bays, one with the hood open and the motor sitting beside it, the other resting on its rims in some stage of a tire rotation.

"Lotty, you out here?" was met with silence.

The phone started again. I walked back to the office and grabbed it. Whoever it was hung up in my ear. That made me mad. I considered taking Number Four and heading home. The ice was getting worse. The greasy dinner was starting to work on my guts. I walked back to the ladies room and knocked again. When there was no answer I tried the knob and pulled the door open.

You know, the first thing I felt wasn't shock; it was pity. Lotty was on the pot, her head thrown back at an awkward angle, her faded jeans and lacy pink nylon underwear around her ankles. One of those movie star tabloids was open, face down on the floor.

"Hey, kiddo? You all right?" I stepped closer. I thought about a heart attack—she was young, but heavy. Then I saw, in the center of her forehead, a crimson hole the size of a pencil and a dark stream of blood that ran across her face and into her hair.

I wasn't afraid at first. I wanted to move her, cover her up. But her rolls of flesh would make that impossible. Why the hell wasn't I at home where I belonged? The phone in the office started ringing again, and I broke into a cold sweat.

Chapter Three

I still needed to use the john and went in the men's room, did my bit and washed up with a sliver of dirty Lava soap that sat on the edge of the sink. My hands shook. My hair was soaked with sweat and my forehead felt clammy. When I reached the front desk, I held on tight to steady myself and ripped open one of Lotty's candy bars. While chewing, I dialed Ralph and Betty's home phone number. I was on the second Snickers when Betty answered.

"It's me, Trudy," I told her.

Betty groaned. "Please don't tell me you're calling in sick. I got George Peters off all week in rehab again and Lester has a court date."

"No," I said. "I'm not sick, I'm down at the office."

"What you doing in town?"

"I came for supper, got stood up and was about to head back home."

"You on the Harley?"

"Yeah."

"Oh," said Betty. "I see. No problem, take Number Four home. Lock the bike up in the garage. I know it's getting slick out there."

"There's another problem."

I could hear her flicking a lighter and inhaling. "What else could possibly go wrong?"

"Lotty's dead on the toilet."

"Trudy," Betty yelled into the phone. "If we have to put you through treatment again, I swear…"

"I'm sober," I told her. "And I'm serious."

"Can you tell what she died of?"

"Gunshot. Right between the eyes."

"We been robbed?"

"I don't know." I hadn't thought of that, but wasn't surprised that Betty did.

She said, "Check."

I tore open another Snickers with my teeth and set the phone down. The back office door was open a crack. I reached for the light string. Ralph's desk was clean the way I was sure he'd left it. He wasn't the type of guy to leave a paper clip out of place. The safe was locked, nothing looked disturbed. Back at the phone I swallowed and said, "We ain't been robbed."

"You called the police?"

"Not yet."

"Do it," said Betty. "Me and Ralph will be there in twenty minutes."

"All right."

I didn't want to hang up. I didn't want to be alone in the building with a dead body. Maybe Betty sensed that because she reminded me of the forty-five on a handmade shelf under the center of the desk.

"See if it's still there," she said.

I slid my hand under the desk, felt around and connected with the forty-five. I pulled it out. "It's here."

"We keep it loaded, so be careful. We're on our way. Call the cops."

My mouth was full. I mumbled, "Right."

Betty added, "And don't touch nothing."

I looked at the gun in my hand and remembered all the *Homicide* reruns on Court TV. Would I be a suspect? If this was the murder weapon, I was screwed. I dialed 9-1-1.

"You need to send the police to the Red, White and Blue Cab Company on North Eleventh."

"What's the problem?" the dispatcher asked.

"There's been a murder."

I finished the candy bars and reached for the plastic pumpkin loaded with Tootsie Pops and Sweet Tarts that sat on the counter. I picked out a grape sucker, tossed the wrapper back in the pumpkin and stuck it in my mouth. My hands were still shaking.

The police dispatcher asked another question. She sounded far away.

I said, "Look, just send the cops," and hung up.

Outside the icy rain was letting up. I wanted to get the hell out of there. If I hadn't told Betty I'd wait for her, I would have gone outside, started the Harley and taken my chances on the slick roads.

The place was unusually quiet. Why weren't there a couple of night drivers hanging around waiting for fares? Lotty complained about the card games and the cussing all the time. But now the place was empty. Where the hell were the drivers?

A wave of nausea hit me. I sprinted for the men's room and barely got my head over the toilet when my gut wrenched and up came an acid mixture of chocolate and chili. The room spun. Stars floated in my peripheral vision. I flushed, moved to the sink, and splashed water on my face. I didn't remember setting the forty-five down, but must have because my shaking hands were empty. I shivered with a needle-like chill, hung on to the filthy basin and took a deep trembling breath.

I heard a noise from the lobby that could have been one of the night drivers back from a fare. Maybe it was the cops or Ralph and Betty. I stood very still and to my horror noticed there wasn't even a lock on the men's room door. Whoever it was walked around. Then the footsteps started in my direction. I covered my mouth to stifle my panicky mewing sounds. The door swung open and I sucked in my breath. All I could see was the gun. I backed up a step and automatically raised my hands.

"Jesus, Trudy, you sick?" said Freddy Walters. "How come you're in here?"

I looked at him, my mouth hanging open. "You scared me."

"Where's everybody at?"

I thought about his wife, a bullet between her eyes in the bathroom next door. I sure didn't want to tell him about that. I answered his question with one of my own. "Why you carrying that gun?"

Freddy was about five feet eight, slender, with dark curls and a receding hair line. The mat on his chest came right to his collar line and made me wonder how he decided where to stop shaving. He was thirty, a kid, really, and would be bald on top within two years. He looked at his piece as if he'd forgotten he was still holding it on me. He lowered the gun, tripped the safety and shoved it in the pocket of his gray work pants.

"Sorry. This is the one I carry in the cab. Lotty radioed earlier that some creep was hanging around out front. The place seems to be empty. No Lotty, no drivers, I figured we been robbed. What you doing here so late? Something wrong with the girls' bathroom? Where's Lotty?"

"Came back in town to have dinner. This is how I found things."

"You check in the garage?" Freddy asked.

My knees felt weak. I headed back to the desk and collapsed in the chair. "I don't think anybody's there."

He walked to the dark doorway and called into the garage. "Lotty? It's me, baby. You out there?"

We both listened to the silence.

"Where do you suppose she's gone?"

I didn't answer, but lay my head on the cool wooden desktop.

Freddy said, "One of the cab's been broke into in back."

I sighed. "Which one?"

He turned and looked at me. I could see him thinking. At length he said, "I couldn't tell."

My guess was he could tell. Here we were, as good friends as people who work together can be, me not telling him his wife was dead in the bathroom and him sparing my feelings about my cab.

"Much damage?" I asked.

"Back glass busted out," he said, turning my direction. "What can you get from an empty cab? Didn't even take the radio."

We were quiet for a moment. Then Freddy switched on the garage light and called for his wife again as he made the rounds, then returned to the desk and gave me a worried look.

My throat felt raw. My mouth tasted of half-digested chocolate, chili, and onion, which is to say awful. I wanted to go home, crawl in bed and forget this. I was just about to tell Freddy that I'd called Betty and Ralph, and leave him to wait for them, when Betty was beside me, her cool hand on the back of my neck. She smelled of stale cigarette smoke.

"You call the cops?" she asked.

I nodded, not raising my head. I could hear Ralph in the back room, Freddy talking to him nervously.

Betty said, "You okay?"

I lifted my head to look at her. She was characteristically braless, sagging a little, wearing a red flannel shirt, faded jeans, and a lined denim jacket.

I asked, "Can I go home?"

"They'll want to talk to you."

"You know what? I don't care."

She smiled. "You had a hard day, ain't you, honey?"

Ralph came out of his office, Freddy behind him. I watched them walk across the lobby toward the front door. They were going to check the cab out back.

Ralph stopped, still holding the door open, and turned to Betty. "Looks like they're here."

I hadn't heard the sirens, but could see the flashing red lights reflected on the glass door. "I don't want to be here when Freddy finds out," I whispered to Betty.

She gave my shoulder a squeeze. "He needs us here. Who else has he got?"

I knew she was right but my guts knotted as two cops approached the desk with Ralph and Freddy a couple of steps behind them.

The phone rang and Betty picked it up, turning her back on all of us. "Red, White and Blue." She listened and said, "I'm sorry. All our cabs are out."

"Where's she at?" the older of the two city's finest asked.

I jerked my head toward the back. "Ladies' room."

Behind me Betty said, "It will be a while. Okay, give me your destination and we'll get there as soon as we can."

"Anybody been in there besides you?"

I shook my head, no, and avoided Freddy's eyes. Betty could have sent him on that call. But I suppose that would have been cruel. The thing was, ever since I found out about my cab being broken into, I'd felt responsible. The key in my pocket and whatever the hell it went to was the cause of all this trouble. If I had given the key to Anita Alvarez, would Lotty be alive? I heard the asshole that opened the bathroom door say, "Jesus, this is a big woman." Then I heard Freddy whimpering like a dog that had been kicked.

The eastern sky was gray by the time I started my Harley and turned toward home. After the ambulance took Lotty out, we all went to the police station and made statements. They really grilled me. Did Lotty have any enemies? Was Freddie the jealous type? They even implied I might have shot her. In the end I guess they figured I was just the unfortunate sap who stumbled on a crime scene. I guess I felt too guilty to mention Alvarez and the key. I would have to find her myself and get some answers. I didn't really believe she would shoot Lotty over a key. Lotty would've let her look in my cab anyway. They wanted to call the shooting a bungled robbery, as if understanding the motive made it all right. We were safe to go on with our lives as long as this act of insanity made sense.

The cold air stung my face. My jacket was zipped all the way up and my stocking cap was pulled down over my ears. I turned into the trailer park where in the early stages of dawn the streetlights were still on and the trailers were dark.

On my own street I could see that Pinky's lights were on. His Weber grill was already smoldering. When I cut my engine, I heard his door slam. I opened my own door for Alex, who was ready for a break. Pinky came across the small lawn toward me. He was a slow moving shadow, barrel-chested and stooped. He had on a plaid hunting hat and the ear pieces curled up on the sides of his face like a debutante's hairdo. He waved at me, and Alex pranced around him, wagging his tail.

"You work last night?" he asked.

I shook my head. "There was some trouble at the office. I promised Betty I'd work tonight. She's shorthanded again."

"You had a visitor," he said. "Pretty late, it was."

"Me? Who was it?"

Pinky shrugged and bent to pet Alex. "I saw a car. Then I heard glass breaking. It was after midnight, I'm pretty sure. Your buddy here was raising a helluva ruckus. Would've called the cops, but by the time I was up, they were gone."

I looked at Alex who was panting, his breath making the air around his nostrils frosty. "What kind of a car were they in?"

"A big one. Dark color."

I shrugged and said, "So, they didn't get in?" I didn't want to worry him.

"Thanks to this guy." Pinky scratched Alex's ears.

"Probably just kids."

"Could be," he agreed. I could tell he was unconvinced.

The trailer was cold with the glass in the front door broken. I cleaned up the mess, cranked up the furnace and covered the hole with cardboard and duct tape. I suppose everything is relative. Had I not just come from a homicide, the broken glass would have upset me more.

I tossed the last of the minute oatmeal in a pan of boiling water and made a cup of camomile tea. The sun was orange on the horizon when I brushed my teeth, stripped to my T-shirt, crew socks and under shorts, and stretched out in bed. Alex curled up at my feet and the last thing I remember was his snoring.

I came awake hearing Betty's voice. The telephone receiver was in my hand.

"Trudy, you awake?"

"No."

She ignored me and said, "I'm back in the office."

I groaned. "So?"

"So, I found something missing."

I shook my head awake and looked at the clock—nine A.M. Why was Betty calling me about something missing? "Why aren't you calling the cops?"

"I did, but I thought you should know."

"What is it?"

"Someone went through the Rolodex. I found it thrown under the desk. Your card is missing. Whoever killed Lotty may have your name, address, phone, social security number—everything."

My mouth was dry. My eyes hurt from lack of sleep. I remembered the late visitor, the broken glass in the front door.

Betty said, "I thought you'd want to know about this. Be careful, Trudy."

"Yeah, don't worry about me." I tried to reassure her. "I got Alex here. No one will sneak up on me like they did on Lotty."

"Good," said Betty.

I let out my breath slowly and said, "I'll see you this evening."

I got up, used the john and then flipped on the thirteen-inch black and white television that sits on the corner of my dresser. I got my house gun out of the bottom of the closet, loaded it and set it on the night stand. I was ready to fall back across the bed when the phone rang again.

"What?" I answered.

"God, you sound cranky," a woman said.

"Who's this?"

"Your sister."

My half sister. "Barb?"

"So are you getting your period, or what?"

"You called me at nine in the morning to ask questions about my cycle?"

"Not really," she said. "The Boys and Girls Club is having a Christmas fundraiser. Jonny is selling candy."

"Oh, put me down for the usual." I'm a soft touch about this stuff. I like the chocolate turtles. Barb's five kids keep me supplied year around.

"But the reason I called right this minute," she said, "is I had the radio on this morning coming to work. They said there was some trouble down at Red, White and Blue."

"Look," I warned her. "Don't say anything to Mom."

"That bad, huh?"

"Our night dispatcher got shot."

"It's on the radio, Trudy. It will probably be in the paper. Accept it, she's going to find out."

My temples were throbbing and I rubbed them slowly.

Barb said, "Are you all right?"

I sighed. "I'm tired. I was up all night."

Barb hesitated. "Maybe I should let you get back to sleep."

"Thanks. It's really been a long night."

"Sorry I woke you."

"I was up. You're not my first call."

"Well, take the phone off the hook, for Christ's sake." She's several years younger, but often falls into the role of the big sister. She seems to like it, and I don't mind. She also runs interference between Mom and me.

"Right," I said.

"And come by and see your nephews sometime before they are all in

24

their forties."

I chuckled softly. "I love you, too."

"Well, good night, then."

"'Night."

I looked at the gun on the nightstand and wondered if I was overreacting. The world seemed to still be spinning on its axis. Barb was at work and Jonny, her second to the youngest, was selling candy for Christmas. I drew my feet up on the bed and stacked the pillows. Before I stretched out, I lifted the telephone receiver and dropped it on the carpet. Then I lay down again and fell asleep watching CNN on a slow news day.

Chapter Four

I asked around about Anita Alvarez, but had no luck. None of the other drivers remembered her. The doorman at the Manor View told me that a woman fitting her description had checked out several days before.

As I made my way up the stairs at the Springfield Funeral Parlor two days later, I was considering contacting the police officers who had asked about her. Lotty was from a family of plus-sized blondes. Five sisters and a brother lined the front row at the funeral home next to their mother, an older version of Lotty herself. Freddy, slim and dark, looked frail and alone in the aisle seat. As I walked past Lotty, who was laid out in an open casket for the evening wake, I looked for the bullet hole in her forehead, but saw only wispy blonde bangs. She was dressed in something silky-pink, and surrounded by pastel arrangements of gladiolus. I made my way from Freddy down the line of family, expressing condolences, and the angry feeling in my guts expanded.

The long narrow room was done in ornate reds and golds. Small circles of people scattered throughout spoke in hushed tones. I found a seat in the back and watched people go to the casket and stare down at Lotty in disbelief. She had done nothing, had hurt no one—her fate was incomprehensible. I told myself for the hundredth time that I would find Anita Alvarez.

Later, feeling too warm and uncomfortable, I decided to go outside with the smokers. Though I quit several years ago when Georgia had been on one of her health kicks, most of the people I knew hadn't, and I didn't want to be alone. On the way out I saw a plate of cookies and a big coffee urn that sat in an alcove next to the back door. A woman in heels, her red hair swept into a French twist, wearing a navy skirt and a matching jacket spoke to me as I passed her.

"Trudy Thomas. How are you holding up?"

I stopped, looked directly at her and tilted my head. She did look familiar. "Have we met?"

She extended her hand. "Toni Matulis. We spoke briefly a couple of days ago."

I remembered her then, the lesbian cop. "Do you smoke?" I asked.

"No."

"I was just going out."

She picked up a store-bought chocolate chip cookie and led the way through the glass doors. I watched her walk. She did the heels like she was born in them, no dykey swagger. Probably with her clothes off, I wouldn't have tagged her as being on my team. Either lesbians were changing or I was getting old, probably the latter.

We were both coatless, wearing blazers. The night was so cold that as I spoke I could see my breath like small clouds in the air. "Did you know Lotty?"

She shook her head. "Not really. Her mother worked with my mother. Mom's in there now, talking to Inez."

I nodded and looked around. A couple of guys from work were huddled under the awning, smoking and passing a bottle back and forth.

"Mom doesn't drive at night anymore," Toni went on. "Her eyes are getting bad."

"I have a question," I said.

Toni's nose was red from the cold. She took a bite of cookie and chewed. She must have realized we were both waiting and said, "Well?"

The best I could do was to blurt it out. "Do you think Lotty's murder is connected to Anita Alvarez?"

Toni shrugged. "Maybe."

"Maybe I agree with you."

"Did you tell that to Homicide?"

I shrugged. "Not really."

Toni blew her nose on the lacy cookie napkin. She frowned and shoved her hands in her pockets, kind of hopping on one foot to keep warm. "Aren't you going to smoke?"

"I don't smoke."

"Then what are we doing out here?"

"I needed some air."

She got a little snippy then. "Well, I need some warm air." She turned, rushed up the steps and back into the building.

I wanted to follow her, but I have this personal policy that had nothing to do with the situation. When a woman turns on her heel and walks away, I never follow. It's cost me a lot as policies go—Georgia for one. But it's an absolute, right up there with voting for all the Democratic women on the ticket and brushing my teeth for three minutes twice a day.

I walked over to the other drivers and exchanged grunts. They were day shift guys who, like me, had been with Red, White and Blue since the beginning. George Peters was just out of rehab. When he offered me a swig from a pint of Calvert's, I raised both hands and said, "I don't drink, remember?" I wanted to say, you don't either, but held my tongue.

"A person needs a swig now and then," said George.

"Damn right," Lester agreed. "Trudy, nobody's going to give you a Boy Scout badge. You might as well relax."

I shook my head and tried to laugh it off. "When I drink, bad things happen."

"Worse than this?" George asked, nodding toward the white, two-story funeral home.

I didn't have an answer and for once kept my mouth shut.

Finally Lester said, "Miss Antinocci says hello."

Old Miss Antinocci was my regular Wednesday morning fare. She got groceries and bought five dollars' worth of lottery tickets every week. She was a smart old broad, worked the numbers with some kind of system. She'd gotten four or five in a row more times than I could count and as a result was a great tipper. The big money still eluded her. She lived on her widow's railroad pension and interest from investments. My dad used to say, "Money goes to money." I figured she would definitely hit it lucky one of these days. Two days and I already missed my regulars.

"How long you going to be on nights?" George asked.

I shrugged. "You think Freddy will be back?"

"What else has he got?" George put the Calverts to his lips and tipped the bottle up. His Adam's apple moved up and down as he swallowed.

I wanted to reach for the bottle, pull it out of his hands and finish it. I was responsible for this whole mess and the guilt ate at me. Maybe Lotty might still be alive if I'd leveled with Toni Matulis, or given Anita Alvarez her damn key.

At length I said, "I need to get back in there," and left them.

French doors opened along the side into the long narrow room where Lotty's wake continued. The crowd had thinned out some. Lotty's sisters were gathered around the casket. They were talking animatedly. Freddy sat alone, his back straight and rigid. I knelt beside him and placed a hand on his shoulder.

"How you doing?"

"All right," he said, "considering." His voice was hoarse.

"You need anything, you let me know."

He nodded and pressed his hand on mine. His thin fingers were cold. I whispered, "I need to leave."

He turned toward me then. "Who is working?"

"Henderson is it until I get back."

He nodded. "Right, you need to go then."

I caught up with Toni Matulis by the coffee urn. Her fingers were wrapped around a steaming cup. Her cheeks were flushed. She was talking to a shorter, thinner, older woman with black hair and green eyes that seemed huge through coke-bottle-thick lenses. Ignoring me, Toni finished her coffee and stepped into the cloak room, emerging with a red coat and a brown leather bomber jacket a lot like my own, only cleaner. She helped the woman I assumed was her mother into the red coat and slid the jacket over her own shoulders. It looked strange with the skirt and blazer. I'd left my jacket at home for that very reason—not the skirt reason, just the good clothes reason.

I was going to have to approach Toni. She was definitely done talking to me. I waited outside and when she emerged touched her arm.

She fixed me with a chilly stare. "I'm off duty right now, Ms. Thomas."

"Can we talk sometime?" I asked.

Toni's mother looked up at me curiously. I nodded hello. "I'm Trudy Thomas."

The old girl grabbed my hand and gave it a firm shake. "Dorothy Matulis."

Toni said, "You have my card."

Dorothy patted Toni's shoulder. "If you have business to discuss, I can wait in the car."

"It's too cold, Mom," Toni insisted. Then she looked directly at me. "You've been withholding information. And now that there's been another murder—"

"Another?"

Toni bit her lip.

So, we'd both been withholding information.

Finally she said, "Why aren't you cold?"

"Scandinavian ancestors," I answered.

She rolled her eyes. "Call me. Tonight. Tomorrow. Whenever. Right now I'm going to take my mother home and pick up my daughter at my sister's."

I nodded, backing away. "It was nice meeting you, Dorothy."

The older woman waved and cautiously made her way down the cement steps.

I had been at the funeral home on my supper break. I drove Number Four home, let Alex out and changed back into my jeans and a sweatshirt.

I couldn't ask for a day off. Betty was dispatching nights and Ralph took the phones days, as well as doing the books. I'd had my broken window fixed and a key lock deadbolt installed. There were iron bars that I could put over the side glass. I'd have to save money for those.

I walked Alex around the neighborhood, the short way again, and radioed in to Betty. There was a fare heading back into town—a middle-aged woman with a yellow beehive hairdo and frosty lipstick who got out at a bar two blocks from the cab stand. There was nothing after that and over the radio Betty told me it was a slow night. I turned the cab around and drove back in.

"How did it go?" Betty asked when I came through the doors.

"Lots of people there."

"Good," said Betty. "That's the only nice thing about dying young. You have a bigger funeral. More of your friends are still alive."

I slung my bomber jacket over the back of a chair and sat down. Betty had a cigarette going behind the counter. She often lets the things burn up while working crossword puzzles. A friend of hers photocopies the ones from the *New York Times*. She refers to them as her nemesis and can go through a pack of cigarettes and the family-sized pack of Juicy Fruit gum in a single shift, answering the phone and digging through three crossword puzzle dictionaries.

Johnny Henderson walked through the door from the garage, removed his cabby hat and ran his fingers through his dark, curly hair. Henderson has been with Red, White and Blue for two years. All the other black drivers work for Clarence at Diamond. But Johnny had got caught in bed with Clarence's wife and was forced to come over to us. His skin was the color of Boston Coffee and his eyes were green with long dark lashes. He was slender, six feet two, twenty-eight years old and always had a girlfriend or two on the string. I'd seen him in action around women. He never really approached them; they came after him. Johnny was a good worker, a big overgrown kid who was eager to please. He took the hard trips, never complained and worked ungodly hours. After Johnny left Diamond, Clarence told Betty he should have gotten rid of his wife instead.

Johnny tossed his hat on the table and unzipped his down-filled jacket. "How was it?" he asked.

I said, "Lotty has a big family."

He nodded. "Her sister, Alma, was in high school with me. We dated, sort of."

"Johnny, you sort of date everybody."

He smiled, showing me his white, even teeth. "Not you, Trudy."

I shook my finger at him and teased, "Honey, if you was a girl, I'd be all over you."

He chuckled. "And if you was a girl, I'd let you."

The room was too warm and damp hair clung to my neck. I was up for the next trip, but sometimes on weeknights that could take a while, so I pulled out a chair and sat at the break table. Henderson lit a cigarette and sat on the other side, sprawling his long legs out toward me. "So how was it really?"

I shrugged. "Okay."

"Wish I'd been here that night."

I studied his expression and tilted my head. "You'd probably been dead, too."

"Cocksuckers," said Johnny. "They didn't have to kill her. She would've let them have anything. Any of us would."

"You want a Coke?" I asked, changing the subject.

"You buying?"

I stood and dug in my pockets. Before I could come up with change, Johnny had four quarters on the table. I took them back toward the machine.

Betty called to me, "You got a couple of messages." She nodded to two red Post-it notes on the message board.

When I came back with two cans of Coke, I pulled the slips off the board. The first was a phone number and an extension. No name. The second was Toni Matulis.

Lotty would have let me use the dispatcher's phone. There was more than one line. But I knew better than to ask Betty and walked to the pay phone in the lounge.

"This is Trudy Thomas returning your call."

"I thought you might have to go back to work," said Toni. "I'm sorry I was such a shit at the wake tonight. I hate funerals."

I thought about the last funeral I had attended. I couldn't go to one without being reminded of my father's. Sometimes I didn't know how bad it bothered me until later when I wanted to get drunk, buy a pack of cigarettes or five pounds of chocolate. Losing my dad had been the worst thing in my life. I'd lost people before and after that, through abandonment and death, but his funeral was the baseline, the hardest one. I wondered who Toni Matulis had lost, and said, "We all have our personal baggage."

She changed the subject. "You wanted to talk to me?"

I checked my watch. Ten-fifteen. "Can we meet?"

"You mean tonight?" she asked. "You're working, right?"

"Yeah."

Toni said, "This is my night off and my daughter is in bed. Can it wait until morning?"

"I get off work at six."

"Well, Doree doesn't go to school until eight-thirty. I could meet you for coffee."

We made arrangements to get together, and I hung up. A call had come in while I was on the phone. I took the slip from Betty and grabbed my jacket. It was three-thirty in the morning before I remembered the other message. I debated about calling so late, then pulled into the driveway of a closed gas station with a car-high pay phone on the corner.

A man's voice came on the line. "Manor View Motel."

The extension must have been a room number. I asked for it and heard the phone ringing again. A black Lincoln Town Car stopped at the intersection. The bass from the stereo was so loud it seemed to shake the pavement. A mirror-tinted window slid down and a black man looked my direction. Then the window went up and the Lincoln rolled through the red light.

"Hello?" The woman's voice sounded far away.

I started with an apology. "I'm sorry to call so late."

"Ms. Thomas?"

"Yes?"

"It's Anita Alvarez. I need to see you."

Her key was at home on my kitchen counter. "I tried meeting you once."

"I know." Her voice softened. "Everything is such a mess."

"I should call the police."

"You haven't, so far," Anita said. "Why is that?"

I thought about Toni Matulis. "What do you want with me?"

"Can we meet?"

"I'm working. I have plans tomorrow."

"Please, Trudy, do you take a break? Can I talk to you now?"

I sighed. The last time I tried meeting her someone got murdered. I was going to talk to Toni Matulis in the morning. But I could gather more evidence. The police certainly didn't know where Anita Alvarez was. Tomorrow maybe I'd be able to take them to her.

I quickly made arrangements to meet Anita in the Manor View coffee shop in twenty minutes. As I set the receiver back, I saw the black Lincoln circle the block again.

Chapter Five

The coffee shop was small, warm and smelled of fresh-cooked bacon. Next to the empty horseshoe counter was a roped-off unlit section of tables. A couple of old coots in business attire filled the first booth, their gestures wide and laughter loud, probably capping off an evening of drinking with a big breakfast. A gray-haired waitress in a black uniform and a frilly apron kept an eye on them as she cleaned the grill.

Anita Alvarez was alone in the corner booth across from a nearly empty pastry counter, a single table-sized pot of coffee and two empty cups in front of her. She looked small and harmless. I had to remind myself that Lotty was dead and this pretty young thing might be a murderer. She wore the same yellow windbreaker she had the night she talked to me in the Red, White and Blue garage.

"Thank you for coming," she said, as I slid into the booth across from her.

"I've got fifteen minutes," I told her. "My break."

"Then I must be quick."

I poured my own coffee and nodded.

She cleared her throat, taking on a serious expression. "I am in trouble, Ms. Thomas, and by association so are you."

I interrupted her. "Look, you can have your damn key. It's home on my kitchen counter. I'll bring it to your room in the morning."

Anita held up a hand. "Please, let me finish."

The coffee was strong. I looked for sweetener and settled on sugar. I wanted to ask about Lotty, but I forced myself to keep quiet and listen.

"Do you know what part of a carcass the vulture starts on?"

That was a damn scary question. My hand shook as I lowered the cup to the table and asked, "Do they have a preference?"

"Oh, yes." Anita leaned toward me. "They go for the soft places. When I was a child in El Salvador, I saw many bodies with the eyes missing." When she spoke of her childhood a slight Spanish accent bled through her perfect English. She squared her shoulders and added, "I've known the mechanisms of terror all my life."

I stirred my coffee and waited. I could see our reflection in the mirror in the back of the pastry shelf, behind three slices of raisin pie. My hair was standing up on top. I ran my fingers through it but it didn't flatten. Anita was sitting perfectly still, watching me.

Finally she said, "We all have our baggage from the past, you are thinking?"

I nodded, wondering if her choice of words was random; hadn't I told Toni Matulis that earlier?

Anita sat her cup on the table and met my eyes. "I have brought my baggage to unpack in front of you. Do you know the history of my country?"

I thought about Antonio and wondered if she knew him. Two Central Americans in a city fifteen hundred miles from Miami—it was possible. I knew very little about Central America. Frankly, I couldn't tell you where Idaho was even if there were money involved. The limits of my geographic knowledge were: Chicago north, St. Louis south, the sun comes up in the east, and the mall is west.

"Revolution?" I ventured. Somebody was always fighting somebody down there.

"My father went to Central America in the Peace Corps. My mother was a young widow in El Salvador at the time. My father already had a wife in the U.S. and after he left the Corps traveled back and forth many times. He'd be gone for months then he'd be back again. My mother had three young children."

Anita hesitated a moment, pushed her coffee cup aside and leaned forward.

I waited, wondering why she was telling me all of this.

"My brother Ricardo joined the rebels. He was murdered by the death squads. I never saw him again." Anita extracted a cigarette from a jeweled case and lit it.

I said, "I'm sorry." And I was, though I secretly hoped this wasn't one of those things my whole race would be held responsible for—like the Native Americans or the slaves. My father told me once that people will find reasons for the harm they need to do. The day I was run out of my home for being a lesbian by neighbors who had once been my friends, I remembered that. My father wasn't an educated man, but he was a wise one.

"Yes, it was very bad." Cigarette smoke whirled around Anita's head. She waved it away from her face. "After Ricardo's death, my mother contacted my father and arranged to have my sister Theresa and me smuggled out of the country."

This was too much information to digest all at once. I asked, "Is your mother still there alone?"

Anita shook her head. "She married a coffee farmer. She and my stepfather have four more children."

I thought about my own mother and my stepfather Raymond. He had been my father's best friend. After the divorce, Mom and I went with Raymond. Raymond hated me. Later, when my sister Barbara was eight months old and Laura was on the way, my real father saw the welts from Raymond's belt on the back of my legs. That was when I moved back home with my dad. I had to take the sixth grade over, but did pretty well the second time.

I missed the baby and Dad made sure that I saw her and, later, saw the others often. I lived with him to the day he died nineteen years later. It was nice, just the two of us. Saturday mornings, doughnuts and coffee heavy with cream at the Harley Davidson repair shop, winter nights over homework and paperback mysteries. Dad liked Mickey Spillane and Shell Scott; I'd liked Trixie Belden and Sherlock Holmes. Later I could see the baby-dyke and old-queen in those characters. There had been this warm feeling of safety and security in my adolescence, at home, anyway. I'd figured some day I'd be giving that feeling to my own children, but by the time I was fifteen I knew it wasn't going to work out that way.

The waitress stopped at our table and shook the coffee pot. "You girls want more?"

Anita said, "No, thank you. We are in a hurry."

The waitress nodded, slapped the ticket on the corner of the table and went on to check on the drunks. I prodded, "So, you and Theresa came to America?"

Anita gently corrected me. "The people in Central America think they are American too."

I mumbled an apology.

She shrugged. "It is a common mistake."

"You and your sister came to live with your father?"

"Not exactly," said Anita. "My father's wife wanted no part of me. My aunt, his sister, took me in. Saw that I was educated. I missed my mother terribly but I didn't make a fuss. Where I come from, self preservation depends on the ability to be obscure."

"What about your sister?"

"Theresa didn't survive the trip."

I cocked my head and waited.

Anita went on. "We took a bus to a village in the mountains to meet my father's men. There had been an earthquake and the water tower was down. We drank water from a river and became ill. Theresa died before our connection arrived. I blamed myself. I was older. I should have known."

I wasn't sure I even believed her story. Maybe she was just trying to get my sympathy. I glanced at the clock above the cash register. I was late already. "I'm sorry for your loss, but what has any of it got to do with me?"

Anita continued, "My father has been investigating the murder of Ricardo. In a place where death came with no reason, where arrests are rumored but never made, my father is demanding a reason and arrests. Recently he came across some evidence, some papers. The day I caught the cab ride with you he had asked me to put them in his safe deposit box."

It made sense—the key, the bank. I asked her about the things that didn't make sense. "Why didn't you meet me that night? I would have given you the key. Why the hell did you need to shoot Lotty?"

"I did not kill your friend," said Anita. "It was because of what happened in my homeland that one must answer for now. Sons disappeared. Children found bodies on the streets in the morning. There are powerful men who do not want their connections with the those death squads known. After our meeting that night in the garage of your cab company, a man with a gun sent by one of those men made me get into his car. I told him about the safe deposit box to escape with my life. That man didn't know that you need more than a key to get to the vault; the bank also has a key and a signature that must match. And, the next day my father told the bank that his key was lost and had the box drilled. He has removed the papers. I did not try to get the key from you because the key is of no use now."

"Then why did you need to see me tonight?"

Anita said, "I wanted to explain that you are also in danger—"

"Wait a minute. Why am I in danger?"

Anita wouldn't meet my eyes. She looked very small sitting across from me. I thought she wasn't going to answer. One of the drunks put money in the jukebox. Garth Brooks started singing a ballad.

"Why am I in danger?" I repeated.

"I'm afraid I told that man that I was to meet with you to get the key."

"So?"

Anita shrugged. "I might have suggested that you and I were working together."

"That explains why they stole information about me and broke into my trailer." I could imagine a movie version of this scene. Garth Brooks, the gray-haired waitress, the drunks, the raisin pie.

Anita swallowed hard. She sounded like a little girl when she said, "I'm so sorry about that. They think you are helping find Ricardo's killers." Then the tears started.

I passed her a napkin to blow her nose and waited. Then I got up to go back to work.

The jukebox was suddenly quiet. The drunks stood, tossing several bills on their table. I wanted to get out of there too.

I said, "I need to get back to work."

"Wait," she said, looking up and wiping her face. "You must work so you can take me to my destination. I am a paying customer. You're a cabdriver. I need a ride."

"Where to?"

Anita dug a piece of paper from her jacket pocket and read slowly, "The Cardinal Apartments."

"You ready?"

She nodded and stood to follow me to the cab. Looking back on this now, I can see there were too many unanswered questions.

"Come on," I said. "I'm parked out back."

Chapter Six

Past a tavern with an unlit beer sign swaying in the wind, the old Route 66 bypass was lined with aging motels that served as living quarters for transients to rent by the day or the week. This area had been nice thirty years ago. But when the interstate was built, many of the small motels went under. The Holiday Inns and Best Westerns advertised on billboards along the new I-55, and though the little motels here had been clean and cost less, travelers who found them were rare. Most of the buildings were left to run down and were converted for the chronically down and out or for those just passing through. Last summer one motel had been closed for city code violations and twenty-nine people went scrambling for a place to sleep. Before that, a fire killed three children who had been left unattended while their mother worked. Crime was high, mostly domestic stuff—somebody beating up somebody else, a woman pulling a knife on her boyfriend, two drunks duking it out, or worse.

Anita Alvarez sat in the front passenger seat, at her insistence, staring straight ahead. Most of the buildings were too far back to see the addresses. She held a small brown traveling case on her lap that she'd gotten from her room before we left the Manor View. She leaned forward slightly, looking for the sign while I let the cab roll forward. Pre-dawn mist swirled in the low places. Trees and bushes appeared to grow out of the fog. The air was cold. It had rained earlier and the sides of the road were mud and gravel.

"Are you sure we're in the right place?"

I nodded. "I know it's confusing. The street stops in the 3100 block and starts again back there." I motioned toward the corner tavern.

The Cardinal Apartments were in the 3300 block. I had been there several years ago when I dated a married woman. Grace had liked the way the carports hid her paneled station wagon from the street. We'd sit naked on the bed, the covers pulled up to our waists, passing a pint of gin back and forth, sharing an ashtray. We talked about our hopes and dreams. We talked about our spouses—her husband and the woman I was cheating on. Grace had been one of the few people in my life who had listened to me. Of course, I was usually too drunk to say anything coherent.

The cabins of the Cardinal Apartments were off the road, down a steep hill—very private. The street looked different now, shabby and rough. I recognized very little. The cab lurched in a pothole and mud splattered up around us.

"Is that it?" Anita asked.

"Where?"

She pointed toward a tree with yellow leaves. A dull white sign with the name "Cardinal Apartments" in chipped red paint hanging crooked by a single hinge was illuminated by a streetlight. The drive seemed to disappear between tangled, gnarly bushes.

I slowed the cab to a stop, looked at the meter and said, "That'll be seven dollars and eighty-five cents."

"Can you wait? I'll only be five minutes or so."

I shrugged. "Sure, why not?" It beat heading back to town empty.

Anita turned to face me and forced a smile. "You could come down with me if you want."

"What for?"

"Just in case there is trouble. Maybe you could pull the cab down the hill."

"If I drive down there, someone could block me in; besides, it looks pretty muddy. I think it's best to wait here."

Anita sighed. "I need your help."

"I agreed to a cab trip," I said. "I agreed to wait for you. When you're done, I'll take you back downtown. What is this place, anyway?"

"Lotty's killers are down there."

I stared at her dumbly. As I said, I should have known. An image formed in my mind—in it, I saw myself putting the cab in reverse and getting the hell out of there. If the murderers were here, I reasoned, I could bring the police.

"I want to deliver my father's bribe money," said Anita. "That's all."

"I don't want to know about any of this."

"Do you have a gun?"

Of course I had a gun. It was wedged under my seat. I'd gotten it before I learned that pulling a weapon on a thief was the best way to end up dead. I never used it. I'd been robbed nine and a half times and I'd never been hurt. Not even a broken fingernail. I looked at Anita and nodded slowly.

"Walk down with me. Hang back and cover me."

"I don't think so."

I could see her face in the pale green lights from the dash. Her eyes flooded and to my horror she started crying again.

"This is dangerous." Even as I said it, I knew I was going down there. I wanted to get a look at Lotty's killers. Maybe fat girls from the wrong side of town didn't rate a real investigation. If a size six college sophomore whose parents were professionals of some kind ended up with a bullet between her eyes, they would have appointed a special task force.

I leaned forward and reached under the seat. The floorboard was smooth. I remembered three days ago, the night I found the key, vacuuming thoroughly. I leaned farther, reached upward under the driver's seat and felt the handle of the Glock. The gun was loaded with the safety on, but I hadn't cleaned it for a few years. Since I had no intention of using it, I wasn't worried about a misfire. I was halfway surprised that the gun hadn't disappeared the night Lotty was murdered and my cab had been broken into.

Anita sniffed.

I reached across her, pulled open the glove compartment and retrieved a couple of tissues.

She blew her nose and stuttered. "Thank you."

"No problem."

"Will you please follow me down there? Just do this one last thing." She leaned toward me, showed me some cleavage. Her voice was almost a whisper. "These guys killed your friend."

I liked Lotty, though I wouldn't really call her a friend. She was certainly as good as anyone else. And Freddy—we were like family, Freddy and me. I sighed. "Oh, all right."

"Good. Turn off the lights and leave the motor running. We won't be long and we may need to leave quickly."

"I don't want the cab stolen."

"Look around you," said Anita. "It's four-thirty in the morning. There's no traffic. The cab will be fine."

Number Four was hard to start when the distributor cap got wet. The last thing we needed was that kind of trouble. I pulled the cab onto the shoulder, killed the headlights and put the transmission in park.

Anita dug in her purse and extracted some kind of 9 millimeter. She placed her purse on the floorboard, tucked the brown travel case under her arm and got out of the cab, letting the door close softly.

I got out and walked around the rear, zipping up my bomber jacket, pulling my black stocking cap over my ears and shoving the Glock in my jacket pocket. The earth was soft and I could feel my boots sinking and sliding as we walked down the narrow tire ruts that led to the Cardinal Apartments.

Someone was playing loud music. On the far end of the cabins a thin blue line in a window could have been from a television set. The air was damp and smelled of burning garbage. As we passed a tree I heard a growl and turned to see a huge, wet, black mongrel chained to a stake, the size of a Lab or a Shepherd. I could barely see his shape, but his eyes and his teeth stood out in the darkness. I hoped he wouldn't start barking, but he did.

Anita rushed past me and around the corner of the first cabin. She called to me, "Hide."

The lights from a cabin halfway down on the left came on as I stooped behind a dripping bush. A branch poked my shoulder.

"Shut up!" a man yelled into the night.

The dog barked tentatively.

"Shut up!"

The dog stopped.

At last my own ragged breathing was all I could hear over the loud heavy metal music. The muscles in the back of my neck were tight. I felt, rather than saw, someone behind me, and the Glock was in my hand and aimed before Anita came into focus with a stunned look on her face .

"Don't sneak up on me like that."

"Sorry."

"Do you know which cabin these men are in?"

Anita nodded and pointed.

I looked around the bush. The tail end of a black Lincoln was sticking out of the carport of number five, directly across from the guy with the dog.

I said, "Go on, I can cover you from here."

She nodded, stood, and brushed off the front of her yellow jacket. She eyed the dog and moved slowly down the row of cabins. The music stopped suddenly, and the night was so quiet I could hear the sounds of her shoes on the wet grass. I watched her step onto the small porch of cabin number five and tap on the door. I could hear her voice but couldn't tell what she said. I assumed she answered whoever was inside. The door cracked open and yellow light spilled out across the porch. The man's voice was soft. I realized then that they weren't speaking English. Anita went in and the door closed behind her.

My jacket was poor protection from the damp chill that seemed to go right through me. I shivered, alternately watching the cabin and the dog on the opposite side of me. The mongrel, of course, was watching me. Knowing a little about dogs, I didn't meet his eyes, didn't challenge him. My palms were damp and I wiped them on my jeans and grasped the Glock, ready for whatever happened next. After several minutes I heard the mongrel growl again. I looked at him. He was showing me sharp yellow teeth. Just when I thought things couldn't get any worse, I heard what sounded like two firecrackers go off. I turned in time to see Anita crashing through the door and running toward me.

She shouted something, probably in Spanish. The dog was barking and pulling at his chain.

"What?" I stood up and watched her run past.

"Run," she shouted over her shoulder.

I ran. My boots were sliding in the mud. I looked back and lights were coming on in all the cabins. A dark man limped from the open door of number five and fired. The bullet hit a stick on the ground a few feet in front of me and splinters shot in all directions. I turned and fired the Glock, aiming over his head. I hoped he would go back inside for cover. I whirled around, giving my ankle a sickening twist. I hate it when the women detectives in the mysteries I read turn their ankles. Their male counterparts don't do it. But a sharp pain jolted through me. I limped on, like a goddamn cliche, and heard another shot whiz by. Then my foot exploded. The pain was so sharp that I fell to my knees. I rolled out of the tire tracks into tall, wet grass under some bushes. My breathing was heavy. All I could hear was the barking dog. I scooted onto my side and tried to look down toward the cabins. The man was gone. I didn't know if he was coming up the hill after me or had gone back into the cabin to reload. I lay perfectly still. That's when I heard the gravel under the tires. That's when I knew that Anita Alvarez was driving away in my cab, leaving me to the bad guys.

My head was pounding. I had sprained my left ankle two or three times before. It didn't take much to turn the damn thing and put me out of commission. Between my weak ankle and the arthritis in my tailbone, I should be getting the senior discounts at the Quonset Hut. I started to get to my knees and a wave of pain washed over me. The sky through the branches of the thorny bush seemed to be getting lighter. My foot throbbed and for the first time I wondered if something was broken. Slowly it came to me that I'd have to look at the damage. My skin felt clammy and cold. My mouth tasted of copper.

I heard the sound of a car and my heart soared. Surely Anita Alvarez was coming back for me. She would be beside me soon. She would help me up the hill and into the cab. I was going to be all right. But the car that sped by was the black Lincoln that had been parked in front of cabin five. The man was going after Anita and my cab.

My boot felt warm and sticky. Though the streetlight was several yards above me, illuminated a patch of ground close by. I sat up and scooted into the light, and then looked at my foot. The left cuff of my jeans, my favorite jeans, was covered with a dark red stain. I had been shot.

I felt dizzy and lay back on the wet grass trying to calm myself. If I passed out, I could bleed to death. I had two choices. I could crawl or roll back down the hill and trust my fate to someone in the cabins below. No one had come out to see what the shooting was about. Even the dog had calmed down. The place was dark and quiet. Or, I could try to crawl to the road, which was maybe fifteen or twenty feet uphill, and take my chances there. I hesitated and felt the corners of my vision grow dark. I shook my head to stay awake and rolled over. Slowly I started pulling my body uphill.

I let my arms and my right leg do most of the work. I slid backward in the mud more than once and learned to grab onto a bush or clusters of weeds and pull. My jeans and bomber jacket were soaked and muddy. Every time my left foot touched the ground the pain was worse. The slope leveled off near the top. The sky was growing lighter. When I reached the road, I held onto a tree and tried to stand. My head spun and I sat down fast. The road was empty and quiet. Near the corner west of the Cardinal Apartments I could see someone on a bicycle coming my direction. As he drew closer, I realized he was a paperboy.

"Hey!" I called to him, waving my arms in the air.

The kid didn't hear me. He turned into a drive and disappeared. In the distance I saw the headlights of a car. Whoever it was, I had to make them stop. I pulled myself to a standing position and, though the pain in my foot was excruciating, I limped out into the center of the road. After gaining my balance I turned. The car that was coming closer was big and dark.

Quickly I made for the bushes, but in the gravel on the side of the road I lost my balance and went sprawling. The car pulled up slowly and stopped. I heard the door open. I struggled to get the Glock out of my jacket pocket. Footsteps were coming toward me. I rolled over pointing the gun with both arms outstretched.

The tall dark figure stepped backward and stopped with his arms in the air. "Trudy," he said. "Is that you?"

I closed my eyes tight and opened them, trying to focus. The voice sounded familiar. My hands were shaking so bad I couldn't hit the guy if my life depended on it. Which in a way it might. Then the gun slipped out of my hands and the figure moved toward me.

"Trudy," he said. "What the hell's happened to you? Where's your cab? What you doing out here?" My eyes focused one last time.

Johnny Henderson was standing over me asking questions. "Were you robbed?" he asked.

I was trying to think of an answer when the world went dark.

Chapter Seven

One of the uncounted humiliations connected to being gay (and child-less, I suppose) is that you never get to grow up. Your parents are always your next of kin. And that's how my mother came to be sitting next to me, reading Martha Stewart's magazine, when I opened my eyes. I was in a two bed room, on the window side. An old woman in the next bed was watching *Hollywood Squares* with the volume turned low; I'd wager my mother had something to do with that. The lights were dimmed and through the rain-streaked windows the sky was dark gray.

"What time is it?" I groaned.

Mom set the magazine down on the window ledge, careful not to lose her place, and stood. "It's two fifteen. Do you think you could eat some lunch? You can have broth and orange Jell-O."

"How long have you been here?"

"Since before you went up to surgery."

I tried to lift my head. I reached for the bed rail and realized that a tube was attached to my left hand. "Help me up, will you?"

"Oh, Trudy, you can't get up."

"I got to pee," I said through my teeth. "Now give me a hand."

My mother said, "I'll get the nurse," and turned and left the room.

Mom isn't really a bad sort. But from the day I was born it seemed like she and I were never on the same page. I wanted a Davy Crockett hat and an air rifle for Christmas; she got me a red crinoline half-slip and a Tiny Tears doll. When I was very young, the bathroom closet had always been full of bright red nail polish, lipstick, Chanel Number 5, scented powders, and hair curlers. Her douche bag hung on the towel rack over the bath tub. Even before I knew what it was, I understood that her territory was marked. To her credit she never colored her hair. These days it's silver. She fought a brave and futile battle with her figure. After my stepsisters were born, she settled into a comfortable size sixteen. She might have given up on a lot of things but she is still determined to marry me off. I suppose she means well. She told me once that if I didn't "straighten up" I'd end up living alone in a high-rise sharing my dinners with a cat.

I happen to know for a fact that my sister Barb would trade her house, five kids and husband for a high-rise and a cat.

The old lady in the next bed stared at me.

I said, "What you looking at?"

She pulled closed the gray curtain that separated our beds.

My eyes felt swollen. I remembered a quick look in the mirror when I'd come in the night before; my lip was split and I had cuts from the gravel down the side of my face. What I knew about the previous night was spotty. Johnny Henderson had maneuvered me into the back seat of his car and had driven me to the hospital. The trip had taken forever. I kept trying to tell Johnny that I hadn't been robbed, but when we got to the hospital I heard him tell the nurse exactly that. He stayed with me until I was admitted. He told them that Red, White and Blue had insurance on their drivers and he even gave them the carrier's name. The truth is most cab companies don't have insurance, but Ralph's younger brother is in the insurance business. So, we we're insured because the commission from the policy stays in the family. Of course, we aren't supposed to really use the insurance.

They were getting ready to take me up to surgery when a policeman arrived and took a statement, mostly from Johnny with me contributing periodic grunts. When we were alone again, I'd extracted a promise from him to call Pinky and ask him to check on my dog. After he took Pinky's number I tried to tell him one last time, that I wasn't robbed.

"Trudy," said Johnny, "what were you doing out in the middle of nowhere shot in the foot?"

"I had a fare," I started to explain. But that's as far as I could get. I wasn't sure what to say.

"You've had too much excitement," Johnny said softly.

"What were you doing out there?" I asked.

"I live just down the way. Got an apartment over Sculley's Tavern. I was on my way in to work. Since Freddy's back driving, Ralph asked me to do the early shift so George could get a day off. You're lucky I found you. Whoever took your cab left you for dead."

"I got shot in the foot. That isn't life threatening. There are no major organs in the foot."

Johnny flashed his perfect teeth. "I need to get to work."

"Did you call Betty?" I asked.

"Soon as we got here."

"Did you tell her I lost the cab?"

Johnny nodded.

"When you get in, tell her not to call my mother, okay?"

"Too late," Johnny said from the doorway. "Your mother is on her way. You need someone here when you go up to surgery."

That had all been several hours ago. Now a nurse in a navy blue cardigan peeked around the gray curtain. "Miss Thomas?"

"What?"

"You're not to get out of bed. Doctor's orders." She held up a bed pan.

So my mother's presence wasn't going to be the most humiliating part of my day. For the first time I noticed my left leg elevated by pillows. Then I felt the pain.

The nurse helped me with the bed pan. And when I complained about the pain while scooting around in the bed, she ordered a painkiller.

When Mom returned she told me she had to get home to cook Raymond's supper. She asked if I needed her to bring anything the next time she came, and I asked her to call Pinky and have him check on Alex. She wrinkled her nose, but I knew she'd do it. After pushing away the orange Jell-O and swallowing the pain medicine, I closed my eyes.

"No, no, no, you got it all wrong," said a voice from a long way off. "If the bread is store-bought, you cut off the crusts; if it is homemade, you leave the crust on."

A huge vase of long-stemmed lavender roses and baby's breath sat on the window ledge. Was I dreaming?

"Look," said the voice, "if you let people bring their own contributions in addition to the caterer, none of the serving dishes will match."

"Maybe we could dim the lights."

Two male voices were arguing. My lips were dry. I opened my mouth and my question came out as a croaking, "What?"

"She's awake. You woke her up."

"Who?" I muttered, forcing my eyes open.

Michael's face appeared above me. He touched my hand. "How you doing, Trudy?"

I said, "What's this about bread crusts? Isn't this your condom night?"

"You got shot in the foot, not the head," said Michael. "Tell me you know what day it is."

I thought hard. I actually didn't know. I'd gone to Lotty's wake last night though it seemed like months ago. The funeral was supposed to be the next morning. Was it over with, then? I'd worked the night shift, so it must be the weekend, or Monday. "I know what day it is," I lied.

Another head appeared next to him. "This is Steve," said Michael. "We're on our way to a meeting about the World AIDS Day reception."

I smiled at Steve who was a younger version of Michael, pale and emaciated, except he wore a black leather vest and sported a handlebar mustache. "So, you've found someone who knows the rules about bread crust?"

Steve said, "Sorry we woke you."

"What time is it?" I asked.

"Five 'til eight," said Michael. "Visiting hours are almost over."

I clasped Michael's hand. "Will you check on Pinky? Make sure he is looking in on Alex?"

"Not to worry, sweetie. Pinky is the one who told me you were up here. He stopped when he was walking that big mutt of yours and talked for a while."

"Alex will be worried."

"Of course," said Michael. "We all are. What in the hell happened, anyway?"

"It's a long story."

"Well, you were lucky someone found you. Honey, you got to get a safer job."

"I've never done anything but drive a cab," I said. "I was stupid to take this fare. I know how to take care of myself most days."

A bell sounded and Steve looked at his watch, then at Michael. I nodded at the flowers on the window ledge. "Those from you?"

"All of us at the Center," said Michael. "There's a card on the night-stand. Everyone signed it."

"Thank you."

Michael's lips formed an upside down smile. "It's time for us to go. You need anything?"

"If you come back up, bring me some junk food."

"Will do."

Steve and I did the nice-to-have-met-you bit and they left.

I started to reach for the card on the night stand and pain shot up my arm. I was suddenly aware of pain throughout my body. The buzzer for the nurse was roped around the bed rail just out of reach. I lay perfectly still and the pain subsided.

Outside the sky was dark. The old woman on the other side of the curtain was watching *Law and Order*. The sound was low, but I could hear the familiar lick that leads to the commercial.

Finally alone, I had time to get angry about Anita Alvarez's betrayal. Questions swam in my mind. Had she thought I was dead when she drove off in my cab? There hadn't been time for her to check. What if Henderson hadn't come along and found me? Could I have made it to a phone?

An aide started working on my roommate, making the bed, giving her fresh water, helping her to the bathroom. I wondered how long I'd have to use the bed pan. How long before I could drive again and how would I get the money to pay bills while I was off work? The cab company had insurance that paid if I was injured during a robbery, but not during acts of utter stupidity. I felt like I'd sunk my life savings in swamp land in Florida.

The nurse's aide started tugging on my sheets. She was young, maybe late twenties with waist-length mousy brown hair that was parted in the middle. Her face was a perfect oval with a light spray of acne on her forehead. Her name tag read "Mrs. Moriarty CNA."

"Are you going to want a sleeping pill?" she asked.

"I'll take all the drugs I can have."

Mrs. Moriarty smiled and pushed her hair back. "I'll tell the nurse."

I asked for a bed pan.

"We have to get you up. I'll put it on the chair."

We? I looked past her. There was only her and me. I was light-headed sitting on the edge of the bed. Mrs. Moriarty put the bedpan on top of a towel on the chair where Mom had sat earlier reading the Martha Stewart magazine. The aide changed my wrinkled cross sheet while I concentrated on keeping my balance on the cold metal rim.

A half hour later I was tucked into bed with a sleeping pill, painkillers and a couple of pills that may have been antibiotics.

The TV droned on, this time, *The Tonight Show*. I listened to Jay Leno's monologue. My foot was elevated and I lay there listening to the rain and my roommate's snoring. Mrs. Moriarty had pushed the gray curtain back and I could see the old woman on her back with her mouth wide open.

The next time I opened my eyes the rain had stopped and the gray curtain was being pulled shut. I could see the outline of long stemmed roses against the dark window. A figure stood next to the bed. I reached for the light.

"Don't."

My skin prickled. "Who's there?"

"I brought your cab back," she whispered. "It's parked out in the hospital lot."

"Anita?"

"I'm glad you're all right. Lotty's murderers are both dead."

"You left me for dead."

"I had to get out of there or I'd be next. I'm sorry."

"Sorry!" I raged. "Sorry? You know what? Just get out of here."

"Not so loud," she said firmly. "Please."

I took a deep breath and closed my eyes. I could hit the buzzer for the nurse. I could scream. What was she going to do? Shoot me, too? I gritted my teeth and said, "Just leave, okay? I've had enough of you and your problems."

"Okay," she said backing away from my bed. "But not until I get a chance to thank you for helping me, and tell you that I am so happy that you got out of there."

"With no help from you."

"I am sorry, Trudy. You were very brave to come with me. Maybe you have more courage than I do. I truly thought you were dead. Please believe I would have helped you otherwise."

"Yeah, well," I said. "I don't believe you!"

She put her finger to her lips to quiet me, and said, "Your keys are by the flowers."

I heard the sound of keys against the marble ledge, and then she was gone. I lay there wide awake for a long time. How was I going to explain the cab down in the parking lot? Why hadn't Anita left it on the street? The robbery story, if I decided to let it stand, would have seemed credible then. My foot throbbed. My muscles were so tight, the anger was actually painful. Finally I buzzed for the nurse.

"I need more pain medication."

She turned on the light, looked at my chart and then at her watch. "It's not time for another hour."

"Please, could you just make this one exception?"

"Sorry. Doctor's orders." She turned to leave.

I raised my voice in anger. "I can't stand this pain for another hour."

The woman in the bed next to me moaned.

The nurse put her index finger to her lips to quiet me and said, "All right, I'll get your shot early this one time. But you've got to promise to relax."

"Thank you," I said. "I'll try to relax."

I did relax eventually and slept.

The nurse woke me when she returned with my painkillers exactly one hour later.

Chapter Eight

The next morning I woke up with no sense of where I was. When a slender black woman pulled the curtains open, the room grew only slightly lighter. Through the window the sky was covered with coagulating dark clouds. The black woman wore silver bifocals and a blue stethoscope looped around her neck. As she took my vitals I decided she could have been my age, give or take.

"This time of year I wonder if the sun is ever going to appear again," the woman said when she saw me looking toward the window. I had been looking at my keys on the ledge next to the vase of roses.

I attempted a smile as she slid a tray of solid food in front of me. Breakfast was hot cereal and a poached egg. The coffee was cold and the orange juice was warm, but I was so hungry it didn't matter. My foot throbbed every time I moved. I asked another pain pill. It must have worked because they had to wake me an hour later for my bed bath.

Around noon a doctor I'd never met told me I needed to learn how to use crutches because I was going to be released. I practiced up and down the hallway one time; my first few steps were surprisingly inept, and I was glad to get back in bed. My mother brought one of her old gray sweat suits for me to wear home. The shirt was snug and we had to cut one pant leg to get it over my foot.

Anita Alvarez' late visit seemed like a bad dream. Yet my keys were there, and when I started gathering my things, I tossed them in a paper sack with the rest of my personal belongings, including a bloody, cut-up pair of hiking boots and the filthy clothes in which I'd been admitted. A whistle of fear stirred in my lungs. The jeans were ruined. How much blood had I lost? Where was my Glock? Was it lying in the mud alongside the road? Had Johnny Henderson tossed it into his car?

Mom stopped at a pharmacy on the way home to get pain and antibiotic prescriptions filled, and when she pulled up to the carport next to my trailer, she turned to me and said, "Stay off that motorcycle."

"No problem."

"I mean it, Trudy. You have to let that foot heal or you'll be limping the rest of your life."

I refused her help and maneuvered the crutches, turning sideways in the car seat. Mom left the car and went inside the trailer ahead of me. I think it took me five minutes to stand and another five to make it up the three steps into the trailer. By the time I got inside Mom was already doing dishes.

"Please," I said, "just leave it."

But she was wound up and there was no stopping her. The place was a mess by her standards, lived-in by mine. I ran the dishwasher once a week and swept and dusted when I expected company, which was next to never. No matter how hard I tried I couldn't keep ahead of the stacks of newspapers, mail and magazines. (really mostly catalogues that kept coming because I hated shopping and ordered what I wanted by mail). Sometimes it seemed like they came every day. Anyway, all those stacks that I needed to sort took up a lot of surface area.

Alex's food and water dishes were empty. I supposed he was over at Pinky's. I would call them as soon as Mom was gone. Neither Alex nor Pinky liked my mother.

"Do you have any food?" She was looking in the refrigerator at some brown lettuce, an almost empty jar of peanut butter and six two-liter bottles of Diet Pepsi.

"I'll get Michael to shop for me," I said.

"I brought some leftover meat loaf, raw carrots and apple juice. You'll have enough for supper tonight."

"Thanks." The answering machine was blinking. I didn't want to start playing my messages until she was gone.

She walked down the short hallway with her hands on her hips and looked into my bedroom. "Do you have any clean sheets?"

"Mom, you're not going to change my sheets."

She turned toward me. "I want to help you get comfortable before I leave."

I was leaning on both crutches in the center of the kitchen, afraid to sit down, afraid I'd never get up without help. "I'll be fine, Mom, really."

She was silent for a moment, staring at me. Then she said softly, "Trudy, you look like hell. Maybe you should stay with me for a few days."

I forced an encouraging smile. "No."

"But—"

"It won't work."

She squared her shoulders. "Well, it's obvious you want me to leave you alone. Let me help you to the couch, at least."

I was glad she helped me. There was barely room to maneuver the

51

crutches between the couch and rocking chair. She put a pillow on the coffee table and lifted my injured foot up. She set the phone next to me, handed me the remote, and said, "You have my number if you need anything."

I said, "Please leave the door unlocked for Pinky."

"Doesn't he have a key?"

"Yeah," I answered.

Mom said, "Stay off that goddamn motorcycle." Then she was gone.

My foot was in a plastic brace with velcro straps that held my ankle stiff and made it impossible to move anything below my knee. I wasn't to put weight on it for several weeks. I stared at the elevated boot and the blank TV screen just past it. What the hell was I going to do now? The answering machine was still blinking, but playing it would require standing and crossing the room. I could hear the wind picking up outside. A moment later soft rain pattered on the trailer's roof.

A tap at the door startled me.

"It's unlocked."

The knob turned and Alex forced his way in, knocking Pinky out of the way. The dog looked quickly right, then left. When he saw me, his tail wagged so fast and hard it almost knocked him off his feet. In a single leap he was on the couch, dancing and panting. I felt a twinge of pain when the couch jiggled, but I held onto him and buried my face in his bristly damp fur.

"Your buddy there missed you," said Pinky, slapping droplets off his baseball cap.

Alex snorted and licked my ear. I looked around him and saw Pinky picking up a plastic ice cream container filled with something orange and brown. He was looking for a place on the counter to set it down.

"What's that?"

"Soup," he said. "I made a batch of vegetable and barley. Want me to heat some up?"

"Are you joining me?"

He nodded.

"Thanks, I'm starving."

An unlit cigar hung from the corner of his mouth. These days he chewed the ends of the things and rarely lit them. He bent and opened the bottom cabinet and pulled out a pan. Three others clattered to the floor.

Alex settled on my lap. I scratched his ears and watched Pinky dump some of the soup in a pot and put the rest in the refrigerator. He brought in a plastic grocery bag from the porch and unloaded crackers, a jumbo-sized jar of peanut butter, store brand white bread and grape jelly.

"How's your mother?" he asked.

"About the same."

Pinky stirred the pot, and I stroked Alex's back and stared out the aluminum-framed window next to the couch. October had brought one chilly, morose sky that followed another. If the rain kept up, it would turn to ice by nightfall.

I needed to talk to Betty and ask if I could dispatch until I could drive again. With Lotty gone she might be grateful for the offer, though she needed me driving as soon as possible. I couldn't stay home—I had no savings and no other resources. I thought about the hospital bills, and considered for the hundredth time letting Betty and the police believe I'd been injured during a robbery. After Johnny Henderson had given the police officer a statement the night I was admitted, the uniform turned to me and told me to come down to the station as soon as I was able to give my own statement. Maybe to avoid the lie I could claim that I didn't remember anything, though that angle would work better if I'd been shot in the head. The insurance company might not be as easy as the police. They had more at stake. A weight of apprehension lay on my chest, as mean as lead. I hate lies, necessary or not. What sort of woman had I become?

Pinky shoved Alex off my lap and handed me a mug of soup and a spoon. He set soda crackers within my reach and went to get his own cup. When he had settled in the swivel rocker, he said, "Is this connected to the thugs who tried to break in here?"

I nodded and started telling him the story between refills of my mug.

After Pinky was gone I struggled to my feet and checked the answering machine. There were four of them—two from the old Mrs. Steiner wanting the lot rent, one hang up and one from Toni Matulis. I shuffled through the papers on the kitchen table and located her business card. On the couch again, with my foot up, I picked up the cordless phone. It rang before I could dial. I hadn't reset the answering machine and quickly realized that I couldn't screen the call. So I hit the button and said, "Hello."

"Trudy?" The voice was familiar. I hadn't heard from her since last Christmas when she'd called and left a message.

"Georgia," I said softly. "How are you?"

"Okay, I guess. I saw Michael at the AIDS Day planning session. He said you'd been hurt in a robbery. He told me he'd been up at the hospital to see you. I tried calling there and they told me you'd been released."

Now, the lesbian community is too small not be friendly to your ex. I don't think there's any way to explain this phenomenon to a straight person. When a lesbian couple splits, there's this awkward business of all their friends being the same people. In a town the size of Springfield with the next large city over a hundred miles away, if you do anything at all social, you're going to run into each other. It's just too painful if you haven't made peace with her. It's a brutal fact of lesbian life, one of the many.

I read someplace the average length of a lesbian relationship is three years, though Georgia and I made it nine. We had something in bed for a while. Then we were good friends for a long time. But gradually that disintegrated. I was drinking. She was screwing around. Nevertheless, I forced myself to take a deep breath, and said, "Yeah, the injury isn't much. My foot."

"Can I help you with anything?"

"That's good of you to ask, but no thanks. I got plenty of help."

"I'm single again."

The words resonated off the soft walls of my heart. I swallowed a hard knot of animosity. Why was she telling me this? I never pretended to understand her. After she left me, she decided to become a witch. She got a tattoo of a pentagram and moved in with another woman on the same day. All I could think to say was, "Too bad," so I said it.

There was an awkward silence. At length she said, "How's Alex?"

"Good."

"I'd sure like to see him."

"Georgia, what do you want?" I blurted it out without thinking, then decided that it was the right thing to say.

She sighed. "I miss being your friend. Whether you like it or not, you and I share a history."

"Do I need to remind you that I'm not the one who left?"

"Are you seeing anyone?"

"I'm too old and set in my ways to start over again. Besides, I've been busy."

"Can I come by sometime?"

"Yeah. Sure. You do that. Look, I need to get off the phone. I have something on the stove."

"Okay."

"Bye."

She didn't answer. I pretended not to notice and hung up.

My hands were shaking as I grabbed a soda cracker left from dinner and shoved it in my mouth. Alex looked up at me from the spot on the floor where he'd been asleep. I motioned for him to come, and he got up on the couch beside me.

The phone started ringing again. I stared at it—three, four, five rings. I couldn't talk to her again. I'm not made of stone. Eight, nine. "Hello?"

"Trudy?" came a woman's voice.

"Who's this?" I asked.

"Toni Matulis. You know I was pretty upset about being stood up yesterday morning. I heard that you had some problems."

"I'm sorry."

"I sat in that damn coffee shop for two hours."

I said. "I couldn't call."

"The report says you were shot during a robbery."

I thought about the insurance company and the bills. I said, "It's hard to remember what happened."

"Really?" she said.

"Well, yes. I was robbed."

"And your cab was stolen?"

"Uh...."

Toni interrupted. "Your cab is in the hospital parking lot. Did the perp return it when he was done? Or was the perp a she?"

I quickly tried to calculate the cost of surgery to remove a bullet and a night in the hospital. "Is my cab all in one piece?" I asked tentatively.

"Looks to me like it's been washed and vacuumed out," said Toni. "Years on the force have taught me that the simplest explanation is bound to be the correct explanation. Have you run into our friend Anita Alvarez again?"

"Look," I said, stalling, "we still need to have that talk. Do you think you could come by?"

"It's time for me to go to work. I have to pick up my daughter in the morning. I don't know when I can come, but I'll try get over there."

"I'm not going anywhere."

She said, "Give me the address then."

And I did.

Chapter Nine

Betty arranged for Johnny Henderson to pick me up and bring me home, and I went to work dispatching nights the following Monday. Basically, I was doing Lotty's job, and I thought about her every time I used the can. I missed her. She'd been my only straight female friend, unless you count Betty, and counting your boss seems pretty desperate. It wasn't like we went to the movies or even to lunch together. But in the evenings, when things were slow, Lotty and I had talked. We knew all the same people. She'd had a wonderful sense of humor and could get me to laugh about anything. Laughter sure made those twelve-hour shifts more bearable.

While I dispatched, most of the time a couple of the night drivers were in the break area, waiting for fares. They played cards, smoked the room blue and gave me the illusion of safety. Maybe they missed Lotty's humor as much as I did. We were a solemn group. I listened to the radio, read a couple of lesbian mysteries and thought about things. I regretted sending Anita Alvarez away from the hospital. I tried to call her number at the Manor View. Her room didn't answer and the desk had no record of her staying there in the past month. The police weren't going to find Lotty's killers. And, if the men Anita said had killed Lotty were really dead, the police hadn't even found their bodies. As far as I knew, no one had even called the police about the shootout at the Cardinal Apartments.

My injured foot was healing and I would have been able to use a special shoe and a cane if the bullet hadn't hit a bone in my foot. The crutches were a constant problem. My underarms were sore, but the foot pain was better, as long as I didn't put weight on it. I was broke, of course. My rent was overdue and my MasterCard payment was late. I had to borrow three hundred dollars from Henderson, and after my first week dispatching, my paycheck came to two-hundred sixty-nine dollars and seventy-three cents. The one thing I didn't have to worry about was food. Everybody brought me a dish of something, including Georgia, who stopped by with my favorite taco casserole. When Alex saw her, he pranced around the trailer happily. He followed her around the kitchen while she heated dinner, and he waited for scraps as if the past two years without her hadn't happened. I have to admit I sat there shoveling in the gooey cheese-covered feast, listening to her chatter on about this one and that one among our old friends, and felt sad that in the end we had failed so miserably.

Betty made her assumptions about my robbery and filed the insurance claim accordingly. Though my silence was dishonest, I kept it. Toni Matulis phoned one day shortly after I'd started back to work and set up a meeting. She came by my trailer the following morning.

"The maid's day off," I said as Toni stepped inside and looked around.

She said, "I imagine it's hard keeping up just now."

I appreciated the benefit of the doubt.

Toni produced a steno pad and said, "I've made some notes, to bring you up to speed."

She was a small woman, her reddish hair swept up in back and clipped in place. She wore faded jeans and a Rams sweatshirt. I put a pot of coffee on, limping around in the messy kitchen, then maneuvered the crutches into the living room and propped my foot up on the pillow that had become a permanent addition to the coffee table. Alex jumped up on the couch beside me. Toni settled in the rocking chair after moving a stack of newspapers to the floor. I nodded to her and she began.

"The investigation started a long time before the local police were involved. There had been an assassination attempt on Governor Wright," said Toni.

"The governor? Wouldn't that have been in the papers, or maybe on CNN?"

"Do you believe that all the news is reported?" she asked.

I shrugged.

"In February he was returning from Chicago and his plane crashed. The pilot was killed and the governor was injured, but managed to walk away. An investigation revealed that someone had tampered with the fuel line. Not many people know. The media reported it as an accident because that's how it was given to them. It was one of those small planes, single engine."

"I've picked up my share of trips at the airport. I know what they look like." I thought I remembered the story. "They said the plane went down near the Des Plaines River."

Tony nodded and went on. "Governor Wright spent a few days recovering, beefed up security and went back to work. Several weeks later, during the night, the mansion was penetrated. A man made his way to the governor's bedroom. You may have seen that in the paper."

I hadn't.

"Anyway, that's when the local police got involved. The governor tripped a security alarm. Executive Security responded as well as us. I never saw anything like it. Guys with guns out crawling all over the place like ants at a picnic. God only knows how, but the guy escaped."

I heard the coffee pot gurgling and started to get up.

Toni looked toward the kitchen and held up her palm to stop me. "I'll get it."

"Mugs are in the corner cabinet."

"Do you take anything in it?"

"No, just black."

Moments later she set two mugs on the coffee table. She'd chosen the mugs with "I have PMS, What's Your Excuse?" and "The best man for the job is a woman" on them. She sat in the rocker and picked up PMS for her own.

I said, "So, the break-in was the first you knew of trouble over there?"

"That's right."

"How does Anita Alvarez figure in this?"

"The executive police gave us very little," said Toni. "They tried to keep local authorities out of the loop. My boss was all right with that. I guess he figured we had enough to do. But the mansion is on my beat. I wanted to know more. So I started snooping around. That's when I found out about Anita. She came and went pretty often."

I nodded.

She sipped coffee and sat the mug down next to my elevated foot. "At first I thought she was a staff member. But when I checked the employee list, I couldn't find her. Custodians are outsourced. I checked with the cleaning service and got nothing. When Pop, my partner, and I had spare time, we staked out the area. Anita seemed to walk past security at all hours. Pop suggested that she might be a member of the family. That's public info and was easy enough to look up. William Wright has three grown sons. All of them live away from home. No daughters. Then I wondered if she was a mistress. But why bring her to the mansion with the wife there? This guy's no Bill Clinton."

"So what happened on October third?"

Toni lifted the mug and sipped again. She looked toward the window and said nothing. I looked the same direction. The morning sky was cloud-covered and gray. The last of the leaves from the walnut tree on the other side of the fence had fallen.

I thought she hadn't understood my question and tried again. "You know, you came to me at Red, White and Blue, and asked if I had picked Anita Alvarez up outside the bank on the third. Why?"

Toni sighed and said, "Give me a moment. I'm trying to decide where to start and how much I can say."

That made me mad. "If you expect the whole story from me, then I want the same from you."

Toni shook her head. "If I say too much, I could jeopardize all the work that's been done."

"Like I'm going to take out a full page ad in the paper."

"The less you know," said Toni, "the safer you are."

She nervously twisted a lock of auburn hair.

"Come on," I urged. "Maybe between us we can find the truth."

Toni hesitated a moment longer. At length she said, "We have a snitch who puts Anita Alvarez at one of the biggest drug buys of this decade."

"Drugs?"

"Sound like a stretch?" asked Toni. "Where do you think the illegal drugs in this area come from?"

I shrugged. "I don't think about it."

"By the time drugs hit the streets, they've been bought and sold several times. The original buyer is the guy who brings the product into the country. That's where our man puts Anita Alvarez."

"So, you're saying that a woman who comes and goes at the executive mansion transports illegal drugs?"

Toni sighed heavily and said, "So it would seem."

"Do you know where she's from?" I asked.

Toni shrugged. "Central or South America. Maybe Colombia."

"She told me she was born in El Salvador."

Toni picked up her mug and drained the last of her coffee. She saw that mine was untouched and asked, "Want me to warm that up?"

"No thanks. Go ahead and refill yours if you want."

She stood and went into the kitchen. When she returned she reached over and let Alex sniff the back of her hand. "What kind of dog is she?"

"He's a mutt. Good companion. Spoiled rotten. He's pretty much the top dog around here."

Toni smiled when Alex let her scratch his ears. "My daughter wants a dog. We live in a trailer too. I figured there wasn't enough room. The yard is so small."

"It's extra work, but he's worth it," I said. "When I'm not laid up, I walk him three or four times a week. He's old and that seems to be enough. He doesn't bark and if I keep the lot cleaned up the neighbors don't complain."

Toni said, "Maybe I should start with an old dog."

I waited until she had settled back into the rocking chair, then asked,

"What happened on October third?"

Toni met my eyes. "One of our snitches was murdered."

"And…?"

"His body was found that morning in a dumpster in back of K-Mart by an employee. He'd been shot one time in the forehead. That sound familiar?"

It did—Lotty. A pang of guilt tugged at me. I still felt responsible for her murder. "How did I get involved in this?" I asked.

"After that, Pop and I asked the captain to put someone on Anita—tailing her. We still didn't know where she lived or what she did besides come and go at the mansion. They picked up her trail that morning and lost her after she got into your cab. I guess it was raining pretty hard. You're a better driver than our boys."

I nodded. It made sense.

"Okay," said Toni, "why don't you tell me how that happened?" She tilted her head toward my foot.

I involuntarily shivered. Now I was the one who didn't know where to start. Toni waited while I tried to decide. Finally I said, "The evening after you and I first met, I checked my cab to see if Alvarez left anything. Among other things I found a key. Believe it or not, as I was leaving for the night Anita approached me. She told me she'd lost something and asked if she could check the cab."

"And you had the key?" asked Toni.

I considered telling Toni that I intended to call and report that I had seen Anita. In the end I just told the truth. I was in deep enough already. I finally said, "That's right. I hadn't decided whether to give it to her or not. But I guess I wanted to hear her side of the story. I needed to get home, and I agreed to meet her later." I told her that when I came back into town Anita stood me up. Right after that I found Lotty's body.

"How did you end up out in the middle of nowhere with a gunshot wound?"

"Anita Alvarez left a message for me. I returned her call and went to meet her at the Manor View coffee shop. At the end of this long story about her childhood, she asked me to take her to the Cardinal Apartments, you know, like a fare. When we got there she convinced me to go with her down the hill and wait for her while she delivered a package."

Toni didn't quite manage to stifle a groan and demanded, "How on earth could you be so gullible?"

I shrugged. "She said it was a bribe. I know it sounds stupid. But she told me these men were the ones who shot Lotty."

"You don't seem like the type to take the law into your own hands."

"If I told you my reasons, you'd never believe me."

"I have to trust you," said Toni. "And to trust you I need to hear everything."

I thought about that. How could I explain the way I felt? Maybe I should just tell her that Anita Alvarez had a nice ass. She'd probably buy that I got involved in this mess because I wanted the young woman's body.

In the end I simply heard myself talking in a measured tone. "My father died suddenly of liver cancer when he was fifty-six years old. We were very close. He raised me after my parents were divorced. When I was a kid, he took me everywhere. He was all I had, and I loved him the way a kid who has been through a divorce will love. You know—with abandonment kind of lurking in the shadows. I was in my thirties when he died, and I had already worked for Red, White and Blue a long time. Georgia and I were seeing each other. When Dad left his house to me, Georgia and I moved in together. It was spring and Georgia made a flower garden, pruned back trees that were overgrown and together we spruced the place up. It was ours. The first thing either of us ever owned. The house was all I had left of my father."

I reached for the now cold mug of coffee and took a swallow. I suppose I was stalling. I hadn't told the story for a long time.

Toni made a face. "Please let me warm that up."

I shook my head.

"I wish there were some way to make this easier…." Toni trailed off and the silence hung there between us.

I took a deep breath and the rest of it rushed out. "The harassment started right away. I'd wake up in the morning and a trash can was turned over. Some of the trash on our lawn wasn't even ours. One afternoon I was sitting in my bedroom, looking out the window across the back yard. It was a beautiful Indian summer day and the neighbor woman was working outside. I saw her hand her ten-year-old several branches that she'd raked up and point to our lot. The kid dragged the branches to the center of our yard and left them. Shortly after that I got a letter from the city instructing me to clean up my yard or be fined—the first of several. Frankly, I always thought someone from the neighborhood association worked there."

Toni interrupted me. "Sounds awful. But I don't see the connection."

I held up a hand and went on, "One evening we were walking after dinner and three or four kids passed us riding bikes and shouting, "Homo." Another time a man, who had been the father of my best friend when I was a child, blatantly glared at us as we walked past him. He was president of the neighborhood association. I imagined him discussing us at their meetings. Anyway, when I realized that the harassment was a united effort on the part of the whole neighborhood and not just one or two bigots, I decided to sell the house. The interest rates were over eleven percent back then. We couldn't find a buyer without seriously underpricing the property. If I could have waited a year or two, I could have gotten eight or ten thousand dollars more. These neighbors had been my father's friends; I grew up playing with their kids. And in the end they ran me out of my home—my father's home. Losing the house was like losing him all over again. Plus, I felt I had failed him."

"Trudy," said Toni, "You didn't fail your father. Your neighbors did."

I shook my head. "I don't know."

"What does this have to do with Anita Alvarez?"

I let out my breath slowly and said, "She told me she was trying to help her father."

Chapter Ten

I knew Anita Alvarez was not a friend, but until I talked to Toni Matulis, it never occurred to me that Anita might be my enemy. I guess even after the shooting, I figured she was a woman in over her head who'd got me in over mine. If Toni Matulis was right, Anita was involved in drugs and two murders, and didn't exactly have my best interests at heart. Anita had convinced me she needed my help, then left me for dead. If she was slick enough to smuggle drugs into the country, deadly enough to murder Lotty and the snitch, why had she asked for my help?

I told Toni Matulis every detail of the events leading up to my being shot. I told her the story about Anita's brother Ricardo, her sister Theresa and their deaths. Matulis took notes; the scribbling on the pages looked like shorthand. She rolled her eyes from time to time in silence. When I told her I left the safety of the cab and went down to the cabins the night I got shot because Anita had wept, Toni smirked.

I folded my arms across my chest and said, "You find this funny?"

"Sorry," she said, forcing a serious expression.

I felt stupid. A few weeks ago I'd been going about my business, driving my lavender cab six days a week, watching *X-Files* reruns when I could and hanging out with friends in my spare time. If I wasn't rich, I managed to own a decent Harley and keep the wolf from the door. Now I was maimed, I couldn't drive or walk, I was deeply in debt, and I'd seen enough television to last a lifetime.

Toni Matulis asked me to contact her immediately if Anita got in touch with me again, though we agreed that she probably wouldn't. Then she left me with strict instructions not to go off on any more adventures.

I figured the best I could do was get better and work harder. My dad used to tell me that money was only money and things were only things, that as long as I was breathing I could replace anything I lost, except for people. Okay, so I'd cut my losses. It wasn't my job to find Lotty's killer. It wasn't my job to help Anita Alvarez, or the police. I'd just forget about this mess and get my life back on track.

That afternoon I took a nap, and after a hot bath in my trailer-sized tub, with my foot hanging over the edge, I felt better than I had in a while. When Johnny Henderson picked me up I watched him handle the cab, thinking that as long as my right foot was in good shape, I could drive. But when I mentioned it to Betty she shook her head and frowned.

"I have to get someone hired to dispatch. You might as well stay on the phones until I can."

"How long do you think it will take?"

She shrugged. "Don't know. I'll put an ad in the paper."

"You haven't got an ad in the paper?"

Betty lit a cigarette and waved the smoke away. Her eyes were a little bloodshot. She stifled a smoker's cough and said, "I thought I'd let the stuff about the last dispatcher being murdered settle down, you know?"

I nodded and dropped it.

There weren't many calls that night and I got involved in a long poker game with Lester, Freddy and Johnny Henderson out in the lounge. The few times the phone rang, Freddy, who was closest, had to jump for it because I couldn't get up on the crutches and across the room fast enough. When Betty came in at six the next morning, all of the ashtrays were full, and I was ahead forty-eight dollars and some change.

On weeknights, instead of parking at the airport for a late flight, at least one of the guys made sure to be in the office. I knew it had to cost them money, especially after an all-night poker game. I was aware more than ever of how many friends I had. To my knowledge no one told them to keep an eye on things or coordinated their comings and goings. No one had to.

On the rare occasions when I was alone, the silence of the darkened garage was eerie. The slightest noise was magnified. The building had once been a small factory. Ralph and Betty hadn't done much to it since they bought the place twenty-three years before. The offices were the factory offices. The garage was unpainted cement block with high windows and hanging fluorescent lights. The bay doors were closed at night; even with all the lights on, the corners were always in shadows. The roof leaked and the concrete floor was usually damp. In the summer the place was like a sauna.

One Sunday morning, Betty told me I would start training a new night dispatcher on Wednesday night. George's daughter Minnie was taking the night shift and by next weekend, if I thought I was able, I could take my cab out. Since I'd been grounded, no one had driven Number Four. After the police released it, which was quickly, as they found no fingerprints or evidence, the lavender cab had been parked in back of the building. I hadn't turned in the keys Anita left at the hospital (though I was damn glad to get my trailer and Harley keys back), so Ralph had another set made from the masters. Betty suggested I start with eight-hour shifts the first two or three nights. I was thrilled. I missed my cab, I missed my work, and I hated being tied to the phone.

The first snow of the year fell. While I slept, a white, silent blanket covered everything. The days were getting shorter and it was almost dark when Henderson picked me up. If I hadn't needed the money so bad, I would have stayed home. Instead, with a generic freezer bag covering my injured foot to keep it dry and the rubber tips of my crutches caked with ice, I maneuvered my way down the slippery trailer steps.

"Are the streets slick?" I asked, tossing my crutches in the back seat and scooting into the car.

Johnny turned toward me. He needed a shave and probably had gotten up only a few minutes before I had.

"It's pretty wet," he said. "I bet it's gone by morning."

I nodded and watched the road ahead. Traffic was sparse, and Henderson's tracks were the first on my street. Even in the main streets weren't cleared—vehicles stuck to rutted paths. The windshield wipers squeaked every time they passed across my view. The noise was irritating. I noticed two magazines on the dashboard.

"These yours?" I asked.

"Had a trip from the airport last night. Woman left them in back of the cab. I saved them for you. I know you already read all those A-B-C mysteries that Betty keeps around."

Not only had I read Betty's four Sue Graftons, but all three of the Jean Marcys that Georgia left for me. I picked up the magazines and examined them. Two *Ladies' Home Journals*. Oh, boy.

By the time we pulled up in front of Red, White and Blue, a low-lying mist had started to form. I could barely see the lights from the Alamo across the street. The floor, already wet and muddy, was hard to maneuver on crutches. I slipped in the mess just inside the door, then moved carefully past the break area and around the desk. Betty looked up from a crossword puzzle and nodded. She picked up a large metal ashtray and tossed about four pounds of butts and gum wrappers in the wastebasket. She said, "Been pretty quiet. Freddy is at the airport waiting for the seven o'clock from Chicago and Lester worked days. Johnny can hang around here."

"We only have two drivers?" I asked, though I could count on my fingers as well as the next guy.

Betty shrugged and pulled her coat off the rack. "I'll be glad when you're back on the road and not sitting in here on your rear end, griping." Then she was gone leaving nothing but the cold wet air as the door whooshed shut.

I tossed the magazines on the desk and slowly lowered my rear end onto the chair.

Johnny grinned at me, flipping the bill of his hat back off his forehead, a toothpick clinched between his white teeth. "She's in a mighty bad mood tonight."

I said, "Be thankful she's on her way out."

"You want a Coke or something?" He dug for change in his jeans pocket.

"I'm fine."

I opened one of the magazines and checked the table of contents. There were lots of Thanksgiving recipes: Grandma's apple-pecan pie, Aunt Mabel's oyster stuffing, ten new ways to use Jell-O, and how to cook a turkey in a bag. My mother was cooking for Raymond and my sisters for the holiday. If I promised to come at Christmas, I got to stay home on Thanksgiving, thus avoiding my stepsisters' kids, ten between them, and Raymond's drinking. Pinky and I usually cooked some frozen pressed turkey and watched the Thanksgiving Day Parade. He made his once-a-year pumpkin pie, which was pretty good though the crust was bought. Later, after the dishes were in the dishwasher, we'd make microwave popcorn. Alex got most of Pinky's. We always watched football until it was time for me to go to work. Thanksgiving was now a week away. Pinky and I were going to eat out this year—take a cab to and from the restaurant. Maybe it was better that way. We could eat real turkey and still watch football, and there'd be no dishes to clean.

Johnny went out on a trip about six-thirty. Even with the snow and fog, there were plenty of calls for two drivers. And I was alone in the office most of the evening. I started reading a column called "Can This Marriage Be Saved?" This woman was forty-three years old and had just sent the younger of her two kids off to college. She felt lonely so she'd joined a women's support group and had taken up with a younger man. Now she wanted a divorce. Then the husband told his story. He thought his wife was having a change-of-life breakdown and wanted her hospitalized. He said how he worked long hours to give her a good home and provide for the kids. He loved her and had never been unfaithful, except one time with the receptionist which went on for three or four years, but that was over. I had just realized that the psychologist was going to have a turn, too, when a scraping sound made me catch my breath.

I raised my head and listened. My fingers moved to the space beneath the desk where the forty-five had been the night of Lotty's murder. Betty had put the weapon back there as soon as she could. I touched the rough metal surface of the handle and I looked toward the door that led to the dark garage and listened again. Everything was quiet. Should I call the police? A cold draft crawled up the back of my neck and I realized the front door had opened. I turned quickly and caught her brushing snow off her coat. I pulled the forty-five from the shelf. I've heard they have a helluva kick and I braced myself.

Anita Alvarez walked toward me. "Have you calmed down yet?"

I didn't answer.

She tossed her coat across the counter that separated the office from the break area. Her hair was wet and I remembered the first time I'd seen her in the cab, combing those short, dark locks down. She rested her elbows on the counter, the way Johnny had earlier. Her breasts pressed against the front of her pale blue sweater. "Are we alone?" she asked.

I said, "A driver could come in any minute."

"Trudy." Anita said my name slowly, like she was talking to a frightened child. "Are you afraid of me?"

"I don't even know who the hell you are."

"I am Anita Alvarez, born in El Salvador, educated in the states. I want to be your friend."

I held up my palm to stop her. "I don't believe you."

She shrugged. "I'm sorry. It really doesn't matter who I am."

"I don't believe you want me for a friend. I want to know what you really want." There, I'd finally asked the question I should have asked in the beginning.

Anita walked around the counter and scooted her butt up onto the desk, shoving "Can This Marriage Be Saved" to the floor. She was close enough that I could feel the electricity from her body. I rolled the desk chair back a couple of inches, the gun still hidden beneath the desk.

"Look at your life." She swept one arm in a semicircle indicating this and that in the room. "Before you met me, you were dying of boredom."

"Before I met you, Lotty was alive," I said. "Before I met you I'd gotten by without a gunshot wound. There was nothing wrong with my life."

"Ah." Anita Alvarez met my eyes, smiled, and said, "You followed the white rabbit much too easily."

I remember that moment clearly, but a long time passed before I understood what she meant. By then it was too late. By the time I remembered a story about Alice, the bored little girl who followed a white rabbit into a hole, I was in jail.

Chapter Eleven

I studied Anita's face. Her eyes were the color of black coffee, her skin smooth and dark. Over her right shoulder, through the front glass, a thick blanket of fog enveloped everything. I could barely see the light over the door. The parking lot was totally obscured. I heard the furnace kick on and the fan rattle as it gained speed. I kept the .45 hidden in my lap, ready. Even though the room was cool, sweat stood on my forehead.

"I'm supposed to call the police if I see you again."

"You're not going to do that." She sounded pretty sure of herself—not cavalier, not particularly happy about it—just sure.

I sighed. "Why are you here? What do I have to do with any of your problems?"

She hung her head like a naughty child, like Alex when he makes a mess on the floor. She said, "I came to say I'm sorry. I tried at the hospital, but you threw me out, remember?"

"Sorry?" I felt anger rise. "Sorry? That's supposed to make it all right? My involvement in your little adventure has ravaged my life."

She looked like she might cry, but this time I wasn't buying it. "I was shot. Nobody in my family has ever been shot! My father and my uncle Ray and my grandfather all fought in World Wars, they never got shot. My step-father deserves to be shot, and he's never been shot. I had a great uncle who ran moonshine in Kentucky and—"

Anita held up a hand. "Okay, I get the picture."

But I wasn't done. "The bills for the hospital aren't even all in yet. I can't drive my cab, so I can't work."

She interrupted me. "My father will pay your hospital bills. Let me know how much it comes to."

I stared at her wide eyed. "Just who in the hell is your father?"

"You wouldn't believe me if I told you."

"That hasn't stopped you up to now." My voice was growing louder. I laid the .45 back on the handmade shelf and reached for Lotty's stash of Snicker bars only to remember it wasn't there, would never be there again.

"William Wright," said Anita.

"What?"

"The governor of Illinois, William J. Wright, is my father."

Pain started above my right eyebrow, as if someone were driving a railroad spike into my forehead. I raised my hand to make sure my brains weren't pouring out. "I don't believe you," I managed to croak.

"Believe what you want." With that she slid off the desk and walked back around the counter.

I studied her with determination, and said, "You left me. I was wounded, and you left me."

"I saw you fall, and I thought you were dead. I'm sorry. It was a mistake."

My voice quivered. "I could have been bleeding to death."

She didn't apologize again. And it wouldn't have mattered if she had. I couldn't reconcile what she had done, yet meeting her exotic brown eyes, I couldn't seem to hold on to my anger. I looked at the floor, and the *Ladies' Home Journal* still open to "Can This Marriage Be Saved?" I wished one of the drivers would come in and interrupt, or the phone would ring and force me to do anything but forgive her. At last I said, "William Wright is a Republican."

The corners of Anita's mouth curled, she sort of coughed, then lost it and laughed. "Good point."

"This is the guy who left you and your family in El Salvador?" I asked, as if Toni Matulis hadn't told me the whole story was untrue.

She said, "It is."

I was thinking that fathers were my Achilles heel and Anita seemed to know that. I said, "Look, you need to leave."

"You're not calling the police, after all?"

I said, "Yeah, I think I might," even though I knew I wouldn't.

She reached inside her jacket, pulled out a card and passed it across the counter to me. "I hope you don't do that. Collect your bills. When you are ready, call this number and talk to Barry Carmichael. If you need anything else, you, and only you, can reach me through him."

I looked at the card and recognized the telephone prefix as a state office number. Had Anita lied to me? Or was Toni Matulis wrong? I started to ask Anita another question, but the phone rang. As I picked it up, she stood and moved away from the desk, then grabbed her coat and with a cavalier wave hurried out the door and disappeared into the fog.

The next morning Georgia called. Mondays are her days off at the beauty shop. She sounded gleeful. "I have some exciting news."

"What time is it?" Even Alex, who was lying next to me, seemed to want to go back to sleep.

"Eleven-thirty, are you still in bed?"

"I worked all night."

"Oh, I'm sorry. I guess I thought you were still off work."

I yawned. "Been dispatching. Tonight is my off night, but if Betty calls, I'll go in. I'm working all the hours that I can."

"I'll tell you my news fast, and then you can go back to sleep."

"Right."

"Remember how I always wanted an SUV?"

I was the one who'd wanted a Jeep, not Georgia. I'd wanted to use it for camping.

She didn't wait for me to respond. "I got one."

That pissed me off. How the hell could she afford it? I'd tried to save the money for a down payment on a used Jeep, but when Georgia left I had the whole trailer payment and lot rent, and then I had to put a new clutch on my bike. The few hundred dollars I'd put aside sort of dwindled away.

I rolled onto my side and threw an arm across Alex. He licked my nose and closed his eyes again. I must have grunted something because Georgia was talking again.

"...a crimson-red Explorer—a one owner, with less than twenty-thousand miles. You should see the leather seats, CD player, four-wheel drive, everything automatic."

"Things going better at the beauty shop?" I asked.

"It's financed to the hilt," said Georgia, "but I just had my fortieth birthday and I decided that I need to start having a few of the things I want in life."

I've always envied Georgia's ability to ignore the price of the things she wants. When we were together and she wanted another woman, I was toast.

"I'm happy for you," I lied.

Her voice softened. "I want to take you for a ride."

"Call me later," I said, though I was pretty sure I'd be working. I did need someone to take me to the store.

As it turned out, the new dispatcher started on Monday night. Betty called and told me she wanted me to drive days on Tuesday. Though I had to be at work at six in the morning on Tuesday, I did have Monday night off. When Georgia called again, I told her I needed to shop for groceries while we were out riding.

The Explorer had running boards that made getting in and out with crutches easier. Georgia demonstrated all the little gadgets as we drove through the wet streets. I hinted for her to let me drive, but she was against it. I didn't push it. The snow from the day before had been salted or plowed aside. Late in the afternoon when we pulled into the supermarket lot, the sun was setting and the sky was clouding up again.

"Let's pick up something for dinner while we're here," Georgia said. "I'll cook."

A home cooked meal sounded pretty good and I agreed.

Georgia was wearing her hair long again, the way she knew I liked it. Her red v-necked sweatshirt showed just enough creamy cleavage. She doesn't own a pair of jeans that aren't stretch jeans. She had on the black ones today. Her round hips looked inviting. She smiled at me, and for an instant I wanted to draw her into my arms right there, but my better judgement stopped me. "Let me handle the cart for you," she said.

I had come to accept the fact that my underarms were going to be sore for a while. Managing the crutches had become second nature. While Georgia checked the calorie count on different brands of microwave popcorn, I wandered through produce. I'm not a vegetable freak. Salads always seem like a good idea, but fresh vegetables bought with good intentions rot in my refrigerator far too often for me to kid myself.

I was standing in front of a display of green bananas when I saw a black Charles Manson T-shirt. I was preparing to call down the parents for letting a kid wear that shirt when I realized the guy in the shirt was a short middle-aged man.

Georgia tossed a box of Smart Pop in our cart and said, "You hungry for bananas?"

I shook my head.

"They look good."

I turned to take a longer look, and a little girl with light brown skin and red hair passed us, touching all the produce within her reach.

"Why do all biracial lesbian couples have mixed-race kids?" Georgia asked.

"Do they?" I shrugged. "Maybe those kids are easier to adopt. What brought that up?"

"It's a thing I've noticed. Look over there, black woman, white woman and biracial kid."

"Where?"

"I think that kid is with those two over there." Georgia pointed and I saw them. The two women looked pretty cozy standing by the salad dressing.

"What makes you so sure they're lesbians?" I asked. "They could be straight friends who are making a salad."

"Oh, come on, look at the tall one."

She was a light-skinned black woman with a great masculine-looking haircut; the shorter woman with the wide hips looked familiar. Before I could discreetly look away she waved at me.

"You know her?" Georgia wasn't doing very well hiding her possessive tone.

I shot her a look that I hoped conveyed: you-were-screwing-around-and-left-me—I haven't-dated-since-we-broke-up—except-a-couple-of-one-night-stands—okay, four—but where-the-hell-do-you-come-off-acting-jealous? Then I said through the corner of my mouth, "A police-woman on Lotty's murder case."

"Well," said Georgia, twisting the knife, "her girlfriend is hot."

To my further chagrin, Toni lifted the kid into the cart, left the taller woman in charge, and came toward us.

She started talking before she got to the bananas. "I'm so glad I ran into you."

I introduced Toni to Georgia and they shook hands.

We all stood there for a moment, then Toni said, "Ah, could we talk alone?"

I tried to gauge Georgia's expression without turning my head. It wasn't hard. I told Toni, "Georgia and I are old friends, you can talk in front of her."

Toni nodded, though I could see she wasn't happy with the situation. "Anita Alvarez is back in town."

"How do you know?" I asked. I was damned if I was going to tell her about Anita's visit the night before. Then I'd have to explain why I hadn't reported it.

"I saw her myself," said Toni, "over near the Manor View. It's on my beat, remember?"

In an effort to stay out of whatever was going on, I said, "What does that have to do with me?"

Toni shrugged. "I thought you may have heard from her. You haven't, have you?"

"Why would she get in touch with me?"

Toni told me to call her if I heard from Anita; she told Georgia that it was nice meeting her, and Georgia said it was her pleasure. Toni went back to the hot girlfriend. The kid by then had climbed out of the cart and was eating a carrot while counting potatoes by taking them off the display one at a time.

Later, while loading the groceries into the back of Georgia's Explorer, we saw them again. They were getting into an old black Jeep, the kind I would have given half my interest in hell to own.

Georgia broiled steaks for supper and by the time our eyes met as we put the dishes in the dishwasher, it was obvious to me that she wanted to top off her big day with sex. I was ambivalent. Of course I wanted her, but she was the source of one of the most painful incidents in my life and that pain was something I did not want. So there I was with my belly full of a good meal, a beautiful woman in my kitchen, and the whole evening ahead of me.

By nine o'clock I had my left hand under her shirt, by ten-thirty we were falling asleep in each other's arms.

Chapter Twelve

When I woke, my fingers were sticky with K-Y Jelly. I clung to the side of the mattress—Georgia's body was behind me, spoon fashion. A long time had passed since I'd let a woman into my bed. Georgia had learned a few new tricks, and it was clear that she hadn't learned them from me. This little tryst didn't mean we were back together—too much time had passed, too many things had been said. I'm not a pushover, not usually, anyway. But the thing with Georgia was complicated. Deep down I felt angry. Was she using me to get over what's-her-name? Even if it turned out we both wanted something more permanent, how could I ever trust her again?

The room was dark and I tried to focus on the red numbers of my digital alarm clock with no success. Alex's nose touched my arm. Maybe that's what woke me. I rolled up to a sitting position, being careful to untangle myself from Georgia, disturbing her as little as possible. I hobbled into the kitchen with the big dog behind me. I hadn't let him out before we'd fallen into the clinch.

I unlocked the door and whispered, "Quiet now, no barking."

There was fresh snow on the ground. The tracks in the street were covered, including Georgia's. Standing at the screen door I looked toward my bike, parked and covered with a canvas tarp. Snow was at least three inches deep. My crutches were where I had left them leaning against the kitchen table. I reached for one and put it under my left arm. Alex was back quickly and I closed and locked the door. That's when I saw the red light of the answering machine flashing. Georgia had turned off the ringer several hours earlier. I thought it might be work calling, so I adjusted the volume low and hit the play button.

The voice was a woman's. "Trudy, please call me." And she gave a number.

Alex lay on the kitchen floor at my feet. I considered resetting the machine and going back to bed. But I had a whole life that didn't include Georgia. If she wanted to hang out with me, she'd have to get used to that. I picked up the phone and dialed what could have been a cell phone number.

"Hello?"

"It's me, Trudy," I whispered.

"Oh, thank God," said Anita Alvarez. "Please come and get me."

"I got shot in the foot and I'm not driving right now, remember? You're going to have to call a cab."

"I'm not in a position to do that," said Anita. "I need your help. Please I'm hurt."

"What do you mean, hurt?"

"I've been beaten up."

"And what's that got to do with me?" I was trying to sound above it all, but something in her voice, a raspy distress, made me hesitate. She sounded hurt.

"Please help me. I have no one else to call."

"What about your politically powerful father?" I asked.

"He's in Chicago. Really, there's no one."

"Call the police," I whispered, but by that time a movie had started running in my head. I could see myself getting dressed, taking the keys to Georgia's Explorer and leaving quietly.

"You know I can't do that. I will explain everything when you get here."

"Look, the police asked me about you. I told them I hadn't heard from you. And frankly, I'd rather keep it that way. Besides, there's three inches of snow on my Harley."

"Can't you get a car?" she said. "I promise. This is the last time. Nothing else."

Silence stretched between us like a yawning pit. My mind was working. I could throw a scare into Georgia and teach her that I wasn't the same old Trudy, the same old sap. Georgia would find out that I had learned some new tricks, too. At length I said, "Where are you?" Then I grabbed a pencil and wrote the directions on the back of my phone bill.

"I'll be driving a red Explorer," I said.

"Oh, thank the Lord," said Anita. "I'll watch for you."

Still in my nightshirt, I grabbed the single sock off the coffee table and pulled it on to my good foot. My underwear was once-worn and a little crunchy from the heavy petting. I left it lying on the floor, grabbed the gray sweat pants and finally a single hiking boot. Moving around on a single crutch, I washed my hands and splashed water on my face, then pulled on a stocking hat and the plaid hunting jacket that was my winter coat. The pockets were full—my gloves, a flashlight I carried to look up addresses while driving the cab, Juicy Fruit gum and a bottle of aspirin. I put the second crutch in place, eased Georgia's keys off the counter and headed for the door. I was sure I'd be back before she missed me.

Alex fussed a little, thinking we were going for a walk. My heart gave a tug as I softly told him no. Maybe Georgia would take him out in the morning.

The SUV had a keyless lock. I clicked the key thing, opened the driver's side door, tossed the crutches in the back seat and struggled up and in. I put the big vehicle in reverse and backed out into the street before the noise of the engine could wake Georgia. I searched the dash for the four-wheel-drive and turned it on just because I could, then dug my gloves from my jacket pocket.

I made my own tracks all the way out of the trailer court and onto the highway heading north. The Explorer sat high, like a pickup truck I had owned once. I liked the feeling.

The address that Anita had given me was near the airport on one of the back roads, which were bound to be slick. The only vehicle I saw all the way to the airport road was a snowplow coming toward me in the opposite lane. The sky was overcast and the snow had settled to a light flurry. Cameron Road was five miles north, closer to the Sangamon River than the airport. In more than one place the two gravel lanes wound near the murky, fog-shrouded bank.

I came to an intersection, saw the sign for Jimmy's Bait Shop and Boat Rental. I turned right and followed a single set of tracks toward the river. An abandoned greenhouse and several small fishing shacks lined the rutted road. The big vehicle went downhill, and I wondered if I'd have to make a run at the steep slope to get back up. In places the road felt soft. I hadn't thought about mud on the tires. But I'd deal with that when I got home. Right now all I had to do was find Jimmy's Bait Shop and Anita Alvarez.

I could see the black river by the time the rising smoke from the chimney of the bait shop came into view. At the end of the empty parking lot a light hung over a small dock with a johnboat secured next to it. The tracks I had been following had come from here. In the snow all around the porch were fresh foot prints. Had Anita found someone else to come for her? Was she even here? There was a dim light through the window of the small shack.

I lowered the automatic window and called out her name. Nothing. The headlights of the Explorer lit the way up to the sagging wooden porch. I hit the horn and waited. By now I was pretty sure I was alone, but I thought I should check the shack to be sure. I rolled the big vehicle as near to the porch as I could get. I needed the headlights, so I left the engine running and reached for my crutches. The whole time I was wondering how I was going to help her, if she were here, since I could barely get around myself. As I got my footing in the parking lot, the crutches sank into the snow and mud. The porch across the front of the bait shop was only twenty feet away, but I moved slowly, thinking the next step would swallow me up. When I reached it, the boards creaked under my weight. As I scraped some of the mud off my boot, I was aware of that tight-in-the-gut feeling you get walking through a dark room.

I called out Anita's name again near the door. After a certain point, the shadow of a tree obscured my view, even with the headlights. The wind was cold on my face, and cut through my sweatpants. I pulled off a glove and rapped on the wooden door. "Anita?" I thought I heard something then. I tried the knob and the door squeaked open.

"Anita? Are you here?" There was a light on toward the back of the room. The place smelled of dust and wood rot. My headlights shining through the side windows illuminated the areas well above the floor. I took out my flashlight and shone it around the room. There were two old refrigerators along the front wall next to a Coke machine, several wash tubs, and a filthy, chest-style freezer. A kitchen table and two chairs were across the room. I didn't really want to go in. As far as I could see, the place was empty. I tried one more time.

"Anita."

I heard a moan and the sound of movement, but I couldn't tell from where. My heart pounded. I didn't really want to find out who or what was in there.

"Anita, if you're here, come on. I have to get this damn truck back before it's missed."

I waited and when I heard nothing further I turned to go.

"Trudy." The voice was weak and definitely coming from inside the shack.

I let out my breath slowly and stepped inside. The heat, what little there was, came from a wood-burning stove. The trap was open and flameless red-hot wood gave off a dim, wavering glow.

I caught her in the flashlight beam near the freezer, on the floor. My feet and the crutches left hunks of mud across the already filthy linoleum like the tracks of an unsteady crab. When I stood at her side and she looked up at me, I sucked in my breath. Her left eye was in the process of swelling shut. Blood was smeared across her upper lip. I couldn't tell if the mess was from the corner of her mouth, which was also swelling, or her nose.

"What in the hell happened to you?"

"I'll explain later," she groaned. "Help me. Let's get out of here."

"Can you stand?" I asked.

"I'll try." Her words were slurred by the swelling lip.

I gave her my arm and braced myself against the freezer chest. She pulled herself up and then dropped back. "Look," I said, "if you can't walk, I'll have to go for help."

"No, I can do it." This time she reached for my right hand, pressed her back against the wall, put her left hand on the handle of the freezer and in a sudden move was standing. Well, sort of leaning over the top of the freezer, but she was on her feet.

I put a crutch under my left arm and held on to Anita with the right. We didn't go in a straight line but managed to get all the way to the door. I could barely hear the engine of the Explorer running, but the headlights were clear and bright. I'd be damn glad to get back on the main road and head for home. I was wondering where I was going to take Anita when I heard a sound coming from the river. The slow putt-putt-putt of an outboard motor grew closer.

Anita groaned. "They're coming back."

When we reached the still open door, wood splintered next to my ear and I heard the sound of the shot a split second later.

We fell back inside the cabin and pulled the door closed.

"We're trapped," Anita whispered.

I looked through the side window at the Explorer waiting several yards away. Neither one of us was in any shape to run. Plus we'd be in full view of the river.

"What in the hell is going on?" I demanded, pulling off my stocking hat and examining the wood splinters that were caught in the yarn.

"Did you bring the gun?"

"Aw, man, not again…"

"Please don't panic," she whispered in a tone that sounded panicky. "Did you bring the gun?"

"No. You didn't tell me to bring a gun. Of course, if you had, I wouldn't have come. Where is your gun, anyway?"

Anita jerked her chin toward the river and the sound of the outboard motor. "Nestor took it."

I raised my voice, "Another Salvadoran gangster?" I needed to sit down. The room was chilly, but dodging gunfire was heat enough for me. My foot and my head were throbbing. We were both breathing hard.

But it was Anita who sank into a chair. She put her bruised head in her hands and said to her lap, "They are getting rid of the bodies. We need to get out of here before they come back."

"The bodies?" My tone may have risen another octave.

Anita motioned toward the freezer chest.

I maneuvered four or five steps and looked. Nothing but dirt.

"Open it."

Foggy cold air rushed out and I waved it away. My flashlight illuminated a dark-haired, thick-built man in a pair of green pajamas who looked up at me with open eyes. On the left side of his blood-soaked pajama top was what could have been a bullet hole. Tiny icicles had formed on his eyebrows and moustache. His skin was the color of dough, with maybe a bit of a bluish cast.

"This one of the guys from the Cardinal?" I asked, feeling amazingly calm.

Anita croaked, "Yeah."

"How did you get him here?"

"A friend helped me," she said. "These guys followed me out here. I set a trap for them—"

"This is confusing," I interrupted. "Are you telling me this happened the night we went to the Cardinal Apartments?"

"Yes."

"You had a friend to help you and you called me?"

"You don't understand," Anita insisted.

"You're right, I don't."

She sucked in her breath. "All right. I admit I deceived you. But that night I had nowhere to turn. My father didn't send me out to the Cardinal. I went with the intention of killing those two. They were making problems for my father and my family in Central America. Large problems."

"That's what you do with people who make problems? You shoot them and put them in a freezer?"

"These are very bad men," said Anita.

"You killed them here?"

Anita nodded. "Several days later, I brought a friend. We cleaned up the blood and put the guys on ice until we could figure out what to do next."

"I don't suppose that friend was available tonight?"

She shook her head. "Chicago."

"Where's the other guy?" I asked, turning toward her.

She jerked her head toward the river and sounds of the outboard motor. "Boat's too small to take them both at once."

"Great, we needed to get out of there." I thought I heard a car door slam. "I only saw one set of tracks, where is the car you came in? Is it out back or something?"

"There were three of them. Another man left a while ago. Maybe he went to get something to tie this guy to."

I nodded, convinced that now there were three men out there and thinking that if I hadn't seen the answering machine, or had simply ignored it, or if I had called the police, I would be home in bed with Georgia. I tried to shake the thoughts away. They weren't helping me now.

Anita said, "These guys found me and forced me to tell them where these two were. Nestor insisted that I come along, on the chance I was deceiving them."

"And you weren't?"

"Not exactly. I didn't really tell them these boys were dead until we got here."

"Why the river?" I asked.

Anita shrugged, then winced in pain. Her voice was shaking. "These men are very bad. They can't afford to be discovered. The first one was tied to a cement log and taken to the center of the river. This one will follow, when their friend returns. And then, we—"

"No, I mean, what is this place? Why did you come here?"

"Family business. My father's second cousin used to run an illegal poker game from here. Jimmy is the guy's youngest son. He was running a legit bait shop and boat rental, but he's in prison right now."

"You have an interesting family."

She grimaced, or maybe it was a painful smile.

"Why didn't you run before now?" I asked. "Surely a little cold and mud beats an execution."

Anita said, "I tried. They caught me and gave me worse than before." She was breathing hard, as if talking was growing painful. "After that, you were my last hope. Jimmy leaves a cell phone here because there's no wire out this far. I tried the taxi office and they said you were off. I called your home and you didn't answer." She started to cry in earnest then and I was ready to join her.

I was telling myself that at least it couldn't get worse when an explosive splashing sound came from outside. I turned to the window. The light over the boat dock reflected on Georgia's red Explorer and for a second I thought they'd moved the vehicle closer to the river. Then tail lights illuminated the dark water as the vehicle floated on the surface briefly and started to sink.

Two men with guns stood on the bank, looking toward the cabin.

Chapter Thirteen

My mouth hung open. Things had definitely hit a rough spot for Georgia and me.

"Now how will we get out of here?" Anita whimpered behind me.

My voice trembled. "That isn't my Explorer, and I didn't have the owner's permission to drive it. I'd just as soon they killed me."

"If we stay here, we will both be dead." Anita struggled to stand. "Come on. The back way is the only chance we've got."

"They're after you," I reasoned out loud. "Why would they want to hurt me?"

"Oh, for Christ's sake. They did this to me and they'll be delighted to do it to you."

I tore my eyes from the window and turned to her. "Out there is a twenty-five thousand dollar Sport Utility Vehicle that belongs to my ex sinking in the goddamn Sangamon River."

"Don't you get it? These guys aren't going to let you go. They sank that vehicle so you couldn't leave."

"Me?"

Anita sat back down on the chair, or fell back down—I wasn't sure which. I weighed my options. Should I help her stand, or take a swing at her? I'd be hard pressed to find a spot that hadn't already been injured. That, and the fact that I'd never hit a woman, was probably the only reason I held on to my temper.

I said, "I think life as I know it is over for me, anyhow."

"Maybe so," said Anita. "But we have to try to stay alive, or these goons will never be brought to justice."

"There's snow and mud out there; we'll leave tracks whichever way we go."

"I prefer that to sitting here and waiting," said Anita. "They'll assume you ran, but they'll come after me because they know I can't."

My voice rose. "Look, I am maimed. They'll track me down like a dog and kill me."

Anita limped toward me and grabbed the sleeve of my hunting jacket.

"We can go out the back. Try to hide somewhere. That could buy us some time."

I suddenly remembered that the police were an option for me, if not for Anita. "Where's the cell phone?"

"There's no one to call," said Anita as she pulled it from her jeans pocket and held it behind her.

"I'm calling Toni Matulis," I said, fully aware that the shortest distance to Toni was 9-1-1.

"The policewoman?"

I nodded and Anita threw the cell phone across the room and deliberately close to my ear. It struck the wood burning stove. By the time I turned to retrieve it, it was in five pieces, two of them still spinning on the linoleum floor.

"You are out of your goddamn mind!"

"I told you, we would not call the police." Her Spanish accent was more pronounced now.

I could hear the voices of the men and glanced out the window. They were closer. I don't think I actually made a decision to run, my body just jerked into motion. I grabbed the crutches and followed Anita though a doorway that led into a cluttered mudroom, with a tiny, dark bathroom off to the left. I shone my flashlight on two waist-high stacks of newspapers that blocked the back door. The lock was the hook-and-eye kind that people used to use on screen doors in the summer, only bigger and rust covered. I reached across the newspapers for the thing. It was stuck.

"Pull the door inward," I said.

Anita grabbed the handle and gave it a tug. The rusty hook moved slightly. I hit the shank hard with the end of the flashlight and it came open. We pushed the door outward. The moon shone on clean snow that was unmarked all the way into the woods. Melting ice dripped from naked tree branches. I looked down. There weren't any steps, just a four-foot drop.

"Shove these newspapers out, they'll break our fall," I said, then turned to see Anita clinging to the wall, vomiting. I gave the papers a shove and they barely moved. But one of my crutches fell over the top and out onto the snow. I shoved again and Anita, still gagging, was beside me on all fours with her shoulder against a stack. The papers, five or six at a time, thudded to the ground.

At length I sat on the last of the stack and let my legs dangle out the door, then shoved my butt off the ledge taking a couple of pages with me. I landed on newspapers, rolled off and ended up lying in the snow next to my crutch.

Anita was still in the doorway, her feet hanging. I stood and reached for her. She put her arms around my neck and I lifted her down, then retrieved the remaining crutch. Together we clung to the ledge, both breathing heavily.

Though our exit seemed to have taken hours, only a couple of minutes had passed. The bad guys could have been at the front door by now. I was hoping they figured we were trapped and that was why they were taking their time, or they thought that I had a gun and was lying in ambush.

"Here," I said, passing her a crutch. "You use one, I'll use the other. Let's try to head back to the main road, through that wooded area and up the hill beyond."

She nodded and took off in front of me. The crutch was the wrong height and she was having a hell of a time. She reached the first tree and stopped. I looked behind us. We were leaving a trail a mile wide.

"Look," Anita whispered. "A car."

I turned and saw the headlights sweep down the hill. "That the third guy?"

"Von." She nodded. "He's come back with the weight."

I watched a long black car come down the hill and into the parking lot. The cold was biting at my cheeks. My nose was running and my shoes, one hiking boot and one plastic with velcro, were soaked from the snow and mud.

Anita turned and proceeded hobbling.

My left foot was throbbing. I wiped my nose on the sleeve of my hunting jacket and followed her into the woods. The night had cleared and subtle moonlight left us in deep shadows. We couldn't see much beyond the beam of my small flashlight, which I used as little as possible because the light made us sitting ducks. The going was rough. I limped painfully over fallen branches and brush hidden in the clean wet blanket of snow.

"I just want you to know," I said between rasping breaths, "I haven't forgotten about that stunt with the phone."

Anita stopped for a moment. Her left eye had completely swollen shut. The nosebleed had slowed and there was this hunk of congealed blood on her upper lip. She couldn't stand completely upright and I towered over her.

"We cannot call the police," she lisped. "My father will make up everything to you."

"Not if I'm dead, he won't! Anyway, I don't believe your father is the governor."

She staggered on ahead of me. "Believe what you want."

We stopped dead at a steep incline. Anita turned to me her chest heaving. She wiped the blood from her upper lip onto her coat sleeve. "We're going to have to crawl up this bank."

"Jesus, it's eight or ten feet straight up."

The image of the Cardinal Apartments and the hill where I was wounded came to me. Why hadn't they discovered our absence? Why weren't they firing at us already? We'd be easy targets on our way to the top.

Anita was ahead of me. She threw herself on the slope and started crawling. I climbed up as far as I could, then gently knelt down to crawl the rest of the way. My sweatpants were immediately soaked with melting snow. I started moving upward, pulling myself along with the aid of fallen branches, clumps of winter grass, whatever I could grasp. I could hear branches breaking under my feet. Balancing the crutch was a big problem; more than once I slid backward, but the layer of fresh snow actually helped me get traction.

Near the top, I looked up to find Anita extending her hand toward me. I sucked in my breath, tossed the crutch I'd been dragging up over the ledge, then grasped Anita's hand and pushed with both feet. One moment I seemed to be dangling, Anita holding all my weight, and the next I was lying face down in a pile of snow at the top.

I rolled over and looked around. We were still a long way from the main road. In the distance, behind us, I could hear voices, men shouting in Spanish.

"What are they saying?"

"You don't want to know."

"What's up here?" I asked, my chest still heaving from the climb. "What can we use to help us? Are there neighbors?"

Anita jerked her chin toward a lone and dilapidated fishing shack. "It's empty. The owners come here in the summer when the weather is warm. We could break in, but with the tracks we're leaving, they'll find us."

"How are you doing?" I asked, gasping.

"Don't worry about me," she said, between gulps of air. "If I can't go on, leave me. I'd do it to you."

"You have done it to me."

"Right." With that she stood and wobbled toward the cabin.

"Where's the other crutch?"

"I lost it," she said over her shoulder.

And that's when I looked back. Through the trees I could barely see the back door of Jimmy's Bait Shop. A man stood with the light behind him. Little more than a sinister shadow, he hopped from the back door to the ground. With a rush of adrenaline, I stood and started limping onward.

Anita tried the door to the cabin, and, when that failed, attempted to look in the front window. There was a lean-to type car port. I ducked under it to see if it held anything useful. In the beam from my flashlight I pulled a tarp off an old rotary push-mower. The earth was dry and the area smelled of gas and oil. A ten-gallon gas can peeked out from under a second tarp that covered something in the corner shadows.

I yanked the tarp back and couldn't believe my eyes. There, leaning on its kickstand, was a 1953 Indian. The gas tank and fenders were rusty. It looked like it hadn't been ridden for awhile. Probably the guy thought he'd restore it someday.

My dad had a 1949 Indian, an old bike even then. He taught me how to ride when I was twelve. I'd ridden the bike around and around the outside of our house in the summer, actually have a track, and must have driven the neighbors crazy. Why was I thinking about that now? Of course, I hadn't seen an Indian since Dad sold his.

"Will it run?" Anita's voice came from behind me.

"I doubt it."

"But you can ride it." Anita's voice was twinged with excitement. "Is there a key there?"

"It doesn't use a key," I said, moving closer. "It's a kick start." I shone the flashlight on the spark plug, and scraped some of the crap off with a fingernail.

"What is a kick start?" she whispered close to my ear.

I pointed to the side and said, "That thing. You put all your weight on it and kick it down. That turns over the motor, and if you do it hard enough, and if the spark plug is still hot, and if there aren't any serious mechanical problems, the engine will start." I reached for the clutch and gave it a squeeze. The cable was rusty but it seemed to work. I was trying to remember the sequence of the gears: two up one down, one down two up, three up, where was neutral? Damn. "What do you think?" Anita asked.

I took hold of the handlebars and rocked the bike back and forth. The fork was unlocked. I could the hear the swishing of at least some gasoline. The lid to the gas tank was stuck and I tapped the butt of the flashlight against the cap and tried again. Several seconds later it came off. I shone the flashlight inside. There was less than a quarter of a tank. God, if I couldn't start it we'd end up at the bottom of the river with the others. Two or four bodies, what difference would it make?

"Check that gas can." It would burn regular or a mix of no-lead and motor oil.

Anita reached for the can and tried to lift it. "There's a little in here."

"Scoot it over here."

She dragged the can across the earth floor.

I opened it and did my best, without a funnel, to hit the tank, spilling almost as much as went inside. I coughed at the smell of the fumes. My head was pounding, and that took my mind off the pain in my foot.

"Can you start it?" Anita's high-pitched voice was grating on me.

I said, "I'll try," though to tell the truth I had doubts. I moved things away from the bike so I could get it turned around. Anita caught on quickly and helped. We were both panting by the time I straddled the Indian and placed my boot on the pedal.

"If it starts," I told Anita, "get on behind me and hold on tight."

She moved to my side.

"Stand back," I warned her, and she did.

One problem would be placing my weight and the weight of the bike on my left foot. I didn't see how it could hurt more than it did already. I squeezed the clutch, turned the throttle to what I hoped was half-way open, threw my weight up and came down hard on the starter pedal. I could feel the spot where the motor turned over and sputtered out. I tried it again. This time the engine rolled a couple of times, then nothing. Without waiting, I jumped on the starter pedal again and heard the ka-chug ka-chug as the motor caught. I turned the throttle open and heard the engine roar to life.

The noise vibrated off the sides of the fishing shack. Bikes don't sound like this anymore, I thought, not even my Harley. I tried to feel the gears with my plastic and velcro covered left foot. Maybe it was one down and three up. I still wasn't sure.

Anita struggled to get on behind me and I reached to help her. She put both arms around my waist.

"For your feet," I said, pointing to the passenger foot rests.

She nodded and I rolled the bike forward and let out the clutch slowly, giving it too much gas, to compensate for the confusion about the gears. I had to look for the headlight switch and when I found it, it wasn't very bright. I'd be glad to get back on the well-lit airport road.

By the time I rolled out of the carport, one of the El Salvadorans was crawling up and over the snowy bank we'd scaled earlier, and I saw the headlights from the long black car speeding up the rutted road toward us.

"Hold on," I yelled over my shoulder, and started up the snow and mud-packed back road.

I had trouble moving very fast because of the bumps and ruts. Again I thought the snow probably helped. The tires on the Indian were a little low and it handled sluggishly, but I could manage. When I gunned the motor and turned onto Cameron Road, I looked back.

"Where are our friends?" I called to Anita.

"Couldn't make it up the hill," she said, close to my ear. "Last I saw they were in the ditch, one pushing while the other one rocked it."

I was so relieved I almost laughed. Of course Salvadorans wouldn't know how to drive in this weather.

We rode toward town. Anita pressed her face against my back and clung to me, sobbing. She needed a doctor. I thought I should take her to the hospital emergency ward. They'd probably call the police, but at least she'd get medical attention. Then it occurred to me that I could be arrested for stealing the Explorer and the Indian, too. However, my friend Michael used to be a registered nurse before he went on disability. He'd wanted to go back to work since he started the cocktail, but was too humiliated by the Krixovan hump. Michael could at least look at Anita's surface injuries. If nothing was broken, he might be able to fix her up. I'd be able to see my own trailer from his when and if Georgia called the police, later in the morning. I wondered if she was up yet.

The wind blew against my face as we rode south on the airport road toward the trailer court. The sky was dark, the full moon set low in the sky, and the morning stars were cold and bright. As I turned toward Michael's trailer, the close escape gave me a heady sense of exhilaration.

Chapter Fourteen

A light was on in Michael's kitchen and, to my surprise, when I pulled the Indian into the drive next to his car, he opened the door and flipped on the porch light. I lowered the throttle and cut the gas. The motor chugged a couple of times and died, leaving a silence that rang in my ears.

Michael called from the open door. "Honey, whatja doing up so early?"

Anita hadn't relaxed her grip; she was clutching my stomach. I gently pulled her arms free and whispered, "You have to get off first. Can you do it?"

She groaned.

"Help me," I said to Michael. "This woman is hurt."

I watched Michael shove his bare feet into the Doc Martins that must have been sitting by the door and come out without a coat. He wore a pair of champagne-colored silk pajamas. If the situation hadn't been so serious, I might have commented on the fashion statement. But I was busy keeping the bike erect.

I heard him behind me say to Anita, "Put your arm around my shoulder."

As she leaned toward him, the bike was harder to hold, but he had her off in a few seconds and was helping her up the three steps into his trailer by the time I put the kickstand down.

I opened the door and limped inside. Michael was making Anita comfortable in the recliner. He turned in my direction. "What in the hell happened to you?"

I shrugged. "Can I use your bathroom?"

"Take off your shoes," he said.

We both looked at my feet.

At length he said, "Oh, the hell with it, go on."

I was sitting on the edge of the bathtub after my shower, wrapped in a colorful beach towel and soaking my feet in cold water, when Michael tapped on the door and came in. He had changed into a nylon jogging suit and tennis shoes. He looked at the pile of filthy clothes and the wet, mud-covered velcro cast in a stack behind the door and passed me a mug of hot Viennese-roast coffee.

"Let me see them now," he said, bending over the bathtub.

I lifted my feet one at a time out of the water for his inspection.

"Your surgery is healing nicely," he said examining the jagged purple scar. "Can you wiggle your toes?"

I tried, and everything on that foot seemed to move, though it hurt like blazes.

"I don't like the color of that little toe on the right," he said. "Put that foot back in the water awhile longer."

"How's Anita?"

"She bathed in my bathroom and is resting on the bed in the guest room."

"In the sunken tub?" I didn't think Anita would have the strength to get in and out of the opulent pink tub with the jet streams. Though I could see how it would help her bruises and aching muscles.

Michael nodded. "I examined her when she got out. I gave her an ice pack to cover her eye. I don't think her jaw is broken—maybe the nose is , but I can't tell. She's taken a pretty bad beating, and I don't like the looks of the bruises around her rib cage. She needs x-rays. I should call an ambulance."

"What did she say to that suggestion?"

"She didn't care much for it." Michael put the lid to the toilet seat down and sat across from me. "Does this have anything to do with your getting shot and losing your cab?"

I nodded.

"There's a black-and-white down at your trailer now. Trudy, what in the hell are you involved in?"

"The police are down the street?"

Michael chuckled. "Georgia has been standing out in the snow cussing like a sailor since before dawn. Does she have something to do with this? I thought you guys were through."

I took a long swallow of the coffee. "It's a complicated story."

"Well, Miss Thing, I didn't figure it was simple. Are you screwing the señorita in the guest room?"

I shook my head. "Don't even go there."

I looked at Michael's sunken blue eyes and tried to find a place to start. Should I tell him about the lesbian policewoman, the Salvadorans, the governor, or Georgia's new Explorer first? What could I say to him that would make any sense? My left foot was throbbing and the right was partially numb. Even with my second cup of coffee I was yawning. Michael certainly had a right to know as much as I did. But at the moment I wasn't sure I knew much of anything, except that Anita was a shifty little number, and Georgia was never going to forget this stunt. Finally, I decided to start with the day before. I told him about Georgia's new Explorer and the dinner and the sex.

"So, are you guys back together?"

I shook my head. "Definitely not."

I told him about letting Alex out in the middle of the night and the answering machine. "I think I wanted to drive that Explorer more than I wanted to rescue Anita Alvarez."

Michael pulled a cigarette pack from his jacket pocket and tapped out a Kool. He held the pack toward me, and I took one. What could a cigarette make worse at this point? He lit his own and then mine.

"So, how do you know Anita?" he asked.

I shrugged. "She caught a ride with me a couple of months ago. Then the police came to see me and I remembered her." I told him how I found the key and came back into town to meet her and discovered Lotty dead on the toilet. The story of the Cardinal Apartments and the El Salvadorans just spilled out. By the time we had finished our cigarettes, Michael was sitting on the stool with his head in his hands.

"Let me see that right foot again," he finally said.

I held the foot out of the water.

"A little better, but you should stay off of it for a few hours. Why don't you stretch out in my bed and take a nap?"

"Will Anita be all right?" I asked, suddenly realizing how tired I was.

"I gave her a couple of my painkillers. She should sleep for a while in peace. But she needs more care than I can give her. She needs to be examined by a doctor."

I nodded to the pile of muddy clothes. "Hand me my hunting jacket, will you?"

He picked it up with his thumb and forefinger, his pinky in the air like the jacket was roach-infested.

My wallet was in the inside pocket. I pulled the card out from the slot behind my driver's license and passed it to him. "Call this number and ask for Barry Carmichael. Tell him that she's here and needs a doctor."

"This her family?"

"In a sense."

Michael wrapped my left foot in an Ace bandage, helped me into his bedroom, situated my right foot under a heating pad and pulled a cover

over me. Though sunlight streamed in his bedroom window, I fell asleep almost immediately.

I woke to the smell of bacon frying and hobbled into the hall. Anita Alvarez was fully dressed, sitting at the kitchen table, eating. She wore a gray sweatshirt and a pair of faded jeans rolled up at the cuffs—Michael's fit her nicely. I, on the other hand, was a few sizes larger than Michael and was stuck in the beach towel.

"Want a sandwich?" Michael called.

Anita looked up at me. Her dark hair was slicked back, and I was surprised all over again by the bruises on her face. Some of the swelling was down, but she still looked like hell. She asked, "How are you feeling?"

I answered, "Suicidal."

And, by God, she laughed.

Michael hurried into the hallway behind the kitchen and pulled open the door to the clothes dryer. "Here," he said, "this was all I could find." He tossed my nightshirt and sweatpants to me. They were still warm and smelled like a fresh dryer sheet. "I'll loan you a pair of my socks."

I looked down at my feet, one Ace-bandaged and one bare. I was damned if I was going to go back for my crutches, wherever they were. I slipped into the bathroom and dressed in my clean clothes. When I came out a few minutes later Anita was standing by the front door.

"Thanks for calling Barry," she said. "He's sent a car for me."

I ducked my head and looked out the window. A silver Buick sat in the drive behind Michael's car. Anita opened the door, hesitated, and turned back to me. "Thanks for your help, Trudy. I owe you one."

"You owe me two," I corrected her. "But don't call me again."

Her attempt at a smile looked comical, with her face all swollen and purple. She reached one arm around my shoulder and gave me a short but fierce hug. She whispered, "Thank you, friend," and then she was gone.

Through the lacy kitchen window I saw that the driver of the Buick was an older woman, older than Anita, anyway—I couldn't say if she was older than me. She had a fashionable, severely cut head full of short white hair. Anita got in the passenger side of the car. They exchanged comments of some nature. The woman covered her mouth (maybe to stifle a scream) and I watched Anita pull the white-haired woman into her arms.

"Who is that?" Michael, at my side, startled me. "Mother, lover, what?"

"Beats the hell out of me." I shook my head. "I think the question is, why didn't she call her last night? Why me?"

I watched the older woman disentangle herself from Anita's embrace and put the Buick in reverse. The big silver car rolled backward into the street. I could see my own trailer at the end of the road and wondered if Georgia was there waiting. Surely she to had work today. So did I, as a matter of fact. I was supposed to be driving. Betty must be furious.

"I called the number you gave me," said Michael. "Maybe this is Carmichael's secretary."

"Could be, I guess."

"Come on," said Michael. "Your sandwich is getting cold."

"What time is it?"

"Almost three."

I had slept longer than I'd thought. My mind was less foggy, but my body was stiff and achy. Just as I sat down at the table the phone rang.

Michael reached for it. "Yeah?"

The bacon was warm and crunchy and good. I reached for the glass of milk, my empty stomach pressing me on.

Michael turned and passed the phone to me. "For you," he said.

Why would Michael, knowing what he knew, tell anyone I was here, I wondered, tentatively putting the receiver to my ear.

"Hello?"

"Trudy," said Pinky, "Is that a 1953 Indian Roadster Chief you rode in on this morning?"

I laughed. "Don't see many Indians these days. What were you doing up so early?"

"What you doing at Michael's? Georgia's been over here looking for you."

"For one thing, I've been avoiding Georgia."

"The police were with her."

"And the police."

"I've been avoiding them too."

"Mind if I come down and take a closer look at that bike?"

"Would you let Alex out for me?"

"Already did," said Pinky. "He's here with me."

I wanted to see Alex, and I wanted to see Pinky, and I made another of a series of mistakes. I told him to come on down. Within half an hour one of the city's finest was reading me my rights as I stood before him handcuffed. Georgia knew I'd be in touch with Pinky, if I was still alive, to make sure Alex was cared for. They had waited around the corner and simply followed him to me.

Chapter Fifteen

By the time I was settled in a holding cell at the county jail, still in my nightshirt and sweatpants with no underwear, I was exhausted. I stared at the beige wall phone, knowing I had to call someone eventually. Michael had loaned me a pair of socks and hightop tennis shoes that were actually comfortable. The shoes were the only thing that had gone well in the last twenty-four hours, and when I got to jail they were the first thing taken away from me. Supper slid through a slot in the beige metal door surprisingly early, a bologna sandwich on dry white bread, greasy potato chips, two carrot sticks and watery tea. There was a large horseshoe desk just outside my door, and the other cells, which were almost all full on a weeknight, circled around it. All the holding cells had huge windows that enabled the staff at the desk to watch the inmates. However, from the inside, most of the glass was a shadowy mirror. I picked at dinner, then set the tray on the floor and stretched out on a hard extension from the wall that passed as a cot. With no blanket or pillow, I pulled my arms inside my nightshirt and lay on my stomach to keep warm.

They would drag me before a judge in the morning, and if I didn't have someone to post bail, I'd be moved upstairs to the regular county jail until trial. I ran through my choices as I stared at my pathetic reflection across the room. I could call my mother. She might come up with bail money, but what she'd put me through when we walked out the door would be worse than sitting in jail. Pinky would be willing to help, though I doubted if he had the resources to get the money. There were, I knew, professional bail-bondsmen; maybe he or Michael could get one—though neither he nor Pinky had any experience in this sort of thing, and I had told them not to do anything until they heard from me. I sure didn't want Pinky to call my Mom. I needed someone who got arrested once in a while and knew the routine. I could call Betty, and probably should if I still wanted my job. Years ago, Betty had bailed out their son a couple of times, against Ralph's wishes, when the kid was arrested on DUI charges. The boy was in AA these days, and he counseled teens with drug problems. Betty would be at home by now, but what would I say to her—how could I explain this mess?

I was charged with theft of the Explorer and criminal damage to property over three hundred dollars—way over. The cops were still waiting to hear from the owner of the Indian. I had been told I would be appointed a lawyer if I couldn't afford one, and I was sure I couldn't afford one if I continued to sit in jail.

I don't know how I dozed off with my mind spinning, but I woke to the sound of a woman hollering, "Billy, you get yo' ass down here."

I blinked my eyes. She was a black woman in net stockings and a tight red dress. She held the phone to her ear, her back to me.

"Honey, you got the money. I gave you the money. Remember? Don' you tell me you ain't got it."

I rolled to a sitting position. The clock over the horseshoe-shaped guard station read six-thirty-five. The cell smelled of some kind of flowery perfume that I found nauseating.

"Call Marcus then. No. No. You call him. I got to call collect and Marcus don't take no collect calls." She hesitated and listened, then stomped her foot. "Billy, you got to call him. They done put me in a cell with some nasty-looking white lady. They put me upstairs if I don't have bail in the morning. If I'm in jail, I can't work tomorrow night. Then where we be? Who gonna buy that rock candy you like so good?"

Her voice became a suave purr. "One hundred dollars, baby. Just bring it down. I make it worth your time. You know I will."

The woman hung up and turned toward me. If my being awake surprised her, she didn't show it. She jerked her head toward the phone and said, "Men, huh?"

I nodded like I really knew what she meant. What made her think women were better?

"So, what they got you in for, sweetie?"

I cleared my throat and said, "Grand theft auto, criminal damage of property and a couple of others I don't remember."

The woman whistled. "They put me in with a bad criminal."

I squared my shoulders as if there were some competition and I had won first prize. "I'm Trudy Thomas," I said.

"Lavonne Winters," she said. "They feed you supper yet?"

"Quite a while ago."

"Damn, I'm hungry."

There was nothing I could do about it, so I stayed quiet.

"I had four hundred dollars they took off me last time I was busted. But tonight I was just getting started. I ax that undercover cop if he was the law and he said no. Lying som'a bitch. I wonder if that's legal?"

"I think they can say whatever they want."

"Well, what good is that?"

I shook my head.

Lavonne scooted onto the other hard bench and pulled her knees up. A closer look revealed the red dress to be worn and held with safety pins in two places. There were holes in her net stockings. Her hair was slicked back in a short ponytail like a WNBA player. Up close I could see the tired lines in her face; she was older than I had originally guessed.

"You make your call yet?" she asked.

I shook my head. "I don't know who to call."

"Honey, you better call someone. You don't want to go upstairs."

I sighed and didn't answer.

At length she said, "You got a boyfriend?"

"No."

"Family?"

"Just my mom," I admitted. "I can't call my mother about bail money."

"You'll have to go before a judge in the morning. What kind of a car did you boost?"

"Explorer."

She whistled. "You steal cars very often? I mean, you work with a ring or something? Maybe they could bail you out."

"I didn't really steal the Explorer. I just borrowed it. I was going to bring it back."

Lavonne chuckled. "Don't say that in front of the judge, honey. They heard it before."

The knot in my stomach tightened.

Lavonne stood and paced the cell. I stretched out again on my belly and closed my eyes. I dreamed about Alex—walking Alex around the trailer park. Stopping at the corner and visiting the little girl with the lavender bike that matched my cab. I dreamed about Georgia, red-faced and angry. I dreamed that Anita Alvarez asked me to go to El Salvador with her and I went.

The sound of breakfast sliding in through the metal door woke me. Lavonne was curled up, still asleep. The toilet and sink were partitioned off by a wall about three feet high. No one could see your bottom half, but it was humiliating enough anyway. I used the john and washed up with cheap soap and paper towels.

"What time is it?" Lavonne said, stretching her arms over her head and yawning.

The guard station clock was behind her. "Six-forty," I told her.

"How come you up?"

I nodded at our breakfast while drying my hands.

Lavonne rolled to a sitting position and stood. She staggered slightly as she reached for a Styrofoam coffee cup. I picked up the opposite tray and took it to my bench.

"You make your call yet?" Lavonne asked.

I shook my head. "I'll call my mother after I finish this coffee."

Lavonne tipped the coffee up and swallowed. "You get used to cold coffee in here. After a few times it ain't that bad."

She was right. The coffee was cold. On the tray was an overripe banana and a glazed doughnut. I polished them off quickly and went to the phone.

Mom would be just getting up for work. I was humiliated to have to call collect, being forty-seven years old and all. What if she wouldn't accept the charges? After four rings the machine picked up. I hung up, tried again and got the machine again. I decided she must be in the shower and waited five minutes. Still no answer. Damn.

At seven-thirty sharp they came and handcuffed us for the trip to court. I still hadn't reached anyone and was resigned to going to jail until I could. The matron who cuffed Lavonne told her Billy was outside, and they took her away. She called, "Good luck with the judge, Trudy Thomas," over her shoulder.

I said, "Thanks," then put my hands on my head as instructed.

Outside of my cell they helped me with my shoes, and I joined about a dozen people who were headed to court. We walked single file through the bowels of the County Building, an armed turnkey at both ends of the line. We passed empty offices and open storage rooms. We were packed into an elevator so tight that I had good-sized men on all sides pressed against me. We had all slept in our clothes and the smell of body odor was strong. On the ninth floor the elevator stopped and we exited into a large hallway that on one side was lined with polished doors to the courtrooms. Across from them were huge windows that looked out over town below. The morning was overcast and all that was left of the snow were spots where it had been piled high by the plows and covered with black soot from the traffic.

What I assumed were family members waited on a bench and stood to follow us in as we marched single file into the courtroom. We sat in the first row on what reminded me of church pews. My handcuffs were uncomfortable, and I was relieved when the two uniforms who brought us up started at each end of the row and removed them. Even the big tough-looking guys rubbed their wrists a little.

The guy sitting next to me, a thirty-something overweight black man in a white T-shirt and house slippers, introduced himself as Herschel Johnson. My thoughts were really elsewhere. I wished I'd reached my mom and had her find a lawyer. The courtroom was intimidating. The other benches filled up as Herschel told me he'd been arrested for holding up a convenience store. He hadn't even gotten any money and thought the judge might go light on him under the circumstances. Herschel was the father of four children by four different women; his fifth baby was due any time. That was what he was doing in the Happy Hen Pantry at three in the morning, looking for a quart of strawberry ice cream. He couldn't tell his girlfriend he didn't have the money. He figured the clerk was just a little bit of a thing—five foot tall and a hundred pounds at best. But the streetwise night shift clerk had hit the alarm, and as Herschel tried to leave the store, she threw a large tape dispenser at his head. No one knew those things were made of cement until it broke in three pieces as Herschel stumbled out the door into the police officer's arms. He seemed to be testing the story on me, and I made sympathetic noises while trying to come up with a story that explained my behavior.

I heard a familiar voice and turned in time to see Georgia staring at me from across the room. She was next to a young woman who I soon would learn was an assistant state's attorney. My head throbbed and sweat ran down the side of my face. Georgia was serious about this.

After a long wait, a judge walked up to the bench and was seated. He was very young with a thick shock of dark hair and rimless glasses. I knew he had to be over twenty-one, but he didn't look it. He started shuffling papers around, then spoke to an old black woman who called the court to order.

Judge Marcolleni called on us left to right. The first guy who went before the bench had been picked up on an outstanding warrant because a previous judgement hadn't been paid. The guy didn't have the money and the judge sent him to jail.

Herschel went up next. The judge asked if he had an attorney.

"No sir, Judge, I don't." Herschel sounded apologetic and respectful.

"These are very serious charges, Mr. Johnson," said the judge. "Were you explained your rights?"

"I know this is serious, Judge," said Herschel, "but I don't want a lawyer." Then he started the story about all the children and the one on the way. He ended up with thirty days in jail and a one thousand dollar fine.

I was longing for my mother by the time they called my name. I stood and walked forward, as did Georgia and the assistant state's attorney.

"Which of you is Miss Thomas?" the judge asked before I could turn around.

"I am, Your Honor." Would anyone who hadn't spent the night in jail come to court in a nightshirt?

From behind me a woman's voice said, "Rosalyn Richards for the defendant, Your Honor."

I gaped at her, and then looked at Georgia who was turning red. I wanted to shrug my shoulders to let her know that I didn't know what was going on either. But she looked away.

The judge read the charges.

Rosalyn said, "We plead not guilty."

My head whipped around so fast a muscle pulled tight in my neck.

They talked about bond and my attorney said I wasn't a flight risk and had strong ties to the community. My bail was set, a court date was assigned, and we were dismissed.

I turned to the woman. "Who the hell are you? I don't have money for bond."

The woman smiled and nodded. "It will be taken care of."

I said, "Georgia is pretty mad. She'll want my hide."

"Oh, don't worry about coming back to court," said Rosalyn, pushing her snow white hair off her forehead. "We will settle out of court."

She said more but I wasn't listening. I finally recognized Rosalyn Richards. She was the woman in the silver Buick who had picked up Anita Alvarez at Michael's trailer the previous afternoon.

Chapter Sixteen

The streets were crappy and the sides of the silver Buick were splattered with dried salt and slush. I had a thousand questions for Rosalyn Richards, but found myself sitting in the passenger seat in silence. When she turned west on Jefferson, I realized she wasn't taking me home.

"Where are we going?"

Rosalyn smiled at me. "Anita wants to talk to you."

"Is she all right?"

"Yes," said Rosalyn. "Thanks to you."

"Well, I don't especially want to talk to her."

"It will only take a few moments," said Rosalyn. "Why don't you count it as time you would have been in jail, had I not come to your rescue?"

I considered that. "You know what? I would be working right now if I hadn't tried to help Anita."

"That may be," admitted Ms. Richards. "But you did get involved and now you need our help."

"Who are you anyway?" I asked. "Who is Anita?" Not that I planned on believing anything she told me.

"I am Rosalyn Richards, a senior partner with the Chicago firm of Barry, Wright, and Richards. Anita is my niece."

"You're the aunt who raised her?"

Rosalyn pulled up to a stoplight, the last one before the road left town. She turned to me. "She told you about that?"

I nodded. Michael's tennis shoe was tight; my foot was throbbing and I wondered if it was swelling. I didn't like the idea of driving out of town with this woman, no matter who she was. "Please take me home."

Rosalyn put the car in motion and said, "You'll be home this afternoon. You'll have everything you need. By tomorrow you will be able to put this all behind you."

"Could you turn the heat up?" I asked, hugging myself.

Rosalyn adjusted the heater and the car grew warmer. My mud-caked hunting jacket was still at Michael's. Though the temperature was in the forties, I shivered in my nightshirt. We drove in silence. I watched out the window, remembering when my father used to read to me about Hansel and Gretel dropping bread crumbs. But I knew the area, at least for the first several miles. When we turned off the main road, I grew worried. We were on some little rural route for a long time; then between a stubble field and a hog farm we turned onto a winding road, and I was lost.

We slowed at a rural mailbox and turned onto a lane that was covered with loose white rock that crunched under the Buick's tires. Trees lined the lane and the winter bare limbs gave the path an ominous feel, like the approach to the house of Usher in the old Vincent Price film. We came to a clearing,but there was no rundown castle looming in the gray sky. The house was a long, low, fifties-style ranch, with lots of windows. We pulled to a stop near the front walk and Rosalyn got out.

I swung the passenger door open and limped behind her to the front door. The house was unusual. I would call it nineteenth century modern. There were antiques mixed with soft, overstuffed contemporary furniture. French doors led toward other parts of the house, but the main section in which we entered was a large single room that served as a kitchen, breakfast alcove, dining room and family room. A long, rectangular, black lacquer dining room table sat near the center of everything, surrounded by no less than ten antique chairs with plenty of room on either side. The blinds were drawn but the room was light and large. The focal point in the family room area was a small fireplace with a bronze hood. The colors were earth tones—gold, rust and beige lots of shades of beige. Everything had the polished look of a good maid. A few book shelves, a rich alabaster carpet, and Van Gogh prints finished off the effect. I scanned the room carefully and didn't see Anita.

A knee-sized mutt came running from another room. She stared at me anxiously while Rosalyn leaned and scratched her back.

"This is Trixie," said Rosalyn. "She owns this place. Just lets me stay here if I keep bringing home the dog food."

I laughed in spite of my nerves and exhaustion.

Rosalyn indicated the family room and said, "Have a seat. I'll get Anita."

Trixie followed me past the shining black table to an olive recliner. When I sat down and extended the foot rest, the dog leapt into my lap. I scratched her back as I'd seen Rosalyn do, and waited.

After what seemed like a long time, Trixie's tail started thumping against my leg. The dog looked toward the dining room, and, like an apparition, Anita appeared there. She wore faded jeans and an off-white, cable-knit sweater. The swelling had gone down around her eyes, but the bright purple color still made me flinch.

"I see you've met the lady of the house," said Anita, limping toward me.

"How are you feeling?" I asked.

She placed her hand on the arm of the couch and lowered herself to a sitting position.

"I've been better."

"Why do you need to see me?"

"I want to make sure everything is taken care of for you."

"Well, I want to go home, take a long hot shower and sleep. I want to go back to work and forget I ever met you."

"And Georgia, you want to take care of her problems, too?"

"I have a feeling I'll be paying for my sins against Georgia for a long time."

Anita smiled. "Michael told me about Georgia. It's really kind of funny when you look at it from a distance."

"Yeah, very funny." My tone was serious, but my face betrayed me, and I tried to suppress a smile.

Anita reached over and scratched Trixie's ears. "And you," she said. "What do you need? How is your foot?"

"Feels good to put it up," I said. "Look, I'll let you pay Georgia off or whatever you want to do. I want to go home and scratch the back of my own dog."

Anita reached for my arm and looked square into my eyes. "Thank you, Trudy."

Trixie jumped down from my lap and up on the couch next to Anita. I wasn't about to say no problem, but I have to admit I felt a little better.

At length I asked, "Why didn't you call Rosalyn from the river? Why me?"

"I left a message for Aunt Roz, but you returned my call first. Pardon me if I decided not to wait. I needed to get the hell out of there."

I nodded. "Who is taking me home?"

Anita smiled. "Are you ready to go?"

"You're damn right I am."

"Aunt Roz has to catch a plane to Chicago in two hours. She'll drop you at home on the way to the airport. In the meantime, can I get you anything? You want some coffee? How about some lunch? I know they don't feed you very well in jail."

I did feel hungry. My joints ached, my foot throbbed and my throat felt raspy. "Something hot to drink or eat would be great."

Anita stood. "Come on, you can sit in the kitchen while I warm something up. I'm hungry, too."

I stood and made my way around the corner to the kitchen and sat at a breakfast bar that separated the dining room from the kitchen proper. Anita placed a mug of coffee in front of me along with some sugar and milk. Then she took a can out of the cupboard and opened it with an electric opener. Soon the smell of tomato soup filled the air.

"So, is this were you were raised?"

Anita shrugged. "Here and there; Aunt Roz has a place in Chicago, too."

"And she is your father's sister?"

Anita nodded and set a bowl and spoon in front of me and a plate of cheese and crackers between us.

I could see out the kitchen window. An in-ground pool sat drained. Beyond that was a two-car garage with wooden steps that led up the side to a door—maybe a second floor apartment door I couldn't tell. Beyond the back lawn was a row of trees that separated the yard from a stubble field dotted with melting snow. I could see a very long way; it was like that on the prairie, flat earth all the way to the horizon. I could see everything but what the heck I was doing there.

"Have I ever lied to you?" I heard someone say and realized it was me.

Anita studied me and finally said, "How should I know?"

"Well, I haven't. And I've helped you."

Anita set her soup spoon down and tilted her head. "What are you getting at?"

"I want you to level with me. I think I've earned at least that much. I've been shot in the foot, my ex-girlfriend's truck is in the Sangamon River and I've spent my first night in jail. Now, what in the hell is going on? What are you involved in? You tell me it's some crusade to find the murderer of your brother, and Toni Matulis says she thinks you're involved in the drug trade."

"The policewoman said that?"

"She did."

Anita squirmed on her stool and checked her watch. "It's a long story, but you are correct; you've earned the right to hear it. Finish your soup and crackers—we'll take our coffee into the other room."

We ate in silence. The soup was the perfect temperature and I finished mine quickly. My mind was oddly quiet. I was tired and my stomach was full and warm. I carried a fresh mug of coffee back to the olive-colored recliner; Anita sat on the couch with Trixie and began. "It is true that members of my family in Central America became involved with drugs and

I would like to help them, but not to continue doing that."

My stomach felt tight. This was about drugs. "So your first story was a lie?"

Anita looked at me sincerely. "Oh no, amiga, that was only the beginning of the story. My stepfather did well with his coffee crop for a long time. I was happy that my mother, three half brothers and my sister were well off. Carlos became a doctor. Grace joined a convent. My brothers Miguel and Manuel went to the university to study horticulture. Miguel married a girl from a neighboring farm and they have two small sons now. Manuel stayed and worked at home.

"But life in the country is hard. Cities have poverty, but the resource-ful can survive. Farmers in the country work hard and if the weather is bad they starve. Of course, as in North America, the farmer gets only a small wedge of the profit pie.

"As you probably know, the price of coffee is way down. Too much coffee in the market. My family was in serious trouble. Manuel started working for the men moving drugs through our country from Colombia. My feelings about that at the time were mixed. You can buy a lot of coffee for what it costs to buy an ounce of cocaine. There is plenty of money to pay bribes. The mountain farms are far from the eyes of the authorities. Manual even decided to risk growing coca. Several months ago my younger sister Grace visited me; she told me that Manuel was living in fear, hiding in the mountains. I guess his new bosses didn't like the competition."

I let this new information sink in. I'd seen drugs ruin people's lives, had a friend or two dead. I think most baby boomers have. I sure didn't want any part of bringing the poison into the country.

Anita didn't seem to be watching me. She was staring at the burnished bronze hood on the fireplace. The room was quiet except for the soft sound of her voice. She stopped for a moment and turned to me. I waited, watch-ing her, and at last said, "What?"

"Oh, I am thinking."

"About how much to say?" I asked.

"Yes, of course. This gets very private."

That made me angry. "Do I have to remind you the price I've paid for the whole truth?" Even as I said it, I wondered how true her story was.

Anita broke my thoughts. "So you must see that my family is suffering from their involvement in drugs. But there is another reason I would not help drug dealers. Back east, in law school, I had a lover who used drugs. Everyone used something or other from time to time to study late or work and go to classes. But Trinket's addiction was more than that. She was a brilliant Asian-American girl. As the only child, her parents expected great things from her. One holiday weekend we had planned to stay at school and enjoy the time alone. We got high together. Her heart gave out."

"Oh…Anita."

Her eyes clouded and she seemed to bite back tears, but immediately shook the emotions off and said in a level voice, "Yes, a terrible event. It stirred up memories of my sister Theresa at the river in Honduras. I was hospitalized from the emotional impact. No one understood my attachment to my roommate. They expected grief, but not so much grief. I could not believe she was dead—we were just having a good time."

"I'm sorry."

"I tell you this not for sympathy, but to explain why I felt a connection to you. That day in the cab, I knew we had one thing in common. Some people I can tell."

As if I'd ever tried to hide it. But I hadn't seen her as a lesbian; she was more feminine than a lipstick femme.

Rosalyn Richards appeared in the kitchen. "I see you girls have eaten," she called to us.

"Yes, Aunt Roz."

Rosalyn walked toward us. "Are you all through talking?"

Anita stood slowly and smiled at me, her eyes glistening. "We are done for now. Thank you, Trudy."

As I stood she came toward me, planted a little kiss on my cheek and whispered, "I will be in touch. You only have half the story and I promise sometime I'll tell you the rest."

"So there is a place where this all connects?"

"Oh, yes."

At that point I believed her. I hugged her awkwardly and could feel her heart racing like a bird's, against my chest.

When Toni Matulis called me later that night, I lied to her. I admit it wasn't a smart thing to do. I was tired, and I had cramps. There's nothing like sex with an ex-lover, getting chased through the woods scared for your life, and spending a night in jail to get a period started. I just wanted to drink some warm milk, crawl in bed with a water bottle, and put the whole damn mess behind me. Anita's problems were hers. Whether she was on the side of the good guys or the bad guys had nothing to do with me. Toni had been taken off the Alvarez case, anyway. None of what had happened the night before was on her beat.

Though Toni tried to argue, in the end she got angry and hung up.

PART TWO

Chapter Seventeen

Some time passed before I saw Anita Alvarez again. The holidays were followed by winter months. I heard from an old bar buddy that Georgia was driving a new Jeep, Grand Cherokee—black, with leather seat covers. The Jeep was only a part of the deal Rosalyn Richards negotiated to get the charges against me dropped. My hospital bills were paid through Rosalyn's office. As Anita had promised, the problems went away, costing little more than frequent night terrors. I dreamed all winter that I was running through the snow with a monster behind me, and my legs only moved in slow motion. When the ice on the Sangamon River thawed, I heard the Explorer was towed out. I'd thought the police might find a body or two at that time, but they hadn't.

Pinky came down with a bad case of the flu that turned into pneumonia in March, and I spent evenings sitting at the hospital with him. A social worker talked to me about a nursing home, or getting a woman to come in and help him. I hadn't realized he was that sick, and the thought of losing him reached down inside me and touched a dark spot of fear I hadn't known existed. Of course, no one had said I was going to lose him, as Michael was quick to point out. Having a friend who is a nurse comes in handy. I arranged with Betty to drive nights for a while longer so I could help Pinky during the day. A private care giver, a friend of Michael's who needed the work, stayed evenings.

Pinky came home from the hospital in a cab with me the last week of March. He'd lost weight. His breathing seemed labored, even with the portable oxygen canister. But when he saw the trailer, the Weber grill and his old Harley 74 under the carport, his face brightened.

I helped him into the trailer. I could have lifted him, but he insisted I pull him in his wheelchair, thudding it backwards up the steps. Pinky's trailer was older than mine and had a personality all its own. Most of his stuff was the original veneer—rust and beige-colored couch and chairs and pressed wood end tables painted an oak color, with a surface that you couldn't damage with a ball peen hammer. The kitchen had matching copper tone appliances that had seen better days, but still worked. I had a bucket of chicken ready for us on the counter.

I put a plate of chicken and biscuits on a TV tray for Pinky and went to fix my own.

Pinky said, "You're like my own daughter. If I had a daughter."

"You've been a father to me for a long time."

"Your dad asked me to look out for you, you know."

I sat on the couch with a plate of chicken balanced on my knees. This was news to me. I must have looked surprised, sitting there, chicken wing in midair, staring at him.

"Now," Pinky was quick to add, "don't get in an uproar. He knew you was grown up and could support yourself. But he told me you was gonna have a hard life and to help you when I could. I done my best."

I swallowed hard, and said, "Dad worried too much."

Pinky's face turned red as he coughed from the depths of his guts. He rattled and wheezed, then put a hand to his chest and said, "Goddamn!"

"Maybe we shouldn't talk so much."

Pinky shook his head. "I'm fine."

I went into the kitchen and returned with Pinky's medicine. I handed it to him. "Go on, it's about time anyway."

Pinky held up a hand. "I'll wait a little. Damn stuff makes me sleepy."

We finished our lunch in silence. Pinky had a good appetite; I counted that as encouraging. When I had cleared the paper plates and trash, I returned to sit next to the old man. "Why did Dad think I would have a hard life?"

Pinky considered this for a moment. "You think he didn't know who you were? He said he didn't want to see you end up alone."

I flushed. We hadn't talked about it. I thought he'd gone to his grave not knowing I was a lesbian.

Pinky turned to face me. "I don't think he ever cared much for Georgia. I told him that some day you'd see the light. But he worried about you. Where could you go and work besides the cab company, wearing your hair like that? Not to say it looks bad. It don't. That would be a good haircut for a boy. You was, and still are, stubborn. It's the trees that can bend to the wind that make out the best."

"I'm not a tree, and I'm not a boy."

Pinky nodded. "Lesbians are women. I seen that on Montel."

My father had known. I hadn't been able to risk losing his love by telling him, and he had known all along. This sense of loss, of what could have been between us, enveloped me. I stared at the blank TV screen for a long time in silence.

At length I felt Pinky's hand pat my knee. I turned to him.

"Why don't you go get Alex now," he said breathlessly.

I nodded and stood.

Later that night I sat in the break area at the cabstand playing solitaire. The woman who'd taken Lotty's place at the phones was soft-spoken, street-wise, and a fence-sitter. Minnie Ballinger, the new dispatcher, was George's youngest daughter. Married twice to men even straight women wouldn't want, she'd been given enough reasons for changing sides once in a while. I only knew about the second husband, Dave, a real maniac, who had hocked all the new furniture and stereo system they'd just financed and gone on a week-long bender.

I don't know about bisexuals. I think we are all just different shades of gray—me being charcoal and Minnie closer to ash, or maybe smoke. And charcoal-gray women have to stay away from smoke-gray women because they will tear your heart out.

So I felt uncomfortable around Minnie. Some of the guys knew her story and expected us, both being single, to become fast friends.

Freddy Walters came in with his dinner, a couple of Big Macs and fries, and sat down across from me. I nodded to him and turned over three more cards. I looked at my options and started to draw three more when Freddy reached across the table and tapped the Queen of Hearts. I saw it then. I could move a whole stack.

I muttered thanks and looked up at him briefly. His mouth was full and he smiled as he chewed, a tiny smudge of ketchup reddening the two day growth on his chin. He appeared to be doing well, all things considered.

"You catch the airport run?" I asked.

He nodded. "Two old ladies who gave me a twenty-five cent tip, and a businessman from Albuquerque who wanted me to break a hundred. I told him if I had a hundred dollars I'd stay up all night watching it."

"So, did you take him?"

"I took him to an ATM machine." Freddy swirled a couple of french fries in a spot of ketchup.

"How you doing these days?" I asked. Working opposite shifts since I'd been back on the road, I hadn't seen much of him.

He gave me a thumbs up and said, "Good. Not great, but good."

Lotty was one special lady. Freddy losing Lotty was a whole different thing from me losing Georgia.

I started moving cards around again.

Freddy laughed. "You're fucked."

"Are you sure?"

He started gathering the trash from his supper. I noticed his small fingers—how he still wore his wedding band. I suppose he didn't consider himself single yet. It would probably take a long time.

He put the trash in a can and started to grab his jacket. I motioned him back to me. He leaned down close to me. "What?"

"The police," I said, "do they have anything new on the murder?"

Freddy met my eyes and sat down again. The life went out of his face. He said, "They closed the case."

"But it isn't solved. How can they just quit?"

Freddy shrugged. "They told me if anything new came to light, they'd reopen it. It's in a cold case file now."

"So," I said, "that's that?"

"Yep."

"God, I'm sorry."

Freddy said, "Yeah." And then turned abruptly and left me sitting there alone. Word was that there'd been no life insurance—he was paying some high interest loan company ten dollars a day to get the bills caught up. Another flight came in at nine. Freddy drove the airport limousine. He was headed back out there.

Early the next morning, as I carried my regulars and took a fare to his job at the hospital laundry, my mind went over and over the events of last fall. Anita Alvarez would have me believe that Lotty's was murdered by Salvadoran mobsters. But something nagged at me—a question I couldn't quite form. The radio was quiet and normally I would have headed east to turn the cab in and catch some sleep before I had to make Pinky's breakfast. But almost absently, I turned the cab south toward town.

A fine rain had fallen during the night and my tires hissed on the wet pavement. At a stoplight I noticed ice glistening off the tree branches and tiny buds preserved on the naked limbs like dripping jewels. Traffic was sparse and little time had passed when I pulled up in front of the governor's mansion. I let the cab idle and stared at the looming structure behind the black iron rails. A semicircular drive made its way toward an awning-covered side door. There were bright dots of purple crocus along the fence line. The gardens would be lush and beautiful in the summer. A separate area behind the brick wall was a rose garden where the governor's wife gave tea parties for any organization that had made campaign donations. The yard was huge and covered with different types of adult trees. The lawn appeared to be raked and tended at this early stage of spring. Living in the same town as the mansion, like most, I took the place for granted.

Some governors had preferred Chicago to the mansion and spent most of their time up there. Others had sojourned here with their families for the length of their terms. William Wright seemed to spend equal time at his home in Chicago and here in Springfield. His wife was a good politician's wife, and I suspected she stayed here more than he did. Wright was two-thirds through his second term and was facing another election. He'd served in several other public offices and his name was known by the time he ran for governor. The party had moved him up to replace an incumbent with a heart condition. He was a big guy, in his mid-sixties, with white hair and a young face. Besides the usual grumbling about campaign finance and budget cuts, I couldn't think of any major disasters.

The sky grew lighter as I sat there. The sun reflected coral on the undersides of gray clouds. A brisk wind rattled the iron gate. I kept going over it all in my mind. Did I need to find Anita Alvarez? Would finding her lead to Lotty's murderer or just make things worse? Would Toni Matulis have any more information? And if she did, could I find out what she knew? I told myself once again that if I'd given the key to Anita when she asked for it, Lotty would be alive. But the key seemed like such a small thing. According to Anita, the key was insignificant. Of course, if that were true, what drew the killers to the cabstand to start with?

If I tried to find Anita, maybe she would have some answers. But where should I start? If I drove around long enough, would I be able to find the house in the country where Anita's aunt lived? If I called the phone number on the business card she'd given me several months ago, would Anita get the message? The number had worked once. But what would I say?

A voice startled me. "Four?"

I picked up the mike. "Four, go."

"You empty?" It was Minnie Ballinger.

"Yep, getting ready to come in."

"Got a call for North Seventh Street, to St. Joseph. A woman in labor."

I put the cab in gear and started rolling. "She alone?"

"Didn't say."

One of our drivers delivered a baby back in the ice storm of seventy-eight when he got trapped between fallen electrical wires on the way to the hospital. Most of us were fast enough to beat the stork. I'd never even had a close call. I'd had a couple of messes in the back seat, but the only one I really minded was when a prospective father barfed during a long contraction. He wasn't in labor. He could have stuck his head out of the window. I preferred women in labor who were alone. They behaved better and they tipped more. This one tipped me a five.

Later that morning at home, after I let Alex out, I started looking through things trying to find the business card Anita had given me. Cold rain had started again, and flecks of ice blew against the trailer. My place was more messy than usual because I was always over at Pinky's helping him. I closed my eyes and tried to concentrate. Michael had used the card the morning Anita and I showed up at his place. He'd given it back the afternoon I got out of jail. I pulled the napkin holder that was stuffed with bills and miscellaneous mail off the top of the refrigerator. The card was down between a bank statement and an application for a new credit card. I dialed the number from the card. I got a recording. The number had been disconnected. I dialed again, more carefully this time, but the results were the same.

Then Alex was back, cold and wet, shaking his coat and tracking mud. He had the routine down pretty well by now. I came home, let him out, fed him and then walked over to Pinky's.

At work later, business was brisk for a Tuesday night and it was close to eight thirty before I could break for supper. There were several cars parked around the tavern when I crossed the street to the Alamo. I could hear the jukebox before I pulled the door open. Cigarette smoke hung in the light over the pool table. Two guys were playing. I was hungry and could smell hot fried food as I slid into a booth.

Almost immediately, Rosa pushed a menu in front of me. "You having supper, Trudy?"

"Chili," I said. "And a cheeseburger."

"Somethin' to drink?"

"Diet Pepsi."

First the drink and then the food appeared quickly in front of me. I didn't see Antonio anywhere. Rosa's brother was behind the bar. Rosa was busy waiting the tables. As I finished my chili, I got her attention.

"Another bowl?"

"Where's Antonio?" I asked.

She looked at me and tilted her head. "He's in the cellar. We had a big order come in this afternoon."

"I need to talk to him."

"Is it something I can help you with?"

As I looked at her, I knew that whatever I said to Antonio, Rosa would hear about, whether he wanted to tell her or not.

"I'll only take a minute of his time."

Rosa slapped my check on the table and left me. I was beginning to think I wouldn't get to talk to Antonio after all when I saw him coming toward me.

His black hair was slicked back into a pony tail. Despite thirty degree temperatures outside, his sweaty T-shirt stuck to him under his arms and down the center of his abdomen. He placed both hands on the table and leaned toward me. "What can I do for you, Trudy?"

"You are from El Salvador."

"Yes, that is right."

"Do you know any others? I mean in this area. Do you know any other people in this area who are from El Salvador?"

"Not many."

"Do you know a woman called Anita Alvarez?"

Antonio slid into the booth across from me. "I have heard the name. She's not from around here. Chicago, I think."

"Would you know how to contact Anita?"

Antonio spread his hands. "I don't know her that well. I have only heard the name. How do you know her?"

"It's a long story."

"I see." Antonio stood and picked up my dirty dishes from in front of me. "I am sorry that I cannot help you."

I reached into my hip pocket for money and nodded. "Don't worry about it. This was a long shot anyway."

I carried my money and the check to the cash register, and I picked up a toothpick and slipped it between my teeth.

Outside the wind was strong, with warm gusts from the southwest. The rest of the night was slow. At four in the morning the engine light came on. The cab was idling rough so I turned it in, letting Minnie Ballinger know that it needed servicing as soon as the mechanic got there. I then knocked off early, rode my Harley home, and started looking for Rosalyn Richards' business card. When I couldn't find it, I dialed directory assistance to find the number of her firm in Chicago. I stayed awake until eight o'clock, and after walking through five minutes of voicemail instructions, left a message for Mrs. Richards to return my call.

She never did.

Chapter Eighteen

Wednesday I spent with Pinky, taking him grocery shopping in the cab. At the store I'd picked up a few things—okay, a couple of frozen pizzas—for my own supper. I was looking forward to watching three or four rented action-adventure movies after I drove around the bumpy rural roads. I had gotten a map from the office and divided it into sections west of town. I figured if I looked when I had a chance, I would find the house in the country eventually. Once that afternoon things looked promising. But a November stubble field is a lot different from spring when the black earth is turned. By the time I knew I was on the wrong country road, it was after four. I made a big black "X" on section one and headed back toward town.

Around six-thirty I was washing a week's worth of dishes. I had already taken a shower, put on a pair of flannel boxer shorts, knee socks and a big T-shirt. I would put the pizzas in the oven and start the first movie soon. I was looking forward to a quiet evening at home.

When the phone rang, I considered letting the machine get it. In fact, many times since then, I wished I had.

It was my sister, Barbara, the one with five kids. "Hi, how you doing?" she started.

"Not bad," I said. "What's up?"

"John is out of town," she said. "A business trip."

"Business?"

"Ever since the merger he has to go to the home office in Chicago for monthly meetings. They put him in a hotel, pay his expenses. I have no complaint. After eighteen years of marriage, it's nice to have time off once in a while."

"Time off your marriage?"

Barb laughed. "Oh, you know."

"Yeah." I really had no idea. I sprayed the silverware with hot water and picked up a towel to dry my hands.

"That's why I'm calling. I wondered if you had plans for dinner?"

I only went to my sister's for dinner on holidays when I couldn't get out of it. But I figured she was feeling lonely with John gone and I hadn't seen the kids for a long time. So I said, "What you cooking?"

"Pot roast."

That was all I needed to hear. I told her I'd be there. She asked me to pick up some ice cream or something for dessert. I had a new half gallon of Rocky Road in the freezer so I putzed around the trailer until the last minute and then put on a clean pair of jeans and a comfortable T-shirt. I tried to comb my hair down. For the bar I spiked it up, but when I was around my family I tried to appear as normal as possible. It wouldn't stay in place and finally I threw the comb on the counter and looked for my hiking boots. There was no reason to think I should dress for dinner.

When Barb opened the door to the yellow three-bedroom frame house, the smell of beef and onions wafted toward me. I stepped in, handed her the ice cream and stood there with my helmet and gloves in my hands.

"Throw your coat on the bed," she said, taking off toward the kitchen.

Down a dark hallway to the back of the house was the master bedroom. A lamp on a walnut-colored night stand illuminated the intricate details of a white chenille queen-sized bedspread. At the foot of the bed was a Lane hope chest that matched the walnut night stand, dresser and headboard. I could see the flicker of candlelight through the open door of the half bath that connected Barb and John's room to the main bathroom. You couldn't call the main bath a guest bathroom because with five sons—ranging in age from seventeen to seven—on a normal day you wouldn't want a guest to go in there.

I tossed my helmet, gloves and jacket across the bed and made my way back down the hallway to the kitchen. Something was strange about the place. I could smell sandalwood incense and vanilla candles. The house was quiet. I rounded the corner to the kitchen and said, "Where's everybody at?"

Barb stood at the sink tearing apart lettuce for a salad. "Kids are at a basketball game with the neighbors."

"Just the two of us for dinner?"

She nervously brushed a strand of hair out of her eyes with her wrist. The doorbell startled both of us. She said, "Actually three for dinner," and stepped around me and went into the living room.

I groaned. She was playing matchmaker. Since I turned thirty, marrying me off had become one of my mother's obsessions. Mom'd surprise me by inviting the son of this friend or the brother of that one to dinner. These guys all had good jobs and were recently divorced or single. Once she'd actually introduced me to a gay guy I knew from the bar. Here was his mother and my mother beaming at us as we talked politely. Later we actually discussed continuing the charade but didn't have the energy. I'd learned to avoid sudden invitations to dinner by my mother, yet I'd let myself get blindsided by my sister.

Barbara was the oldest of the four children my mother had had with one of my dad's best friends, her second husband. All those kids were my half sisters and brothers, really. But when they were little, it was too complicated to explain. Even living with my father, I'd babysat them, gone to their birthday parties, and had them over to spend the night. I was ten years older than Barb, but with two brothers before another sister, she'd attached herself to me early and hard. We'd never talked about my sexual orientation. Sometimes I told myself that she knew. After all, Georgia and I bought the trailer together. But she'd probably been too young to think much about the arrangement back then. So much for assumptions. Maybe Mom put her up to this. I wanted to give Barb the benefit of the doubt.

"Put your coat on the bed," I heard my sister say. "It's this way."

I felt sweat break out on my forehead. The kitchen was too warm. I shoved my hands deep in my jeans pockets and closed my eyes. When I opened them, Barb, who was five foot three, stood before me. The guy behind her was a head taller with brown hair going gray.

"Trudy, this is Eileen Sheridan. Eileen, my sister Trudy."

Eileen? I blinked. She was one of those "Women's Studies" types, the kind we used to call "wine and cheese" lesbians. Definitely not a bar dyke. Her hair was straight, parted on the left, shoulder length and cut shorter on the sides so that the ends framed her neck and chin. She wore a cowry shell necklace, a poison-green crinkled-cotton shirt, matching pants and sensible shoes. Her hands were large and unadorned, nails short and clean. She reminded me of a mature Sigourney Weaver, a real *Gorillas in the Mist*, no-mistaking-for-a-straight-woman woman. Not really my type, but—

Eileen extended her hand. I wiped the sweat off mine and took hers to shake. Maybe she looked more like an *Alien III* Sigourney Weaver. "Your sister has told me so much about you."

I looked at Barb quickly, then back at the Amazon. "Hello," I finally croaked.

Eileen chuckled. Her voice was deep and throaty. "My God. Your sister didn't tell you I was coming."

We both looked at Barb, who flushed. "Well, it was a last minute thing."

I couldn't think of a damn thing to say.

Eileen said, "Oh, dear."

I excused myself and hurried down the hall. In the master bedroom I sat on the chenille bedspread next to the coats and tried to regulate my breathing. My helmet rolled toward me. The implications of this whole thing were amazing. My sister knew about my lifestyle, though we'd never discussed it—and was trying to fix me up. Her kids were gone, so she either didn't want them to see this, or wanted privacy for this little act of civil disobedience, or both.

Suddenly Barb was beside me talking. "I'm sorry. I didn't think this would freak you out. It was John's idea, really. Eileen moved into the old Philman house across the street. She doesn't know anyone, and we thought—I mean, not to date, but so she knew someone."

"John knows about me?"

"Good God, Trudy, he's the one who told me."

"What? When did he tell you?"

"About fifteen years ago," said Barb. "Remember the time Mom invited you over for a family dinner and to meet Alan Johnson, and you brought Georgia, and Georgia got mad?"

Fifteen years. Was there anybody who didn't know?

"I wouldn't believe him at first," Barb went on. "But remember the time at Robby's track meet you told me about fighting with Georgia about the thermostat setting?"

Georgia liked it warmer than me.

"I realized that day that you were fighting over the same things with Georgia that I fought about with John. I made the connection. I wanted to talk to you when Georgia moved out. But you pulled away from everyone."

Eileen was leaning against the bedroom door frame. "I think I should leave."

"No, please," said Barb.

I took a deep breath and squared my shoulders. "Please don't go. My sister makes a wonderful roast. If she'd told me you were coming, I might have combed my hair or put on a T-shirt with no cuss words. But believe me, there's no reason for you to leave."

Barb laughed. Her eyes sparkled in the light from the lamp. Maybe tears were in her eyes. I couldn't tell.

Eileen remembered to ask Barb if she needed help with anything, and we both helped. I set the table while Eileen finished the salad. After the initial crisis, dinner went fine. Barb and Eileen talked like old friends. When they were laughing about something one of the kids had done, I admit I wondered if Eileen was there for Barb.

I reached for the last dinner roll and Barb took the basket into the kitchen to refill it. The woman from across the street and I were alone briefly.

"Your sister tells me you drive a cab," Eileen said as she scooped up a second helping of gravy. "That must be interesting."

I watched her dubiously. Most of the time I think people like her look down on people like me. Was she putting me on, or sincere? I finally decided to take her at face value, and said, "I like it. I meet all kinds of people and can keep up on my reading during the slow periods."

"What do you like to read?"

"Oh, mystery, science fiction, most of the lesbian stuff I can find," I said. "I'll read about anything." I buttered the roll, and asked, "What do you do for a living?"

She sat back in her chair and seemed to consider this. How many answers could there be? At length she said, "I used to teach. I loved it, but being on my own—I just reached an age, I guess, when I started thinking about how much money I was putting aside for my old age. So I got a state job and recently transferred here. After Chicago, and the community up there, I feel totally lost."

"What did you teach?" She didn't look like a gym teacher to me.

"High school math and Spanish and German."

The only thing I did worse than math was spelling. I looked at Eileen and thought that if I'd had a high school teacher who looked like her, I would have been the star pupil, somehow.

Eileen didn't wait for a response, but asked, "Tell me, where do the gay people go in this town, besides the bars?"

I smiled and said, "There are four gay bars."

"Oh, I was sure there were bars. But aren't there other groups?"

Wine and cheese lesbian, I thought. I'd made her at first glance. This woman doesn't meet her girlfriends in bars. She's a different kind of animal. Though I have to admit she made me consider changing sides, I couldn't imagine life without a belly-rubbing slow dance at the Crones' Nest, or a game of pool at Jamie's. What made this woman want to get up in the morning?

Barb came back in the dining room, set the rolls down near my plate. "Isn't there a social group? One that meets for dinners and the like?"

I looked at my sister, frowning. How the hell did she know about that?

She saw my expression and laughed. "Psychology of Women. I'm taking classes at the community college. A lesbian visited our class."

I saw Eileen out of the corner of my eye, enjoying the way my sister and I were trying to communicate. Actually, the way I was struggling. My sister was doing just fine.

"A lot of the classmembers were startled. But I told them that I had a sister who was a lesbian and she wasn't any worse than anyone else."

This really amused Eileen. She kind of choked and put her napkin in front of her mouth to hide the smile.

"I'll tell you what," I said. "I will find out when that group's next meeting is, and I'll take you and introduce you to them."

Eileen said, "That would be wonderful." She rooted around in her shoulder bag, extracted a business card and passed it to me. "My phone number."

I didn't have a chance to look at it because the front door opened and the boys burst in, all noise and confusion, the youngest with red coloring all around his mouth from cherry soda, the oldest tossing the car keys on the counter like a grown man.

They were just in time for ice cream.

Chapter Nineteen

By the weekend I had gone through two more sections on the county map with no luck. Nothing looked familiar. Once I would have sworn I turned on the right road, but in the end I was lost.

Saturday evening during a quiet spell, I was alone in the office with Minnie Ballinger. I don't know why I felt so awkward talking to her about gay stuff. I started a game of solitaire. Later, when I looked her direction, she was watching me, and she smiled.

I returned the smile nervously and said, "Have to cheat to win more often than not."

Minnie shrugged. "Life's like that, I think."

I nodded and pretended to concentrate on the game. The phone rang and Minnie answered. When she hung up, she said, "Got a trip from K-Mart on the east end. You want it? Or you want me to radio one of the guys?"

I gathered the cards. "Need the money."

"Boy, who don't?" she agreed.

Minnie seemed to be in a friendly mood so I stepped to the counter and screwed up my courage. "I have a question for you."

"What?"

"You know that social group for lesbians?"

"LESA?"

"Yeah, that's the name."

"What about it?"

"I was wondering if you knew anybody on the mailing list. I have a friend—well, my sister has a friend—who just moved here and wants to meet some people—you know, not at the bar."

She reached for her purse, a big, brown, leather deal with a shoulder strap and one compartment where everything got dumped, and started digging things out. "I have the newsletter in here somewhere. They meet on the first Wednesday and the third Sunday every month."

I watched her set a wallet, nail polish, makeup, hair pick, tampons and several items I lost track of on the desk. A tube of lipstick started rolling toward the edge and I caught it for her. She stuck her arm in all the way to her elbow. Fluff chick, I thought. Finally, she pulled some folded lavender sheets of paper from the bottom and handed them to me.

"There's a number to call. This is from last month, so you can keep it."

I folded the newsletter over one more time, and shoved it in my jeans pocket. "Thanks."

"You ever go to a meeting?" she asked.

"Dances sometimes." I didn't want to talk, really, but felt I owed her something for the newsletter. I didn't understand Minnie with her red nail polish and streaks of blonde. I suppose I could have accepted that—there were lipstick lesbians—but sleeping with a man every now and then baffled me. Anyway, I added, "When I was with Georgia, she liked the dances."

Minnie took her arm and shoved all the stuff on the desk back into her bag. Without looking at me she asked, "She the woman with the Explorer?"

I looked at her directly then. "You heard about that?"

"Hell, Trudy, everybody heard about that. What I want to know is how you bought her off on a cabdriver's salary."

I stared at her dumbly.

"You can buy yourself out of a big mess like that, but you have to go to the bad end of town for a trip because you need the money. I don't get it."

I said, "I don't mind the bad end of town," and walked away. Let her assume I had something lucrative going on the side. There were ways to make more money with less effort. Working girls. Drugs. I told myself that I didn't care what she thought. When I slid behind the wheel of my cab, I was cussing my sister for getting me involved in that conversation.

I found Rosalyn Richard's place the following Wednesday, in section four of the now scribbled-up county map.

That day, when I turned off the main road, it felt right. I drove several miles looking for the side road. The day was sunny and warm, no rain since the weekend; the grass was turning green and the trees were budding. With the windows open, the smell of a hog farm assaulted my nostrils. At ten in the morning, the rough-running lavender cab was the only car on the road. The mechanic at the office had told me it needed a ring job and to watch the oil level. The ancient Plymouth was over fifteen years old, and I don't know how many times the gauge had turned over the one hundred thousand mile mark. Maybe three. I nursed the cab along, not really wanting to switch to another. No one else wanted to drive Number Four and I could take it for personal use whenever I needed. Even if I drove another cab, it would be a cold day in hell before Ralph and Betty painted another Red, White and Blue cab lavender.

Anyway, that morning when I accelerated too fast, black smoke boiled of the tail pipe on the road behind me. When a road looked familiar, I slowed and took it, figuring I could use it to turn around. But the dirt ruts wound right and then left, and next to a familiar-looking rural mail box I found the white rock lane. It looked different; trees were no longer bare. The horror movie effect was lessened by the blue, cloudless sky.

The drapes were closed and from the driveway it appeared that no one was home. I got out of the cab and went up to the door. My heart was thudding. What did I want from Anita Alvarez? What did I think she could or would tell me? I rang the bell and waited. I remembered the little dog and listened. If someone rang my door bell, Alex went nuts. But the house was quiet. I knocked on the door, waited, then pounded.

No one answered.

At least I had found the place. I went back to the cab, got the map and drew a circle around the spot. I could check on the place any time I wanted. I threw the map in the passenger seat and walked around the corner of the house and toward the back. I could hear birds and found an abandoned feeder and a birdbath that still contained rainwater sitting in the center of what appeared to be an overgrown garden. No one had started turning its soil yet this year. But it was early. I walked across the back yard and around the dry in-ground pool. The stubble field that I had looked across from the window that day was freshly plowed, and the scent of damp earth drifted toward me. Several robins scratched around in the newly turned soil, digging for worms. Everything looked different, but this was the place.

As I turned back, I noticed a kitchen window with only a sheer set of curtains. I walked close to the house. From the outside the window was high, but I could stand on my toes and see in well enough, just resting my chin on the window ledge. Kitchen cabinet doors hung open. I could see across the dining area. The long black table was gone. The room was empty. The cabinets were empty. I had a sinking feeling. I wasn't going to find Anita this way.

I made a date to take Eileen Sheridan to a LESA social at the Olive Garden that evening. A social meant that whoever wanted to met for dinner. Someone would reserve a large table and everyone who came would crowd around. I was nervous about running into Georgia, who sometimes went to LESA socials, and wondered how many of the women I would know. I definitely didn't hang around with these folks, but some women from the bar did.

We had agreed to go on my bike, weather permitting. The sky was fairly cloudless, but the air was cooling when I dug Georgia's old helmet out of the bottom of the closet and strapped it to the back of the seat. I was nervous as hell. Would Georgia be at the LESA social? I could imagine walking in with Eileen, carrying our helmets, and Georgia recognizing hers in the hands of the Amazon. She might make a scene. On the other hand, if she wasn't there, I wondered if I would recognize anyone. Plus, there was the business of what I would talk about with Eileen all evening. I went back into the trailer for a roll of antacids before I started the bike.

Eileen came to the door in a pair of faded jeans and a long-sleeved Bull's T-shirt. She pulled on a denim jacket and I noticed she'd had sense enough to wear boots. I handed her the helmet and started the bike. When she climbed on behind me, she didn't hesitate to slide her arms around my waist. Normally I don't notice the vibration of the seat. But with the warmth and scent of this woman I hardly knew behind me, I was aware of all kinds of stimulation.

Pulling into the Olive Garden parking lot, I looked around for a black Grand Cherokee. Though I didn't see one, Georgia could have ridden with a friend. As usual, the lot was packed, but I managed to pull the bike close to the building. Eileen threw her leg over the back and, with a short skip, was standing beside me unbuckling the helmet.

We made our way through the crowd of waiting patrons, none of whom looked like our party, to the check-in hostess. She appeared young, about sixteen, and, when she flashed us a smile, had a mouth full of braces.

"Are you with the LESA party?" Sixteen years old and she had us spotted.

I nodded.

"Several of your group are here already." She pulled a couple of menus from beneath the counter and said, "Follow me, please."

We followed the girl through two or three dining rooms to what seemed like the back of the restaurant. She pointed toward a long table with half a dozen women already seated and drinking. I recognized none of them.

A woman with long gray hair stood and held out her hand. "Hi, welcome. I'm Maggie. This is Agnes, Sally..." and she went around the table. We introduced ourselves and I chose a seat where I could see out a window. To my relief I could also see my Harley.

Agnes, a butch-looking woman with spiked hair, noticed me looking and laughed. "We saw you two pull up and were hoping you were with our bunch."

I stared at her dumbly. But Eileen recovered for me and said, "Thanks."

"Have you been to LESA before?" asked Maggie.

"I've been to the dances," I said. "This is Eileen's first time. She just moved here from Chicago."

Maggie nodded knowingly. "This must be a real culture shock."

Eileen put her hand on my shoulder. "Actually, everyone I've met has been very nice. It's just a little harder to find you folks here than it is up there."

"Well, now that you've found us, maybe you can help us do something about that."

Then the waitress was standing over us asking for our drink order and four more women were led to our table by the hostess with braces. Our introductions started all over again and I forgot to worry that Georgia might show up. I started to relax.

Eileen took the lead with the social stuff, but I held my own. Several women were very interested in the Harley, and I think if I had been alone, I might have been asked for some rides. Why hadn't I thought of this group before? They were all friendly. Eileen had a knack for getting the women to talk about themselves and I found they weren't all professionals or Women's Studies teachers. One woman worked in a laundry and another managed a convenience store. A forty-year-old attorney named Carol had just had a baby by artificial insemination and was thrilled to get out of the house alone for the first time since her daughter was born. The new mother passed around pictures and I have to admit the little tyke was cute. Some of the women started talking about childbirth and teething. Agnes said her first son didn't sleep through the night until he was six months old. The new mother looked worried, but others quickly assured her that was extreme.

Close to ten the group started to break up. At one time I think there were twenty-three of us. The money on the table for the waitress was enough to make me to consider a career change.

The food was good and I drank so much coffee that I had to make a pit stop before we left the restaurant. Outside the wind had picked up. The sky was starless and I counted that as a bad sign.

"Thanks for bringing me with you tonight," Eileen said, fiddling with the straps on her helmet. "Would you like to go get some coffee or something?"

I looked at the sky and frowned. "I better get you home. Looks like it's going to rain."

"I have a coffeepot at my house."

Before it occurred to me that she'd extended an invitation to come into her house, I said, "If I have another cup of coffee, I might not sleep for a week."

The Amazon didn't seem too disappointed. If she felt rejected, she hid it well. As we pulled out of the parking lot, she slid her arms around my waist. Lightning flashed, then above the sounds of the Harley I heard thunder. A cold gust of wind rippled my jacket. Eileen held on tighter. The warmth of her body against my back was soothing. I reminded myself that women like her didn't mate with women like me.

At the corner of MacArthur and Laurel the sky opened up. We were northbound and the worst was driven against our backs and left side, though we were completely drenched by the time we traveled the next block. I squinted my eyes against the rain.

"Want to pull in somewhere?" I shouted over my shoulder.

"We're wet now." Eileen laughed. "If it doesn't bother you, let's keep going to my house."

She was right, we were both soaked. I didn't mind taking her home. Needles of rain stung my face and pelted my chest. I was cold, but not bone-chilling cold. The big Harley handled well on the wet pavement. Traffic seemed to make way for us. We got splashed just before the entrance to the subdivision by a passing car.

When I turned onto her block, I checked my sister's house to see if anyone was up. A light was on in the living room. I'd decided to dry off over there and wait out the rain.

"Pull into the carport," Eileen hollered as I slowed near her house.

Anyone who's ever tried to argue on a Harley will understand why I simply pulled into the carport.

She threw her leg over the back and pulled off the helmet. "Turn off the bike and come in. I'll make some herbal tea, hot chocolate or something."

"I'm going across the street to my sister's to dry off and wait out the rain."

"Don't be silly. I want you to come in." She flashed a warm smile. "I am not going to take no for an answer."

What could I do? The rain beat down. Cold wind whipped around the side of the house. I shut off the bike and dismounted. I looked longingly one last time at my sister's light across the street and followed Eileen through her back door.

Chapter Twenty

We sat in front of a gas log, tea mugs in hand, and listened to the rain. She wore a pair of light gray sweatpants and a red flannel shirt. I was in her heavy terry-cloth robe with a towel kind of hanging off my head. Eileen had put my wet clothes in her dryer. I was waiting for them to dry and for the rain to stop. I felt sleepy and was quiet for a long time.

"Are you warm enough?" she asked at some point.

"Yes, very comfortable, thanks."

"I had a great time this evening. You were wonderful to take me."

"I enjoyed it myself," I admitted. "I wouldn't have gone if it weren't for you. So, thank you too."

The living room was about the size of Barb's. Most of the sixties-style ranches in this area were alike: small eat-in kitchen, living room/dining room combo, one and one-half baths, two regular size bedrooms and one very small one. John and my sister had branched out into the basement, converting a large space next to the laundry room into a fourth bedroom for the oldest boy. This meant privacy, and his younger brothers were counting the days until he went off to college or the military and they had their turn.

Eileen said, "Tell me about yourself."

I shrugged. "Not much to tell."

"You drive a cab, own a top-of-the-line Harley, and have a nice sister. Surely there's more than that."

I sat my mug on the floor, leaned back in the overstuffed chair and looked at her. "This is a two-way street, you know? If I tell you about me, you have to reciprocate."

"That sounds fair."

"Okay," I started. "I am forty-seven years old. I have a dog named Alex and I've never done anything but drive a cab."

"A lavender cab."

"Yes, lavender."

"How on earth did you get that kind of paint job?"

"My boss, Ralph, wanted an American-sounding name for his new company. He's second generation from some little country in Eastern Europe, I forget which one. Anyway, he named the company Red, White and Blue. But he'd bought all these cabs from the old Springfield-Yellow Cab owners. So, with his last dime, he hired this body shop to paint the cabs red, white and blue. Ralph ran out of money before the guy was done. They had words about the price of the paint jobs. The body shop guy showed Ralph the contract. Ralph pretended to not understand. At least that's what I think he does when it's convenient. The body shop guy saw he wasn't going to get more money, so he poured all the colors together on the last cab. That's the one I drive."

Eileen laughed. "That's a great story."

"It's true."

"Even better."

"Now it's your turn."

Eileen drew her feet up under her and looked at the ceiling for a moment. "Well, I told you that I used to teach high school. But I wasn't honest about why I left."

"They find out about your secret life and throw you out?"

Eileen shook her head. "No. It was the kids. I just couldn't stop getting close to them. Especially the ones who were struggling. People live some pretty strange lives. I had kids whose parents were abusive, drug abusers, in jail, on the streets. School was the steadiest thing they had. Do you remember high school?"

"The worst time I can remember," I said. "I thank God every day that my life didn't turn out to be like high school."

"Imagine that being all you had. Kids today are exposed to a lot of violence, but the problems go much deeper than that." She was quiet and I waited. At length she said, "I just couldn't spend another weekend wondering if a kid was going to commit suicide or not. I couldn't take it anymore. I loved teaching, but I wasn't one of those teachers who left it at the door. I had to quit."

A green plant stood next to her chair, a Mother-in-law's tongue, the biggest one I'd ever seen. Beyond that was the front window. Through the vertical blinds I could see the rain in the glow of the streetlight. I could hear the thudding of the clothes dryer.

"I know it's hard," I said, "to let go of something you love."

After a moment she said, "What have you let go of that you loved?"

"Enough."

"Reciprocation, remember?"

I sighed and counted on my fingers. "My father, the house I grew up in, a lover of many years…"

"Georgia?"

"Who told you about Georgia?"

"I heard your sister say her name the other night."

I rubbed the towel on my damp hair and tossed it to the floor next to the mug. I leaned my head back. "We forgot how much we loved each other, at least that's what I'm telling myself these days. I guess it happens. Love is really unfair, you know?"

Her voice was low and husky. "How is love unfair, Trudy?" The way she said my name made my heart leap.

I suppose I stammered a little—then heard myself say, "We don't realize when we're happy, and that's unfair. All those years with Georgia, I thought we were struggling, but that when we got money saved, or she finished beauty school, or we got the trailer paid off, then we'd be happy. My eyes were always on the next goal. Time seemed to pass quickly, though we went through some pretty tough stuff together.

Then she told me she was leaving, and suddenly I knew how much I loved her. It wasn't something I thought about every day. But I knew at that moment that it was true and had always been true. I've also realized since I've gotten older, that when we were young and struggling, when she was in beauty school and I was working extra hours to help pay the bills, we were happy. It's not fair that I didn't know at the time; I would have savored it. But I kept thinking this one happy moment would come, and it didn't."

Eileen finished my thought. "Because it was already there."

"Yeah."

"You're right. That isn't fair."

I felt close to tears.

"So," Eileen gently prodded, "how come she left?"

"She found someone else."

"You find someone else."

"I'm too old and too tired to start over."

"Oh, you're not so old." She ducked her head, trying to meet my eyes, trying to get me to smile.

I yawned. "Then just too tired."

Eileen laughed. "Well, I didn't mean right this minute. Tomorrow, after a good night's sleep, or the next day. This weekend."

I felt exposed, somehow. I hadn't talked to anyone, not like that, since I could remember. Companionship was another thing that had gone with Georgia. Sure, I had friends, but none as close as the woman I used to come home to.

Gradually I realized the storm had passed and the rain outside was softer. Eileen's living room was quiet and cozy. The buzzer from the dryer startled us.

Eileen checked her watch. "It's late, and we could be up all night waiting for the rain to stop. I have a guest room with a sofa bed. Why don't you stay?"

"I can't," I said, relieved to have an excuse. Suddenly I wanted to be home in my own bed. "I have a dog, remember?"

She didn't try to argue, but stood and stretched. "Well, those warm clothes ought to feel good for the first block or so."

I carried my cup into the kitchen and set it in the sink, then stood looking out the window at the carport and my Harley. The rain had turned into a fine mist and the wind had died down. The ride home wouldn't be too hard. When I turned, Eileen handed me my things and I headed toward the bathroom where I'd taken them off.

Next to the bathroom, the door to Eileen's bedroom stood open. This trip the light was on, and I glanced in. The king-sized bed, with a brass headboard was more wrinkled on one side than the other—on the non-slept in side were a couple of stacks of magazines. When you're single you notice those things. The walls looked, at first glance, schizophrenic. The base color was an off white, but patches of different shades of blue went every direction, as if the paint job was started, the color still undecided and left unfinished. The top of the single dresser was covered with clutter; two drawers were partially opened. A bookshelf sat near the only window. The books were stacked around it, but not on it. I stared at the contents of the shelves for several seconds. Everything was there: goddess statues, hand cream, knitting needles, and audio tapes. The bottom shelf was lined with shoes and in the center of the top shelf was a gun. I started to back away when I noticed the night stand. In addition to a white phone, a lamp, and an alarm clock, there was an eight by ten photo of two women. I recognized Eileen, tall and dark, her arm slung over the shorter woman's shoulders. I looked behind me, making sure that I was alone, and then stepped through the doorway. The shorter woman in the picture was Hispanic. She had long dark hair and wore large sunglasses. Something about her looked familiar, and I was creeping closer when Eileen said from behind me, "Are you finding everything you need?"

I jumped and let out an involuntary squeal.

"Sorry to scare you." She was laughing. "I apologize for the mess in there. I'm remodeling."

"Interesting use of the bookshelf."

She shrugged. "You know how it is when you move. I should throw half that stuff away. I was trying to sort out the magazines and ended up reading them all."

"You should see my place," I said. "And I haven't moved for a long time."

Several minutes later, when I came out of the bathroom, Eileen was waiting for me. She took the robe and tossed it into her bedroom, and we walked together toward the kitchen.

She stopped me when I was ready to go out the door. "Thanks again for taking me to that dinner. I had a great time."

"Me, too."

She smiled. "Let's seal the evening with a hug."

I didn't move as she stepped close and embraced me. My arms went around her automatically. Her hair was still damp. She smelled good. I was about to pull away when I felt a wet kiss on my cheek. I turned toward her and accidently brushed her lips.

I pulled away awkwardly, and said, "I'll call you."

"Good. Thanks again."

I tried to study her expression, but it gave up little. I said, "Good night, then."

She reached past me to open the door.

I could feel her body pressed against mine and her moist lips on my cheek all the way across town. Between that and the images of the center-piece on her bookshelves—the Virgin Mary, the Spanish girlfriend and a handgun, I didn't even notice the rain.

At home I let Alex out and fixed him fresh water. As I walked through the trailer to the bathroom, I stripped off my damp clothes. I let the hot needles of the shower beat against my skin until I looked like a very butch lobster. In bed, wearing only a T-shirt and clean underwear, I tossed and turned for a long time before I fell asleep. Alex, who usually had the patience of a saint, grew weary of the ordeal and got down and curled up on the floor.

I woke to the sound of the alarm clock. My sinuses were swollen shut, my head ached and every muscle in my body felt stiff. Even with two over-the-counter ibuprofen, I moved slow. By the time I was dressed and at Pinky's, he was up and fixing his own breakfast. Alex did a little dance and the old man broke off a piece of bacon for him.

"You must be feeling a lot better this morning," I said, opening the refrigerator and reaching for the apple juice.

"As late as you come in last night, I thought I might starve before you got over here."

"Got caught in the rain on the bike."

"Never knew that to keep you from getting home."

I poured juice in the glasses that Pinky had already set on the table, then pulled out my chair and collapsed.

Pinky set a plate of bacon covered with a paper towel on the table. He put two slices of toast in the toaster. "You want me to cook the eggs?" he asked.

"How many you want?" I stood slowly and went to the refrigerator again.

"Two's fine with me. Cook yourself some. You look like hell."

"Yeah, yeah." I cracked three eggs, dropped them into the bacon grease, pitched the shells and reached for a coffee cup. It was then I remembered how much coffee I'd had the night before at dinner. No wonder I hadn't slept.

We ate quietly for a while. I watched the old man. He was better. His color seemed good, his breathing less labored. I wanted to tell him how much I loved him, how scared I'd been and how glad I was to see him improved. Instead I said, "When's your next doctor's appointment?"

He looked at me and smiled. A drop of egg yoke glistened on his whiskered chin. "I love you too, honey."

We had our own language, Pinky and I. My heart did a little flutter, and I said, "I met someone."

"Where? How?" I had his attention.

"Barb introduced us."

"Barb?"

"My sister."

"Son of a gun." Pinky poured milk in his coffee and reached for the sugar. "Tell me about her."

"She's from Chicago. Used to teach high school. Moved here to work for the state. We're very different, but I like her a lot. She's nice." I told Pinky her name and about getting caught in the rain.

He listened, nodding from time to time. In the end he said, "Good. I don't like to see you alone."

I thought about that for a second. "I'm all right alone," I said. "I have you and Alex."

Pinky chuckled. "An old man and a dog."

We ate in silence. I was so hungry I don't even remember chewing.

After a while, Pinky asked, "You have to leave early again?"

"Nope, I found the house yesterday. It's empty."

"They weren't home?"

"They've moved."

"You had a chance to see today's paper?"

I shook my head. "Why?"

"It's over there on the chair," he said. "Take a look at the front page."

I stood and reached across the recliner. When I turned the paper over I was struck by the headline: "Police Officer Killed in Line of Duty." I sat down hard. A gray picture of the front gates at the governor's mansion, an ambulance and two police cars in the rain stared up at me. A body covered with a blanket lay in an area cordoned off by police tape. I didn't recognize the officers standing near the squad cars, but I knew whose beat it was.

I read the single column below the picture:

> Springfield Police Officers responding to an alarm at the YWCA, 415 East Jackson, were engaged in gunfire. One officer is dead and a second is seriously wounded. Security from the executive mansion was on the scene. Names are being withheld pending the notification of families. Police, at this time, have no suspects. Homicide detective James Harris claimed that several commercial alarms were set off during last night's electrical storm. Police had been checking them out when the incident occurred.

When I looked back at Pinky, my mouth hung open. Was Toni Matulis dead? My next thought was did this have something to do with Anita Alvarez? It was at the governor's mansion, after all. Could the governor of Illinois have something to do with a drug operation? Why did I feel so damn guilty, anyway? I hadn't killed anybody, and catching bad guys was not in a cabdriver's job description.

Pinky's voice cut through my thoughts. "What do you think?"

I stood there with the paper in my hand, at a loss for words.

At length Pinky nodded and said, "Yeah, me too."

Chapter Twenty-One

Toni Matulis had been moved from intensive care earlier that morning. Her family a sister and Toni's child—had been weary and solemn. The kid, who had one front tooth half grown in and the other missing totally, had stayed home from school to sit with her mother. Toni's sister worked hard to convince the cranky little girl that her mama was all right, or else the hospital wouldn't have moved her out of the ward for the "very, very sick people."

"I know it was intensive care," the kid said. "And I know why they moved her, though she doesn't look better to me. I just want to know when will my mother be able to come home? When will she be that much better?"

The aunt stooped to meet the little girl's eyes. "Sooner than you think."

Nevertheless, the child was crying, from fatigue as much as fear, when Toni's sister finally swept her up and carried her out of the waiting area.

The room was too warm. Sweat stood on my forehead as I looked out through the windows beside the bed. The spring equinox sky was azure with a few feathery clouds. Somewhere women would be sitting in a circle on the new grass drumming, thanking the Goddess for another rebirth. The time was three fifteen in the afternoon; I would be pressed to leave the hospital room for work in another hour or so. But I'd held back until after her sister and daughter had left.

Once Toni had gotten settled in her room and her family had gone home, she'd been given a pain killer and had fallen asleep. I grabbed a couple of magazines from the waiting room and took them to the softest chair next to her window. I read and listened to the hospital noises in the hall and the hum of the IV machine.

Looking at the sky, I remembered my own hospitalization several months ago and the visit from Anita Alvarez in the middle of the night. Until the moment Pinky showed me the newspaper, I realized that I had put aside my fear and confusion. Time sure takes care of a lot of stuff. When I let myself think about the night I escaped with Anita from Jimmy's Bait Shop, my blood ran cold. Now another person was dead and Toni was in that hospital bed, injured far worse than I had been. Most officers, I'd heard it said, went an entire career without a gunshot wound. This was Toni Matulis' second—second and third, I should say—she had taken more than one bullet.

Toni slept on, unaware that I was waiting. I opened a magazine. There was nothing for me to do but wait. I wasn't going anywhere until she talked to me, or I had to go to work, whichever came first. I looked through the magazine and must have nodded off when a voice startled me.

"You're the cabdriver, aren't you?"

She was a tall black woman. I looked at her, puzzled. "Huh?"

"I saw you that day in the supermarket," she said. "Toni talked to you about one of her cases while I watched Doree."

I held out my hand to shake hers. "Trudy Thomas."

"Bertha Brannon." Her hand was large and warm. She was big and powerful looking, dressed casually in faded blue jeans and a yellow sweatshirt. She pulled the hard chair near me and straddled it backward. "You are the cabdriver who works where that woman was murdered."

"You've got a good memory."

"I don't know if I want you here or not," said Bertha.

I held up a hand. "Wait. You don't understand."

"You're here about the murder, right?"

"Right."

"Then I do understand," said Bertha. "What you need to know is this—Toni was wounded two years ago. This time it's much more serious. She's scared the hell out of all of us. Plus, Pop Wilson, a man I've known since I was a little girl, is dead."

She stopped abruptly, as if she needed to collect herself, to swallow her feelings back down.

I waited, watching her.

Finally she said, "Toni is through with the police force. She's going to law school."

"I can't afford law school." Toni's croaking voice interrupted.

We both turned.

Bertha stood and moved next to the bed. "I have a relative who can spare the money."

"I don't want your mother's money."

"And I don't want you dead," Bertha said. "You know I can't raise that kid on my own."

Toni's only free hand had an IV needle taped to it. She reached for Bertha and looked toward me in the same motion.

Bertha brushed a blood-crusted strand of auburn hair back and bent to kiss Toni's almost fish-belly-white skin. Lotty's face floated up in my mind. The crimson red stream of blood from the pencil-sized hole had contrasted against her pale forehead, too.

"I'm sorry to intrude," I said.

Toni asked, "What is it, Trudy?"

"I just want five minutes," I said. "I've been waiting all day, and if you feel up to it, I'd like to talk to you."

"About your old friend Anita?"

I nodded. "I thought we could share some information."

Toni sighed. "I shared information with a homicide detective earlier today. I don't think it would be wise—"

A male nurse entered the room, and Toni stopped talking. He unceremoniously pulled the bed curtain closed and said, "I need to get vitals and check her dressing, if you will excuse us."

I stood, and Bertha and I walked out into the gleaming hallway. An old woman, wearing a red housecoat, moved slowly past us pushing an IV stand.

"What's on your mind, Trudy?"

I stammered, "Maybe I shouldn't have come. I understand your protective feelings."

With an openness I found disarming, Bertha said, "I can't lose her. She'll be off the job for a while this time. When she is healthy enough to work, I'll have convinced her to not go back. She told me once that before Doree was born she'd wanted to go to law school. Then the baby came and she couldn't manage it. The kid is in school now. Toni can do that or anything else she wants to. I'll tell you one thing I know for sure, she will not finish this investigation. Let somebody else figure it out."

"They closed Lotty's case."

"The dispatcher?"

"Yes."

"Well, a policeman is dead now. They'll open it again. If you know anything you haven't told them, I suggest you contact the Springfield Police Department. Detective James Harris in homicide caught this case."

"Do you think they've made the connection?"

Bertha considered this. "Are you sure there is a connection?"

"No, but Toni told me that Anita Alvarez spends a lot of time at the governor's mansion. Anita told me once she was the governor's daughter."

Bertha's eyes widened.

"Illegitimate daughter," I added quickly.

The old lady walked past us again. Bertha watched her, waiting. The male nurse came out of Toni's room. I wanted to get back in there and talk to her. I suppose I didn't because I wanted Bertha's permission. That way if anything went wrong I wouldn't be totally alone in the blame. I noticed the clock over the empty nurses' station read five twenty. From somewhere I could hear the clatter of dinner trays, and the smell of institutional food drifted in the air.

"Did it occur to you that Anita lied?" Bertha asked at length.

I nodded and shrugged.

"What do you need to talk to Toni about?"

I drew in a long breath. "I wanted to tell her that the night my ex-girlfriend's Explorer sank in the Sangamon River, Anita Alvarez was with me. Anita told me that her family grows cocaine. There were other men at the river. Some of them were alive and one or two of them weren't."

"The police know none of this?"

"I don't think so. Anita had left by the time I was arrested. My attorney advised me to say as little as possible."

"Then tell them now."

"I want to find out if there's more that Toni hasn't told me."

"Go away, Trudy," Bertha seemed to plead. "Call Harris at Homicide."

"But—"

"No." Bertha shook her head firmly. "I've taken Toni off of the case."

I looked longingly at the door to Toni's hospital room. Bertha stepped in front of me and that was that. I shook hands with her and told her I was glad to meet her, though I was not. I asked her to give my best to Toni, which I meant, and I headed toward the elevator and to work.

That night was a busy one. The engine light came on in the cab about nine-thirty when I was on the east side of town at a supermarket. I dropped off my fare and went inside to get a case of oil. When I checked, the oil mark wasn't even on the stick. I poured three quarts in and the warning light went off. I wondered how long I could keep driving the lavender cab before the motor was gone. A different cab seemed like a bigger change than I could manage—a stressor right up there with death and divorce.

Trips were steady until the taverns closed. There was always this slow time between the late-night people and the early-day people when I sat in the train station, the airport or the office. I pulled up behind Johnny Henderson at terminal "A" around three-twenty. Johnny leaned against his cab, smoking and sipping from a Styrofoam cup of coffee. When I shut off my engine, he looked my direction and waved.

As I walked toward him, I could see his white teeth flashing in a grin.

He shoved the bill of his cap back with his thumb and said, "You have black smoke coming out of your tailpipe."

"Rings," I said, leaning against the side of his red, white and blue.

"You gonna get it fixed?"

"I don't know."

"Always something, ain't it?"

I nodded. My mind was on Toni Matulis. All evening I'd been thinking about Bertha's plea. I agreed with her to a point. But Toni could talk to me and still leave the police department. I couldn't see what one thing had to do with the other.

"Ralph'll want to junk it," Johnny said.

"I know. It's got more wrong with it. Rear seal. Shocks. Heater don't work half the time. It stalls out when it rains."

"Hell, they all do that."

I chuckled. It was true. There wasn't a cab on the lot that didn't have some problems. A couple of years ago Ralph'd had a mechanic who did engine work like it was nothing. These days he relied on Lester more often than not. Serious problems require a specialist and they don't come cheap.

Johnny tossed his cigarette butt on the sidewalk and stepped on it. "Maybe you could check a junk yard. You know, replace the whole engine."

"That might cost less."

"Ralph would fix it if you helped pay for it."

"It's his damn cab."

"Trudy, Number Four is your cab. He'd let you trade easy enough."

I sighed and looked past the terminal to the blue lights on the runway. We had half an hour before the St. Louis flight came in. More than an hour for the one from Indianapolis. The night was quiet and clear. A breeze from the southwest ruffled my jacket. I dug in my pocket for change.

"I'm going to get a soda. You want anything?"

Johnny shook his head. "I'm good."

I crossed the sidewalk and pulled open the door to the empty terminal. The snack machines were about thirty or forty yards down a worn-out carpeted hall. Standing before them I considered my choices: four kinds of coffee, three kinds of tea, Pepsi and all of their products and bottled water.

The lighted machines and the solitude were mesmerizing. I felt as if I were standing at an altar asking some higher being for help. I started thinking about Bertha and Toni again. I remembered the sleepy little girl who only wanted her mother to come home. Bertha hadn't been much different. What was I hoping that Toni could tell me? I had been up all day with only the sleep I'd gotten at the hospital. My own thinking was distorted and slowed by fatigue. My eyes burned and my back was aching. I turned the change over in my hand until the quarters felt warm. What I hoped to learn, of course, was what had happened the night that Toni was shot. Had she seen Anita Alvarez? What had she and Pop Wilson encountered at the gates of the governor's mansion, and how did it connect to Lotty's death?

I was wondering how my knowing something like that could harm Bertha and the kid when the terminal started to fill with people. I looked toward the gates and realized that the St. Louis flight was in. I'd either stood in front of those machines for half an hour or the flight was early. I fed my quarters into the Pepsi machine and got a plastic bottle of diet. By the time I was back outside, Johnny was loading suitcases into his trunk and an elderly woman was looking at Number Four hopefully. I tossed the unopened soda in the front seat and helped the old girl with her bags.

I'd made a decision. The next day when I went to visit Toni Matulis, I'd do my best to avoid Bertha Brannon.

Chapter Twenty-Two

I woke the next afternoon with a dull headache and Alex panting hot dog breath at my face. He saw my left eye open and woofed softly. I rolled to a sitting position. The room was warm. The way the sun slanted through the bedroom window, I guessed it was about three hours past noon. The last couple of weeks when the sun reached the top of the dresser, that had been the case. Standing, I caught a blurry reflection in the dresser mirror. My hair stood on end and my face looked puffy. I wondered if I was coming down with something, though that wouldn't account for the hair.

Because my knees ached, I knew it had rained or was about to rain. Alex did a little dance as I limped through the kitchen to the front door wearing nothing but a red music festival T-shirt and a pair of boxer shorts. I'd have to shower and dress right away if I wanted to make it to the hospital before work.

Again, I asked myself what was the use? Nobody wanted me to talk to Toni. Even Freddy hadn't asked me to do more. Sure, I wanted to know what was going on. But sometimes life didn't work out that way. Sometimes loose ends went untied. I felt torn. I could make a pot of chili and have a big supper. In fact, I could eat chili for a week if I cooked today. If I stopped at the hospital, I'd have to settle for a couple of peanut butter sandwiches, or fast food.

I rinsed three ibuprofen down with a swig of orange juice from the jug and went back to the door for Alex. When I didn't find him on the porch, I leaned out. Little Wendy from down the street was playing on a small silver scooter. The air was fresh and damp. Puddles stood in the street. Alex marched along next to the child. I called him. He looked my direction, but otherwise ignored me. I couldn't really blame him. He would be inside all night alone. I hadn't walked him in a long time. I left him to play and got dressed. Then I grabbed the leash, went outside and took him for a walk. That's how I ended up not going to see Toni Matulis before work. Alex and I walked all over the trailer court. He inspected every mud puddle and hiked his leg several times. I noticed trees in blossom and tulips several inches above the black soil in the neighborhood flowerpots. We made our way down one street and up the next. I'm not sure how long we were gone, but by the time we reached our own steps again, we were both out of breath.

Back inside, I threw some hamburger in a pot and cut up an onion. While walking with Alex, I'd decided I could stop by the hospital later that evening if things were slow. If not, there was always tomorrow.

I phoned Eileen Sheridan and, when she didn't answer, left a message asking her to return my call. I didn't want to let too much time pass before we connected. I wasn't sure what I'd have said if she'd answered.

I drained about half the fat off the browned hamburger and onions and added the beans and tomatoes. Alex was right under my feet when the can opener whirred several times. I stirred the pot and left it all to simmer while I showered and washed my hair, then sat in a bathrobe and ate chili while Alex crunched on his own supper.

Around five-thirty I kicked over the Harley and headed for work. The afternoon had been warm, but like other spring days, the evening was starting to cool. I let myself enjoy the wind and sun on my face. When I pulled the bike inside the first bay and shut off the engine, I felt great. I had a belly full of my favorite food and the smell of sunshine in my hair.

The evening was slow. Johnny Henderson and I started a game of hearts and when Freddy came on at eight we dealt him in. Minnie had a soft rock station on the radio and they were doing a tribute to the Mamas and the Papas. At one point the four of us were tapping our feet to Creeque Alley singing, "…and no one's getting fat, but Mama Cass."

We didn't really get busy until around ten-thirty when a tractor pull at the convention center broke up. Several of the ole boys were meeting at a country and western bar on the north end. After that the folks from out of town rode to their motels. Considering all the big trucks parked in the lots, it was hard to believe that anyone needed a ride. But they kept us busy and they tipped well, and they would tip even better coming back from the bars.

So, it was after three in the morning when I came back in to the office. Freddy and Johnny were at the airport.

I got a Coke and some corn chips from the vending machine and started a game of solitaire. Toni Matulis had slipped my mind completely until then. The image of Bertha Brannon's face as she stood between me and the door to Toni's room flashed in my mind. In the morning, Bertha would be at work. Some instinct told me that Toni would level with me, that she wanted my help in spite of what Bertha said. I remembered the night Anita and I had encountered gunfire at the Cardinal Apartments and all that had followed. I sat there staring at the queen of diamonds as my mind spun off on the events since I'd met Anita Alvarez.

Minnie had turned the radio down and was reading. After a while I lay the card down and drew again. The room was growing stuffy, and I got up and went to prop the front door open. Outside the night was cool. This time of year it was too early for the flies that buzzed around the dumpster across the street, moths that circled the lights out front or the mosquitoes that bred in the deep ditches and puddles between here and the main road. I looked across the street at the Alamo. The lights were off, but there were four cars in the dark parking lot. One parked toward the back looked familiar, though I wasn't sure from where.

"The fresh air feels good." Minnie's voice startled me.

I turned toward her. "They having a private party across the street?"

Minnie shrugged and came around the dispatcher's counter. "What do you mean?"

"Those cars." I pointed. "Lot's usually empty this time of the morning."

"Maybe they're cleaning or doing inventory." She had a cigarette between her fingers and stepped outside drawing on it. "Man, it was getting hot in there."

"Wait 'til this summer," I said.

"So, how'd it go at the LESA dinner? You have a good time?"

I stepped outside and leaned against the rough cinder block wall. "It was very nice, actually."

"They are a good group," said Minnie. "a lot of older women."

"Yes," I said stiffly. "There were several women my age."

Minnie laughed and slapped my arm. "Aw, I didn't mean nothin'."

I nodded and took a deep breath. I would have gone back in, but she flicked her cigarette across the drive and went back in herself. So, I stayed where I was, looking at the Alamo parking lot and the cars. From where I stood the car nearest the fence looked like a silver Buick.

There wasn't much traffic on the road out front this time of night. Except for us and the Alamo it was mostly a residential neighborhood. The sky was clear and there was a cool breeze from the southwest. I was considering taking the cab to the train station when a long dark car came around the corner. I stepped to the left out of the light from the road. Standing in the shadows, I watched the car pull into the parking lot across the street and kill its headlights. Two dark figures got out of the front seat and one from the back. What the hell was going on over there? The three people tapped on the tavern door. It was quickly opened and the figures slipped inside.

I called inside to Minnie, "I'm going to park at the train station and wait for the five-fifteen."

"Right," she answered.

I walked around the side toward my cab, then changed my mind. Staying low, I crossed the street toward the Alamo. My heart raced when I saw a car at the corner, but it turned the opposite direction and the taillights disappeared into a driveway several houses down.

Wet grass had soaked my shoes and pantlegs by the time my body was pressed against the rough wood siding of the Alamo. The car was a silver Buick, all right. I was sure it was the one I had ridden in several months ago, upon being let out of jail.

I inched around the back, away from the street. A patch of uncut weeds, about three feet wide, stretched between a neighbor's fence and the building. I could hear muffled voices. There were two windows. The first looked promising, but when I peered in, I found myself looking into the unlit, dark kitchen. I could see a dim light coming from another room.

I moved slowly to the next window, up higher, also the kitchen, but closer to the light. My foot encountered an object and I reached down to find myself against the gas meter. I put my foot on top of the thing; it was wet with dew and slippery. The weathered ledge of the window was covered with cracked and peeling paint. I grabbed with both hands and pulled myself up, standing on the unsteady, rounded top of the meter.

I could see through the kitchen to the office where people seemed to be gathered, although no one was directly in front of the open door. I could hear their voices, and I realized that they were speaking in Spanish.

My foot slipped and I grabbed the window ledge to get my balance. A sharp splinter drove itself into my palm. I gritted my teeth and bit back a curse. I heard a chair scrape and a woman looked out of the office doorway toward the kitchen. I recognized her immediately. Her short white hair shone in the dim light. My attorney, Anita's aunt, Rosalyn Richards, was looking my direction. I ducked. Seconds later I heard the door close.

When I stepped down off the gas meter, my knees complained. I moved slowly through the damp weeds and around the building, hoping that no one had heard me. I figured walking would attract less attention than running. I thought my heart would burst out of my chest before I was safe on the cab stand lot.

Back in the office I headed to the first aid kit.

"I thought you were going to the train station."

"Didn't make it."

"So I see." Minnie didn't seem too concerned. She leaned over her paperback, dismissing me.

In the bathroom, after washing the area, I managed to pull a hunk of wood out of my palm even with my short fingernails. I then covered the spot with antiseptic. Back at the dispatcher's counter I asked for the clip board.

"You signing out?"

I nodded.

She passed it to me and the blue ink pen that was tied to the metal loop with a piece of dirty string flopped and struck my hand. I swore and Minnie looked at me questioningly.

"Got a splinter a while ago."

"You get it all out?" Minnie seemed interested. "You'll get an infection if you didn't."

I hesitated, then stuck my hand under her nose. She inspected it and pronounced it a good and thorough job. I turned to head for the door and heard Minnie say, "What should I tell Ralph and Betty?"

"Tell them I was injured on company property," I said over my shoulder.

I had no intention of going home. I pulled Number Four around the side of the building, backing into the first parking space, and watched the Alamo.

Johnny and Freddy had returned from their airport trips and the sky was growing light when the first people left the meeting across the street. They were the three men that I'd seen arrive in the limo several hours earlier.

I waited for another fifteen or twenty minutes. Two more men came out of the tavern. I didn't recognize either of them. Then came Rosalyn Richards and Anita Alvarez. I swear they both looked toward the cab stand. I ducked out of sight, though I doubt if they could have seen me where I was parked. When I raised my head moments later, they were gone.

Chapter Twenty-Three

The concrete steps to the hospital glistened in the white sun. Across the manicured lawn and street, people were drifting out into the heat from the other medical buildings and the university. Overweight women in cranberry-colored scrubs drew on cigarettes while standing in patches of shade; cigarette smoke drifted upward and was swept away on the balmy spring air. Three young people in white jackets opened paper bags and stood around a partially shaded picnic table.

Visiting hours didn't start until two. I was early and therefore hoped to find Toni Matulis alone. I'd stopped at a greenhouse near home and picked out a purple African violet in a plastic pot, then balanced it in a box on the gas tank of the Harley all the way into town. I held the plant in both hands as the cool, quiet elevator rose.

Toni's room was on the east side, down an antiseptic-smelling corridor to the right. A uniformed police officer sat on a folding chair to the right of the door to her room. He was a young guy, fit-looking, with a ruddy complexion. He watched me approach.

"Is Toni allowed visitors?" If I used her first name, I thought I might seem like a close friend.

"Only family." The policeman's expression was grim.

"I'm her cousin." The lie rolled off my tongue like butter.

"Your name?"

"Trudy Thomas," I said. "Would you tell her that cousin Trudy is here?"

The officer looked at a clipboard and then checked his watch. "No Thomas on the list. Plus, it's not visiting hours yet."

"I'm from out of town. I've come a long way. Would you just ask her if she'll see me for a few minutes?"

The officer considered this, and then stood and went into the hospital room. When he returned minutes later he held the door open. "She wants to see you."

I hesitated in front of the opened doorway, then stepped inside. The curtains had been drawn and my eyes took a second to adjust. She was sitting up in bed, a tray of food before her.

"I thought I'd see you yesterday," she said.

"Your friend, Bertha, asked me—no, told me—not to come."

"Yes," said Toni, "I know. But you needed to talk to me."

"Right."

Toni looked at her plate and pushed some macaroni around with a fork. "So, what's on your mind?"

I sat the little plant next to her tray and scooted a chair closer.

She examined the purple flowers and said, "Thank you."

"I think it needs some water."

Toni stuck a finger beneath the fuzzy green leaves. "Run a little on it from the sink." She nodded toward the bathroom door. "And set it on the window ledge there with the others."

The others turned out to be a huge arrangement of white roses and a large green plant in a brass pot. I watered the violet and set it in a narrow strip of sun.

"Beautiful," said Toni.

Settling into the chair, I got right down to it. "Did the shooting the other night have something to do with Anita Alvarez?"

"Well, if you mean did I see her there, the answer is no. But I'm sure she was involved somehow."

"What happened?"

"My partner and I…" she hesitated for a moment, perhaps remembering that he was now dead, then swallowed hard and continued. "Pop and I were checking out an alarm at the YWCA that had gone off during the storm. We rolled up to the building without flashing lights. We were pretty sure nothing was wrong, but we had to investigate anyway. We walked all around the building in the pouring rain. Pop radioed back in and asked dispatch if the building contact had been called. Someone was on the way, so we got back in the car to wait. We were parked there on Fifth Street."

"You were facing the mansion?"

"Yeah. There wasn't much traffic. Then Pop started cussing. I looked across the Jackson intersection as a streetlight flickered and went out. There was a security camera on the northeast corner—attached to a pole. Someone was sitting on the chain-link fence, messing with the device. Whoever it was obviously hadn't seen us."

"Visiting hours do not start until two o'clock." A voice startled us.

I turned to find a plump woman in a white uniform standing at the foot of the bed. Her dark hair was pulled straight back in a short ponytail. A couple of loose strands fell at the sides of her round face. She looked mad.

Toni recovered first. "This is my cousin from Chicago. She has to catch a train at two thirty."

"Nevertheless—"

But Toni wasn't having it. "Let me talk to your supervisor."

I was surprised to see the woman in white change her approach. "You have to understand, Ms. Matulis, I have treatments to do. You are supposed to get out of bed this afternoon, doctor's orders. And look, you haven't even touched your lunch."

Toni eyed the woman. "Loretta," she said, probably reading the name from the woman's tag, "I will finish my lunch while I talk to my cousin. You can get me up now and I can sit in the chair while we visit. Surely you understand the train schedule problem."

Loretta considered this and finally, with languid indifference, said, "Okay, I have two more patients to do. I'll put you last. Do try to finish your lunch and get some liquids down. We are supposed to disconnect the IV today. Your doctor is going to want you to drink lots of fluids."

"I will," said Toni. "Thank you."

The round little woman in white turned and left.

Toni said, "Now what the hell are we going to do with this lunch?"

"What you got?"

"Macaroni and cheese, green Jell-O, vegetable soup and a brownie."

"I will help you with the brownie."

"Back off, Trudy. That's the only thing I want."

Like a couple of conspirators, we scooped the food together, and I quickly flushed it. Toni unwrapped the brownie and poured hot water over a tea bag.

"Now where was I?"

"The guy on the pole."

"Right. I called for backup as Pop got out of the car. I was right behind him, maybe twenty feet. I heard him holler, 'Police—get down on the ground!' and I saw a flash. It came from the front drive, not the guy on the fence. Pop started forward, but the second shot got him. I couldn't leave him in the open. I pulled my own weapon and fired a couple of rounds and ran to him. I just kept firing while I helped him crawl to cover. I honestly don't know how I did that. Rain was beating down; it was dark. I didn't realize I was hit until we were behind the car. Then everything went black."

"But you didn't see Anita Alvarez?"

"I don't think Anita was there." Toni sighed and sipped her tea. She made a face and reached for a packet of sugar. "But think about it, Trudy. Anita coming and going at the mansion. Anita in the center of everything.

Not only your troubles last fall, but a lot of things that I can't ethically tell you about."

I listened to the spoon clink against the cup as she stirred. Finally I said, "Last night—well, really early this morning—there was a meeting at the Alamo Tavern."

"The Alamo?"

"This place across from the cabstand. It's owned by a Mexican woman who has a Salvadoran lover. I was convinced that they knew nothing about Anita—hell, he told me they didn't. Then I saw her over there at a meeting of some kind."

"So, she is in town," Toni said thoughtfully.

"She was a few hours ago." I went on to tell Toni about the other members of the meeting, especially Rosalyn Richards, the woman who had been introduced to me as the governor's sister.

"Of all the places they could have met," said Toni, "why would they choose the Alamo?"

I shrugged. "I was hoping you could tell me."

She didn't remind me that I had been less than forthcoming with her in the past. "Help me lower this bed and I'll tell you what I can."

I rolled the lunch tray to the foot of the bed, set the hot tea on the side table and searched for the down button. When she was comfortable, I scooted my chair closer. I could see she was tired and probably in some pain. Thanks to me she was last on the treatment list and would be last to get her pain pills.

"That interstate highway out east of town," Toni started. "The DEA calls it the pipeline. We are on a direct route from St. Louis to Chicago. Drugs come from Central America, across the border and go north. Chicago, then Detroit, wherever. Everything passes by on the pipeline."

"And Anita is probably involved in that drug trade," I finished for her. Toni had given me this information the last time we'd talked. Surely she knew more than I did at this point. I thought about the stories Anita had told me—her father, her family back in El Salvador, her brother hiding from gangsters. Then I remembered her sister Theresa, dead from drinking river water, her brother Ricardo, taken by strange men and shot, the girl she loved in college, overdosed.

Toni said, "In one way or other, Anita's in up to her neck."

"Who were the guys who shot at you?"

"Officers tend to know the local criminals. I got a good enough look to know they weren't from around here, which leads me to believe they are connected to the drug trade. I connect them to Anita because they were at the mansion. That's been her territory." Toni's voice was flat, hollow; her skin was pale as she changed the subject. "Pop Wilson was close to retirement. He'd been on the force since the seventies. He was my partner and my friend."

"I'm sorry for your loss." What else could I say?

"It's not just my loss. The whole community will miss him. The force needs about thirty more like him. It's a different world these days from the one Pop came up in. His particular combination of talents and skills, as well as street smarts, just doesn't happen anymore. He was one of a kind. We'll never replace him."

I said nothing. Toni reached for the teacup, and I jumped to help her. She sat up slightly and sipped the amber liquid, then dropped her head back suddenly. She was growing more uncomfortable. My visit was too much for her.

I stood to go. "I'll find the nurse on my way out."

"One more thing."

I leaned close. "I'll do whatever you need."

"Pop and I had an informant, Ramie Malone. I need to get word to him. I want to see him." She reached awkwardly for the drawer in the bedside table and moved some things around. "I've tried calling and paging him. He doesn't answer. Maybe he just doesn't recognize the hospital number on his caller ID. Maybe he's left town since Pop's murder." She pulled a small red address book out from under some get-well cards and opened it.

And that's how I ended up, in the early evening, just before time for work, over on East Pine Street, looking for Ramie Malone.

Small children were playing in the narrow roadway as I turned the bike and wove back and forth between parked cars on either side. I passed children slowly—they were in no hurry to move. The neighborhood consisted of small houses that were little more than shacks built close together, with littered and muddy front yards. A tree stump lay uprooted near the driveway that led to Ramie Malone's address. Its roots were a cluster of thin threads and clods of mud.

I stopped in front of a gray-shingled, shotgun-style house and dismounted. Ramie's front windows, set in frames of painted wood, were protected by rusty iron bars. The lot was covered with patches of grass and mud. A chain-link fence separated Ramie's narrow lot from the neighbor's. An old car seat, foam stuffing spilling out, sat at an awkward angle near the high front steps. The roof was dark green shingles, edged with moss in patches. The great brick chimney was soot-darkened and amazingly high.

As I approached the house I could see a rickety garage in back, the door padlocked.

The neighbor's pit bull, chained to a tree that looked too small to hold it, barked viciously at my approach. I climbed the steep steps and looked for a doorbell. Seeing none, I knocked and waited. This seemed to piss the pit bull off even more. After the third try, I descended the stairs and walked around the side of the house. There was no driveway to the garage, though patches on the ground indicated there once had been. The earth and the side shingles emitted a heavy, dank odor. The basement windows were opaque with dirt. On the back porch was a trash can overflowing with beer bottles and pizza boxes. The wooden steps gave a little when I stepped on them. I noticed immediately that the back door was open; three dead bolts and a special security night lock were all unfastened. The skin on the back of my neck prickled. The air seemed close and too warm.

I turned and looked across the lot. An apple tree blossomed innocently in the back corner; a pair of jeans was thrown across a low-hanging clothes-line, and an abandoned doghouse leaned against the weathered garage. Turning back, I put my face to the open door and called out, "Ramie." I hadn't expected a response and didn't get one.

I pushed the door further open and called, "Ramie," again. I stepped across the threshold into a tiny kitchen. The walls were bright yellow, the dusty beige curtains were edged with red embroidery and ruffled. Someone, at one time or other, had made an effort. A heavy, cobwebby dampness hung over everything. Up on the ceiling the mold looked ancient. A double sink was overflowing with dirty cups and glasses. Greasy pans were stacked on the stove. Near the doorway to the next room a filthy patch on the floor indicated that something had been moved. My guess was the refrigerator.

"Ramie." I didn't expect to find him home at this point, but I wanted to make sure that anyone I encountered knew my reason for being there. My plan was to check a couple of rooms and leave. A center bedroom was large and messy, empty beer cans everywhere. I saw my dark reflection in a full length mirror that was mounted on an open closet door. An unmade king-sized waterbed was across from a plush entertainment center that blocked the only window and most of the light. The TV screen, too large for the room, silently flickered on a sports station.

When I approached the arched doorway to the living room my heart sank. I put my hand over my nose and mouth. The smell was strong.

I surveyed the crime scene with a strange detachment. I should have been scared to death. I should have been puking or running or both. But all I felt was a childlike weariness.

The placement of the refrigerator told a horrible story—pushed up against the front door, it sat askew and the scrape marks on the inside of the steel door indicated that someone had pushed their way in, pushed the refrigerator aside. I realized I was standing on something hard, moved my foot and looked down at two shell casings and a dark, sticky pool of blood. My eyes followed the stain to the green sofa. I assumed it was Ramie. He was lying on the couch looking up at me. The entrance wound wasn't bad, right in his forehead; gunpowder burn marks spidered across his face. The exit wound had opened up the back of his head—blood and tissue oozed down the arm of the couch and onto the shag carpet. Ramie had been a good-looking boy—brown-skinned, Latino, with a narrow moustache and thick, shoulder-length, dark hair.

Whoever came, Ramie had been expecting them. Bars on the window and a refrigerator against the door hadn't kept them out. The bullet in the forehead was execution-style, too much like Lotty's to be a coincidence. The back door was probably open because they left that way.

I turned and made my way out, gasping for air, realizing only then that I'd been holding my breath. I slumped on the back steps and put my head in my hands. I don't own a cell phone and was on the bike, rather than in the cab, so I had no radio. I was damned if I was going to walk next door, past the pit bull, to call the police. Finally, I wiped my sweaty palms on my jeans and stood. I was going to work. I could call Toni from there and let her contact the police. Hopefully, she'd be able to tell me what all of this meant.

Chapter Twenty-Four

Red, White and Blue was busy when I checked in. There was no time to use the phone. I had done two trips and a regular was waiting when Number Four died. Red lights on the dash came on and I coasted into a filling station, as far from the pumps as I could roll. I sat there staring across the hood, watching faint smoke rise. Wonderful—a dead body and a dead cab in the same day. After a few minutes I tried the starter. The engine turned over slowly, but wouldn't catch. I picked up the mike and called dispatch.

Minnie Ballinger's silky voice was distorted by static. "Four. Go."

"I'm broke down."

"How bad?"

"Bad."

"What's your twenty?"

"Lucy's Standard on the corner of Ninth and North Grand."

"Roger that. You need a tow truck?"

"If you please."

"Freddy's on his way in. I'll send him your way when he gets in. Could be forty-five minutes."

I asked Minnie to have Johnny Henderson pick up my regular waiting on North Seventh Street. That was my trip and my tip, but I couldn't cover it. Inside the station, I used the john and bought a cold bottle of root beer. On the way back to my cab I noticed a pay phone and checked my pocket for change. The phone book was missing but I knew the main number of the hospital by heart. I asked for Toni Matulis' room and knew immediately that the woman who answered was Bertha Brannon. I hung up and dialed 9-1-1.

A man answered. "9-1-1, what's your emergency?"

I gave the guy Ramie Malone's address and said, "Please send a car. There's been a shooting."

"Someone is injured?"

"A man is dead."

"Who is calling please?"

As if this guy could see me, I shook my head. I wasn't going to get involved in this one. I had enough trouble. I said, "Just send a car," and hung up.

The evening was growing warm. Gray clouds gathered in the sky. I sat in the driver's seat with the door open, one leg sprawled on the pavement, and reached for a paperback mystery I'd started reading the night before. When the first large drops of rain splatted against the windshield, I realized I'd nodded off. I pulled my leg into the car and closed the door. The sky had grown dark. Without further warning rain beat down so hard I could barely see the door to Lucy's station. I thought about the rain the first day I met Anita Alvarez, a storm no worse than this. I checked my watch. I had radioed in over two hours ago. I checked the rear view mirror. If a tow truck was there, I wouldn't be able to see it. My stomach felt hollow. It was way past my suppertime.

I reached for the mike. "Four."

No answer. The battery was probably low. I tried again.

Finally I heard Minnie's staticky voice. "Four. Go."

"Where's the truck?"

"Trudy?"

"Yeah. It's me."

"You're breaking… bad. Can you… a phone?"

I looked toward the pay phone. "If I swim."

"Say again?"

"It's raining. I'm in the cab. Where's the tow truck?"

I heard a bunch of static and a word or two I couldn't understand. Between the battery and the storm all I could make out was "…not there."

I tossed the mike on the seat and waited. Every once in a while I saw red taillights from cars at the pumps. A lighted beer sign from inside the station looked inviting, but very far away. I was kicking myself for not pushing the cab under the awning.

A noise startled me. I looked to my left; a face was at the window. It was Johnny Henderson under an umbrella. I rolled down the window.

"You stranded?" he asked.

"Isn't that obvious? Did you bring the truck?"

"Nope," he shouted over the rain. "Minnie asked me to pick you up. We can get the cab after the storm."

"Can you push me into a parking space or something?"

He looked around and nodded. "You need to roll forward and to the left about ten yards. That'll put you by the back fence, next to the dumpster."

I squinted. I could make out the dark object. Johnny disappeared and I pulled the gear shift into neutral. Seconds later, the cab lurched as Johnny's bumper tapped mine. As I started to roll, I fought the powerless wheel, aiming for the space between the Dumpster and the ladies' room door. I did the best I could, knowing that I wouldn't get a second chance. Finally I threw it in park and grabbed the cashbox and the keys. The rest could wait.

Johnny appeared at the side of the cab under a multi-colored golf umbrella. He carried it for customers on days like this. I had a smaller version in the trunk somewhere. I got out, locked Number Four and let him escort me to his passenger door.

When we were both settled and he had started driving toward Ninth Street, I said, "What took so long? What happened to Freddy and the tow truck?"

Johnny shrugged. "He was coming in, but never got there. I was a couple of blocks away. Minnie called me to come and rescue you."

"But what happened?"

"Beats me." Johnny ducked his head to look at the rearview mirror and turned to check his blind spot before changing lanes. "Radio is fucked. Maybe he picked up another trip. Maybe he's broke down, too."

By the time we reached the Red, White and Blue office the rain had eased to a steady drizzle. Johnny left me under the awning and took off. He was two trips behind. I walked into the office. Minnie was alone. Beyond her I saw the open door to the garage. The tow truck was still parked in the first stall.

"What happened to Freddy?"

"I wish I knew," Minnie said, moving behind the counter. "There's Number Six and Number Twenty-one."

"You want me to go back out right now?" I hadn't considered this. I was ready to go home for dinner.

"Please," she said. "With this rain, the phones have been ringing off the hook. I have four trips in addition to the ones Johnny is taking care of. Freddy left us. I can't reach him at all."

"I hope he hasn't had an accident."

"With this weather, who knows?" Minnie shook her head. She met my eyes with a pleading look.

"What direction are they?"

"One north, one train station, and two west."

"Where is north going?"

"Airport."

"I'll take the north one and stop by home to grab a sandwich. If I eat in the cab, I can get to the others in thirty-five, forty minutes. Call them back, though, you know how people get when they have to wait."

Minnie let out her breath slowly. "Thanks, Trudy. So are you taking Six or Twenty-one?"

Twenty-one was the limo. It was big and boxy, but rode nice in bad weather. It was after ten. There'd be shoppers, movies getting out, the bars, and later I could try to catch the train station and airport. At this point I needed to make up for lost time. I grabbed the keys for Twenty-one and Minnie logged it.

The Red, White and Blue limo was parked on the south side of the building. As I settled myself behind the wheel and adjusted the seat and mirrors, the odor of stale cigarette smoke assaulted my nostrils. No one smoked in Number Four, not even the customers. George drove Number Twenty-one days and the ashtray was overflowing with brown Kool filters. I yanked the thing out and took it around to the trash to empty it. Back in the cab, the clean ashtray didn't make much difference. The windows were automatic and I buzzed the back ones down halfway.

The big car seemed to glide over the wet streets. Sometimes I forget how much I put up with in Number Four—the loud muffler, the squeaky brakes, the rough idle. I settled back into foul-smelling luxury and tried not to worry about my cab and Freddy.

When I finally headed home to take care of Alex and grab some dinner, it was after eleven-thirty. Alex bounded out of the trailer almost knocking me down the steps as soon as I opened the door. Inside I hunted for something to make a sandwich out of.

Alex was settled on the couch with a Milk Bone and I was on my way out the door with my dinner in my hand when I noticed the flashing answering machine. I stopped and watched the red light blink. Two messages. Setting the bag on the counter, I hit the play button.

The first message was from my sister Barb. They were having a cookout Saturday and wanted me to come. I could bring a "friend" if I wanted. Dinner at two. Bring potato chips or something, nothing fancy, just family.

How much family, I wondered? What kind of "friend" did she mean? Was I to invite Eileen Sheridan?

Before I could think it through, the machine beeped again. There was silence, and then a familiar voice said, "Trudy, if you're there, pick up." Toni Matulis waited and then said, "I know you just tried to call here. Visiting hours are over. I am alone. Call me back no matter what time you get this message."

I checked my watch. I had two fares waiting on the west end and the flight from St. Louis was due to come less than an hour from now. I had to be at the airport. I couldn't afford to miss the opportunity to make up for the hours spent sitting at Lucy's Standard.

Alex looked at me expectantly. I shut the door, crossed to the phone and dialed the hospital number. When the recorded message picked up, I punched in Toni's room number. Back in the days when people answered the phone, you'd never get them to ring a patient's room this late at night.

"Hello," came Toni's sleepy voice.

"Sorry to wake you," I started. "You asked me to call whenever I got your message."

"I'm all right," said Toni. "Don't worry about it."

"Well, I can't talk long. My cab broke down tonight and I'm way behind on everything."

"I just wanted to know how things went with Ramie. Did you find the place? Was he there?"

I hesitated. "Uh, he was there." Why couldn't the police have told her? Surely they'd found the body by now.

"What's wrong?"

"I'm sorry to tell you this," I said. "But there was a dead body on the couch at Ramie Malone's house. I'm figuring it was him."

"Oh, God."

"I called the police when I couldn't get you and gave them the address."

"How bad?"

"Isn't dead always bad?"

Toni stammered, "Could you tell if he, he suffered?"

She wanted to know if he had been tortured. I thought about the skid marks on the carpet, the young man watching the refrigerator being pushed back as the front door was shoved open an inch at a time. "He got it right between the eyes, like Lotty."

"Damn, damn, damn," she whispered.

"I'm sorry," I said. "This is all related somehow, isn't it?"

"So it would seem. Could you tell how long the body had been there? I mean, was he cold?"

"I'm no expert. But there was a strong smell. It didn't happen today, would be my guess."

"Probably before Pop and I ran into the bastards. By the way, how did you get in?"

"The back door was standing open."

"Wonderful."

"You know, maybe you need more protection. The police still keeping the guard at your door?"

She said nothing, but a soft sound told me that she was crying. I considered trying to reach Bertha, but what could I tell her that wouldn't stir up a hornet's nest? I couldn't just call the police and tell them that Toni was probably in danger. How could I explain that?

"Are you going to be all right?" I asked at length.

"I'll be fine."

"Call your superiors and ask for more protection," I prodded. "Enough people have died."

"Thanks for your help, Trudy."

"I mean it."

"I know," she said. "I appreciate your concern, but I'm fine."

The clock over the stove said it was twelve. "Look, I've got to run. I'll check on you tomorrow. But think about what I said."

Silence.

"Toni?"

"I'm here."

"Think about it, okay?"

"The guard is still out there. I'll be safe as long as I'm in the hospital."

"Good. I'll talk to you tomorrow."

Just above a whisper, she said, "Okay," then hung up.

Chapter Twenty-Five

On Wednesday I rode by the Ramie's house and saw crime scene tape across the porch. At least I knew they'd found the body.

I had driven Number Twenty-one on Tuesday, but that wasn't going to be a permanent solution to my taxi problems. I wanted Number Four fixed, no matter what it cost. I talked to Ralph about getting a new engine for the cab, as Johnny Henderson had suggested. Ralph told me he would consider it, if I could find one. So after riding by Ramie Malone's house I headed for the first of the two junkyards in Springfield. Central Iron didn't have anything that would work. A guy took my number and promised to be on the lookout for me.

Tangler and Thompson Salvage on the north end of town was my second stop. One of the owners, Harold Tangler, was a boy I'd gone to school with. He'd sat next to me in my seventh grade science class, and I think he liked me because he used to shoot staples into the tips of his fingers and show me the blood. I'd sometimes wondered what masochistic thing he'd done to win the woman he eventually married.

I hadn't seen him for a long time. His reddish blond hair had thinned on top and turned white at the temples. His skin was still freckled and fair. He was in his late forties, and there were pictures of his grandchildren, three little redheaded girls, on his grimy metal desk. He'd been in the office alone when I came in, and he seemed glad to have company. We shot the breeze awhile before I got down to business.

Harold shook his head slowly. "I could call around. Did you try Central?"

"Yeah, they don't have anything."

"Les Jones might be able to help you." He explained that the address and phone number belonged to a stock car driver who rebuilt motors on the side. Evidently Jones always needed money and would give me a reasonable price.

"Thanks." I took the paper, shoved it into my back pocket and ran my fingers through my hair.

"No problem." Harold grinned at me. Behind him the phone rang. I waved and turned to go as he reached for it.

Outside the azure sky and a cool breeze made for almost perfect spring weather. The days had grown longer and warmer. Soon it would be summer. Tropical regions have nothing on the Midwest in the summer, with temperatures in the high nineties and humidity that renders the atmosphere dense enough to lean on. Brutal summers and winters made me appreciate the good days.

That evening, after a long nap, I called Eileen Sheridan. She didn't answer, so I left another message. She hadn't returned any of my calls so far. I was puzzled. What that about?

I called my sister to RSVP about the cookout and told her I was going to bring Pinky if he felt up to it.

Barb said, "I don't mean to pry, but what do you think of Eileen?"

"She's nice."

"Okay, okay. I get the picture," said Barb. "I'll butt out."

I'd put a frozen pizza in the oven around six and was settling in for the evening, with the local news on television and a rented movie waiting. I put a bottle of Diet Pepsi and a paper plate on the coffee table. When the phone rang, I picked it up, thinking it might be Eileen.

Minnie Ballinger said, "Thank God you're home. Freddy didn't come to work. Betty told me to call you. Can you drive tonight?"

I opened the oven door, determined that the pizza was done and turned off the oven.

"Did you call him?" I asked, remembering that Freddy had disappeared in the middle of the shift Monday night, along with his cab.

"He doesn't answer. George stayed over. He said he'd work until you can get here."

Betty had known I would come in. I always did. Sometimes I complained more than the others, but she'd even called me at the last minute on Christmas day and I worked. "I haven't eaten yet and I need a shower."

"When can you be here?" Minnie asked anxiously.

"I'll be there as soon as I can. An hour, give or take. Is Twenty-one available?"

"George is driving it, but he wants to leave when you come in. So I guess it is."

I'd only had a few hours sleep and I was tired. But I was also glad for a chance to make the extra money. George was waiting out front when I parked the Harley inside the garage doors.

"Minnie said you wanted to drive the limo," George called to me as I walked toward him.

"How's it been?" I asked, as I opened the passenger door to toss a liter bottle of Diet Pepsi and the paperback mystery in the seat.

"Not bad."

The passenger seat was full of junk. "What's this?" I asked.

"Oh," said George. "just toss that stuff in the trunk. Throw it all in the blue bag."

I spotted a half empty pint of gin. "You wanna take care of this yourself?"

"Sure," he said nervously.

He stepped in front of me, grabbed the blue bag and started throwing stuff inside. In addition to the bottle of gin, I saw a couple of packs of cigarettes, a pornographic magazine, an open bag of potato chips, a deck of cards and a two-way radio. "You see anything you want to use, speak up," he said. "This radio is a cheap one, but I have a crystal for the police band. It's a nice little scanner, except the battery is low."

"I've got what I need," I said. "What's that on the floor?"

"What? Oh, that." George reached to the floorboard and retrieved what looked like a baby food jar full of pale yellow liquid. He blushed and stammered, "H-had my appointment with my probation officer this morning."

"So?"

"So she drops me at random."

"Urine?"

George nodded. "A clean drop."

"Are you fucking with me?"

George tossed the jar in the blue bag. "That woman finds out I been drinking and I'm in jail. Then where would Ralph and Betty be?"

"Listen, you dumbass," I said. "They watch you pee when they do a drop." I knew a thing or two about treatment. I knew about random drops. I'd done a couple myself.

George flushed. "I know, but I have a shy bladder and a very busy female probation officer. The first time she dropped me—"

I held up my hand.

"What?"

"I'm almost afraid to ask, but where did you get a clean drop?"

"My grandson, you see—"

I shook my head. "Don't tell me any more. Just get that stuff out of the seat so I can drive. I'm gonna go check in."

"Sure, Trudy. Thanks for working."

"Open the windows," I said over my shoulder, remembering the smell of the cigarette smoke I'd dealt with all week.

There were three calls waiting and I was busy for a couple of hours. Finally empty around nine, I turned the limo toward Lincoln Street and Freddy's little blue bungalow. I was worried about him. He may have gone on a bender or ended up in jail.

Freddy's house sat back from the road on a tree-lined lot. On the dark porch, a couple of off-white lawn chairs sat near a small glider. The mail box was full. I tried the front door and found it locked, then rang the bell and waited and pounded with my fist. I descended the steps and walked around an overgrown bush to the driveway side of the house. I couldn't see anything from the window as the rooms inside were dark. The back door was locked up tight.

I heard a noise and my heart leapt. Someone was dragging something. The back porch light at the neighbor's house was on. Slowly I crept toward the noise. Then I saw her. An elderly woman in a pink duster was dragging a garbage can down her walk toward the alley. Her back porch light fell across Freddy's driveway in front of his garage. As the old woman returned to her porch, I called out, "Hello."

She grabbed her chest and looked around.

"Over here." I waved to get her attention.

"Who are you?"

"I'm a friend of Freddy's," I said. "I'm looking for him."

"Lord, you like to scared me to death."

"I'm sorry."

She took a few steps toward me. "I thought I was all alone out here."

"My name is Trudy Thomas. I want to make sure that Freddy is all right. He hasn't come to work the last couple of days."

"Come to think of it," said the old woman, "I haven't seen him either. He was supposed to cut my grass yesterday."

"When was the last time you saw him?"

"Monday, before he went to work. He told me if he didn't get to the grass on his day off, he'd get it on the weekend." The woman shrugged and her voice took on a worried tone. "I just assumed something came up."

"You're probably right," I tried to assure her.

"Do you think I should call the police?"

"They can't do anything at this point. He's an adult. Adults have a right to disappear if they want to." I didn't want the old girl to worry.

I made a note on a scrap of paper. "Would you give me a call if Freddy shows up, or if you see anything suspicious over here?"

The woman nodded and shoved the piece of paper in the pocket of her duster. I said, "Good night," and started to walk away when the old woman asked, "How do you know Freddy? Do you drive a cab too?"

I pointed toward the street where the Red, White and Blue limo was parked. "Yeah. We've worked together for a long time."

"Then you knew Lotty?"

"Yes," I said. "Her death was a terrible thing."

"Those two were so much in love." Her voice took on a wistful quality.

"Well, if he shows up, please call me." I turned to go.

"My name is Sylvia, by the way."

I waved my hand. "Good night, Sylvia."

By morning Ralph would have the police looking for Freddy's missing cab. After seeing Ramie Malone, I was ready to believe that something bad might have happened to Freddy.

As I started the cab, I heard Minnie paging me.

"Twenty-one, go."

"You been out of the cab?" she asked.

"Pit stop," I lied.

"You have a PR at the Manor View." A PR meant the caller had requested me specifically. I had my regulars on days, but rarely got personal calls working nights. When I heard the word Manor View, I immediately thought of Anita Alvarez.

"You have a destination?"

"Alamo, across the street."

"Ten-four." I put the limo in drive and pulled away from the curb.

Chapter Twenty-Six

I pulled under the awning at the Manor View Motel. My heart pounded as a small dark figure hurried toward the cab. The passenger door opened and Anita Alvarez slid into the seat next to me. Casually, she turned toward me and said, "Long time no see."

My mind whirled with images of the past week—the empty house in the country, Toni Matulis in a hospital bed, Ramie Malone with the refrigerator askew in front of his door, Freddy's empty bungalow—I couldn't think where to start. Finally I said, "Where to?"

"The Alamo."

"Right." I put Twenty-one in drive and turned north onto Fourth Street. I missed the light at Capital and turned to her. "I—"

She interrupted me, "You're in a different cab."

"Mine broke down."

"I see."

"Aren't you going to tell me what the hell is going on?"

Dark hair framed her face. She wore khaki safari shorts, a black tank top and black Reebok tennis shoes. I could see a tattoo on the side of her leg, but couldn't make out the image in the darkness.

She said, "What do you want to know?"

"You started to tell me a story six months ago," I reminded her.

"Yes," she said, "of course."

"A police officer was killed near the mansion, right over there." I pointed. "Another cop is in the hospital, wounded and probably needs protection, though I couldn't say from who. A police informant was executed a couple of days ago, bullet right through the forehead, like Lotty. Now Freddy Walters, Lotty's widowed husband, is missing. He hasn't worked since Monday. I went by his house—"

"Hold on a minute, Trudy," Anita interrupted, "one thing at a time."

The light turned green and I continued north on Fourth Street. "Okay, then tell me why are you headed to the Alamo and what you were doing last weekend at there last weekend?"

"Antonio and I are old friends, we were children together," she answered. "We played together, went to the same missionary school. When he came to America, he contacted me."

"He told me he didn't know you."

"Yes, I'm afraid he had no choice."

My head throbbed. We headed east on Carpenter for a few blocks and rolled into a filling station lot. I felt old and tired. I chewed my lower lip thoughtfully and asked, "What was the meeting about?"

"I told them it was foolish to meet so close to your place of work, but we couldn't go to the mansion. We should have rented a room somewhere."

"You are avoiding the question. What was the meeting about?"

"It's a long and involved story." She rolled down the window on her right, scooted sideways in the seat, faced my direction, and flashed me a one-sided smile. "I see you've whittled out a couple of minutes for us to talk, but I need to get to the Alamo."

"Why did you call for me?" I asked. "You asked for me specifically. Surely you knew I would want some answers."

"Okay, I asked for you because I did want to see you."

"Let's take care of my questions first."

"All right." She folded her hands in her lap, her posture erect and prim. "We met last week because we came onto some information that a load of processed cocaine was on the way north. This stuff had not gone through the Mexican middleman. One less man to pay, more money for the traffickers involved. The druglords where the cocaine is grown, know of my father's connection and my brothers' farm. When my father started looking for Ricardo's murderers, they found out about his political position here in Illinois. First they tried to blackmail him with his second family in El Salvador to keep him quiet. Look at the news; you can see what that would mean for a man in public life. My father was already married when he had three children with my mother. He also believes his political career would be over if he were publicly associated with my mother and her son's connection to drug trafficking. We were trying to come up with a solution when they tried to kill my father. "

"So you killed them."

"You don't really want to know the truth, Trudy," she said, settling back into her seat and looking straight ahead.

I waited. A large woman with three little boys pulled into the parking space next to us, and they all got out. As she marched in front of the cab, her tan cleavage bulged over the top of a bra-like halter the colors of the American flag. The littlest kid smacked the cab's hood. His mother grabbed his arm and pulled him away, then smiled and waved to me.

Anita said, "I miss my family."

"Your aunt has moved."

"Yes. How do you know?"

"I drove past the place."

"A little out of your way, wasn't it?"

"Okay," I admitted. "I've been trying to find you."

Anita flashed a smile. "Well, now you have found me."

I coaxed her. "The last time we talked you told me about your friend's death at college. What happened after that?"

"I came home to Chicago," she said softly. "I stayed with my aunt and worked at her firm. First I did clerical work, then paralegal. A year later I finished my degree and started law school."

"So you are an attorney, too?"

She shook her head. "I have a law degree. I wanted to go into politics, like my father, and I started working for the district attorney. I did a year there. Worked my tail off for very little money. Then I met a woman and, as you Americans say, everything went to hell."

"Still living in Chicago?" I asked, when her words seemed to trail off.

Anita nodded. "It's a big city. We shared an apartment right under my father's nose. Even if he'd figured out that we were living together, I doubt he would have known we were lovers. He wasn't governor then."

"State treasurer," I interjected.

"Yes. Anyway, she worked for the state police and loved her job. I could see how my education could be very useful in her line of work. Plus, it paid more than working for the city. Anyway, I applied and was accepted."

"You work for the state police?"

She nodded.

"So you come and go at the mansion because you work for the state police?" I wasn't convinced, and I'm sure my voice betrayed that. The whole thing sounded far-fetched. Of course, everything that had happened recently was light years past normal.

A man and woman were arguing at the gas pumps. I couldn't make out the words, but they sounded drunk, each trying to out shout the other, their voices like stainless steel. The woman with the little boys returned to her car, shoving lotto tickets in her purse and brazenly carrying a quart of 8-Ball. The kids trailed along behind, each holding a can of unopened soda.

I turned toward Anita. The night was warm and perspiration dotted her nose and upper lip; the faint smell of warm Oriental spices hung in the air—her cologne, I assumed. She met my eyes, her face expressionless. I lowered my window, hoping for a breeze, but it only seemed to let in more heat. The atmosphere had changed and every little thing stood out; each movement was distinct and seemed vastly important.

"Look," I said in an even tone, "tell me the rest or I will call the police as soon as I let you out of the cab."

Anita continued to stare ahead.

"You know," I said, "it's late. I'm losing money sitting here."

Anita pulled a tube of lipstick and a hand mirror from her bag. She touched up her lips, then turned to me with a hard vermilion smile.

I recoiled somewhat, my right temple pounding, anger like lava surging through me. I started the cab and put it in gear. We were on the street headed north before she spoke again.

"Trudy, the law is an imperfect mechanism."

"I'm still not sure which side of that imperfect mechanism you are on," I said, my voice low and dispirited. I had decided to let her off at the Alamo and call the police. Pop Wilson was dead and Toni Matulis was out of commission. Who else knew about Anita?

Toni had told me they'd been warned off the case several months ago because Executive Security had taken it over. The state police hadn't wanted interference from the city police. The only reason she kept working on it was the mansion was on her beat. Should I tell the police that Antonio had said he didn't know a woman who it turns out grew up with him? No laws broken there. Did I tell them that Anita was connected to the shootings at the mansion? But was she? And what would happen when the governor himself turned out to be involved? My whole story was as thin as the gold on a weekend wedding ring.

"Why don't you come into the tavern?" she said as we turned onto North Eleventh Street. "We can talk where it's cool. I called you for a reason. We can go over it there. Then I will tell you whatever you want to know."

Why had she called for me? Was I getting too close? Asking too many questions, looking for her? "There's something I have to know right now." I didn't look at her, not even a glance. "Did you have anything to do with the murder of the police officer a few days ago?" That was certainly something I could report to the police.

The cab was silent. I waited, a cold chill spreading across my neck and shoulders. Finally she said, "I didn't shoot him, if that's what you mean."

"That's not what I mean." My voice rose as I repeated, "Did you have anything to do with it?"

"We set up a sting. Several things went wrong—"

"Did you have anything to do with the murder?"

Anita sucked in her breath. "Yes."

I pulled Number Twenty-one into the Alamo's narrow lot and put it in park.

Anita dug in her purse and pulled out a ten. She opened the passenger door, got out, walked around to the driver's side and passed the money to me. Her movements were as graceful as a panther. "Keep the change."

I nodded, looked behind me to see if anything was coming and put the cab in reverse.

"Wait a minute." Anita held onto the door as if she could stop me.

I kept my foot on the brake and waited.

"Come in, Trudy," she said. "Let me buy you a drink."

"I don't drink."

"Some chili, then. Have you had your supper yet?"

"I'm not hungry." Which was a lie, because I'm always hungry for chili.

Anita smiled confidently. More than anything, I wanted the truth. She turned in the direction of the Alamo and strolled languidly toward it. Her hand on the door, she turned back and looked at me seductively.

An inner voice reminded me that following Anita was always dangerous. I knew she had killed the men from El Salvador. Would she hesitate to kill me if she thought I knew too much? Maybe she had even intended me to die when she took the cab and left me stranded. Now she could finish the job.

But the Alamo was a public place, after all, not a dark alley. I put the limo in park and radioed Minnie that I was taking a break. She didn't sound thrilled with this, but since I'd come in on my night off, she held her tongue. I rolled up the windows, locked the cab and followed Anita Alvarez into the Alamo.

The place was fairly lively for a Wednesday night. Two couples were playing pool. Several men lined the bar and the jukebox was blaring. Anita approached the bar and spoke to a couple of men I didn't know. I waited, watching her. When she looked up and saw me, surprise registered on her face. She said something to the men and they looked my direction too.

"Thank you for changing your mind."

I shrugged.

"Sit down a minute." She indicated an empty booth along the wall. "Let me buy you a Coke or something."

"I'm fine." I slid into the booth on the side that faced the door.

"You want some dinner?"

I shook my head.

Anita looked at her watch. "We're going to have a meeting. A couple of people are late."

Rosa crossed the room and asked, "You two gonna have anything?"

Anita said, "Bring me a Coke."

Rosa looked at me and I said, "Coffee."

A slow song started on the jukebox, Kris Kristofferson, I think. A man and a woman from a booth down near the pool table got up and danced, moving together as one, shutting out the rest of the world. Rosa sat a coffee mug in front of me, gave Anita a Coke in a highball glass, and waved her off when she started to pay. I lifted the hot coffee to my lips. The liquid was strong and bitter. The door behind Anita opened and a woman with white hair entered. She looked around and her eyes settled on me. She smiled and came toward us.

"What a pleasant surprise," said Rosalyn Richards. "So nice to see you again, Trudy."

"One person is late," said Anita. "Antonio is in the back."

Rosalyn looked toward the two men at the bar. "I see Executive Security is here."

Anita nodded.

"And has Ms. Thomas agreed?"

Anita quickly put her finger to her lips and Rosalyn stopped mid-sentence.

I sipped the coffee again. The second time it went down smoother. I needed to get back to work. I had to let Alex out in a couple of hours and make Pinky's breakfast in the morning.

Rosalyn said, "I'm heading to the back room. See you both soon."

"Have I agreed to what?" I asked, as soon as the older woman was out of sight.

Anita reached across the table and placed her hand over mine. "A small thing. You will gain a lot of information and the price will be one little thing."

I was shaking my head, about to refuse, when the door to the Alamo opened again. A tall woman with dark hair stepped inside and looked around. Her eyes rested almost immediately on the table where Anita's hand still covered mine. I started to say "hello" when I realized that she hadn't seen me. She was looking at Anita, who at the same time noticed that I had been distracted and turned. Anita then slid out of the booth, crossed the room and embraced Eileen Sheridan.

Chapter Twenty-Seven

The backroom had been used for storage and a long narrow folding table was open in its center. A rattan chair covered with newspapers was at the far end of the room. Cases of ketchup, potato chips, canned red beans, chili powder, crackers and other cooking supplies lined the walls. It was an internal room with no windows and a single door. Eight of us gradually settled on an assortment of stools and folding chairs around the table. A man who introduced himself as Barry Carmichael was directly across from me at the head of the table. Along my left side were Anita, Eileen and Antonio. Along the right were Rosalyn Richards and the two older guys who'd been at the bar. Phillip Roach wore a pimento-colored baseball cap backward; Ryan Andrews had gray hair and an iron smile. Both these two were with the Illinois State Drug Enforcement Unit. Barry Carmichael was the man whose number Anita had once given me if I needed to reach her. The morning after our adventure at Jimmy's Bait Shop, he had sent Rosalyn Richards to our aid.

Carmichael opened a green folder and read from the top page. "The shipment came through Tijuana successfully and is currently across the border. Barring anything unforseen, it will be here for delivery late tomorrow night. The traffickers will contact our operants and a meeting will be set."

"So," said Anita, "tomorrow."

Carmichael nodded.

Eileen Sheridan said, "Has Trudy agreed to work with us?"

Everyone turned to me.

I heard Anita say, "We haven't discussed it yet."

Carmichael swore and slapped the green file against the table.

"We don't need her," Roach said. "We can rent a cab from Red, White and Blue or one of the other companies. We'll be better off with one of our own people driving anyway."

Anita said, "Won't work. One of their guys knows her."

There followed a long silence during which I squirmed in my chair. The room was warm and with eight people crowded in, the air seemed heavy and close. My mind was racing. Every cabdriver knows drug dealers. I suppose it follows that they know us. So what?

Finally Carmichael said, "Ms. Thomas, Anita has suggested that you might help us with a sting. We intend to shut down a local drug operation. These guys have figured out a way to cut out so many middlemen that the profits for them are astronomical. That, of course, involved many obstacles, and so far they've overcome all of them. We've been working on this for several months."

Anita leaned forward. "Because of my connections in Central America—more specifically, my families' connections—I have been able to ferret out information on drug shipments. I've been working in the background in state law enforcement for years. We've made some arrests, but never been able to get anyone this high up in the operation. There is so much money involved that most of these guys just pay off the police. Eileen and I have been working on this particular sale for a while."

"Is this related to the men at the Cardinal?" I asked.

Anita nodded. "Those men worked for a man in Central America who is beyond the law. They had the nerve to contact my father, Governor Wright. Because of his connections to my family they thought he might grant them safe passage. But things don't work the same here as down there. So they tried to kill my father."

"And you killed them," I finished for her.

"I-I—" Anita sat back in her chair while the others watched her. "I was just going to talk to them. It was self defense. They shot at us."

There was an awkward silence. We all knew it was a lie.

At length Eileen spoke up. "My job with the state police is to head up Operation Valkyrie. We came across the information about this particular shipment through an arrest made on the highway north of here. We convinced a trafficker to give us information in exchange for amnesty. We've invested a great deal of time and expense. Naturally we want a successful outcome."

Antonio, who I had almost forgotten was there, spoke up. "Who on their end would ask for Trudy?"

"The only people I know who sell drugs," I said evenly, "work the street corners. Any cabdriver can find those guys."

"You know someone higher up in the food chain than that," said Anita.

"Who?"

"Freddy Walters."

My mouth dropped open. Suddenly I was mad. "Who the hell are you guys? I want to see some identification." What happened next was sort of stunning. Badges came out of everywhere. They all had badges, except Antonio.

Anita tossed her identification on the table in front of me. "They want you as bait. They figure if we are who we claim, local drug kingpins, we won't care what happens to you. Real buyers wouldn't be concerned for your safety."

Barry Carmichael said, "Of course, we are concerned for your safety—for everyone's safety. You will be wearing a vest. We will have Andrews here in the back seat with the money. Twelve million dollars, in cash."

I said, "You'd need a pickup truck to carry that much cash."

Carmichael smiled. His voice, his demeanor, everything gave an impression of complete docility. "Most of it will be in large bills." He turned to Eileen. "Two leather bags?"

Eileen nodded.

"And what if I say no?"

Anita spoke up. "You can do that. This is dangerous. If we can arrest these local gangsters, the Springfield community will benefit." She looked around at the others.

I actually started to imagine it. "Do I carry a gun?" I asked, feeling less like a cowboy than I sounded.

Everyone looked at Eileen. So she was the head guy. I was surprised again. She said, "Do you know how to use a gun?"

"I do."

Eileen said, "Carrying a weapon could put you in more danger—if you don't intend to use it."

I wiped sweat from my forehead and ran my damp hand through my hair, my mind spinning. How the hell was Freddy involved in this mess? Had Lotty been killed because of drugs, instead of because of my screwups? I looked up at the others. Everyone seemed to be waiting.

I said, "Tell me more about Freddy Walters."

Carmichael said, "I'm afraid we can't. His involvement and your participation has been a last minute wrench thrown into the works. The first time we heard his name was a couple of days ago."

"Monday?"

Carmichael shrugged. "Maybe, why?"

"That's when he disappeared in the middle of his shift."

Carmichael nodded. He leaned back in his chair and looked at me.

Eileen spoke up then. "I say we scrap the whole thing. Something is wrong. We can't afford to risk lives, or the money."

Anita turned toward Eileen. "The money is the most important thing to you, isn't it? If that much cocaine hits the streets in a town this size, the current drug problem will seem goddamn small. Cocaine ravages people's lives. Crime increases. People die."

"I know Valkyrie and other operations like it are doing little more than putting a Band-Aid on stage-three cancer," said Eileen. "But this time the risk is too high."

"So?" Anita challenged her.

"Twelve million dollars, 'Nita. I work with a budget, not a cornucopia. We'd never be able to crawl out of the hole if we lost the money."

Antonio said, "The bottom line here is, will Trudy help us? I think we could still pull this off if she will."

Eileen said, "I'm not convinced."

I looked at Anita Alvarez, Antonio and the others. The whole thing seemed too Hollywood to me.

Carmichael said, "With something this big we have to expect a little of the unexpected."

"Can I sleep on it?" I asked, wanting to just get the hell out of there.

Anita looked at Carmichael. "What's our drop dead time?"

"We really need to know tonight," he answered.

"Drop-dead time?" Anita demanded.

Carmichael considered the question. He looked at the two Drug Enforcement guys and asked, "What's your bottom line?"

"I'd say noon tomorrow," said Ryan Andrews.

Carmichael said to me, "How does that sound to you?"

"Good." I looked at my watch. "I've got to get back on the road. We're shorthanded tonight. I'm supposed to be working."

In the next few moments I excused myself and went back to the cab. I radioed Minnie, who was glad to hear from me, and she gave me three trips stacked end to end. By the time I was free to think about the meeting at the Alamo, it was very late. I considered calling Toni Matulis and running all this new information past her. Could two separate agencies, the city and the state, be working on the same thing, unknowingly? It happened all the time on *Miami Vice* reruns, but their vice cops still used Commodore computers. It was an old show.

The next morning Ralph and Betty had two new drivers starting days. Lester would be working nights with Johnny Henderson and me. Betty offered to let me have the night off but seemed relieved when I didn't take it.

At home I let Alex out and went to make Pinky's breakfast. He'd been awake for quite a while and seemed to be feeling well. I made coffee and sliced bananas over two bowls of Cheerios. While we ate, I told him about the meeting at the Alamo.

When I finished, Pinky asked, "Did you ask them about Ramie Malone?"

"No."

"Do you think there's a connection?"

I said, "Maybe."

"Sounds like everybody involved only knows a piece of this mess," said Pinky. He peeled another banana and gave Alex a bite, then looked back at me. "The state guys hadn't heard of Freddy Walters, they don't know about Ramie Malone, and what's left of the city guys don't appear to know about the state guys."

"Well…" my voice trailed off.

Pinky refilled his coffee cup and offered me more.

I held up my hand. "Better not, I need to sleep."

"One more question," said Pinky. "How is the governor involved in all of this? No one has explained that. What did Matulis and her partner come across at the gates of the mansion?"

Of course he was right. I felt Pinky's hand on my shoulder and I placed mine over his. "You need any more help from me?" I asked. "I have to sleep fast this morning."

"Alex and I are fine," said Pinky. "But if I get a vote, I say stay out of whatever is going on tonight. You've been shot once already. You don't want to make Alex and me orphans."

I nodded. "You're right. I'll call them as soon as I get home and tell them that I won't be helping."

"Good."

At home I stripped, tossing my clothes in the laundry basket and showered. I put on a fresh pair of boxer shorts and an old red T-shirt. I felt clean, tired and ready for a good sleep. The trailer air was warm and I kicked the air conditioner on and closed the shades. Then I sat in the easy chair and dialed Barry Carmichael's number.

I got a machine and was almost relieved. I left a message: "This is Trudy. I've thought over your request for help tonight and talked it over with my family. I've decided to decline. I'm letting you know early, and I'm sure you'll work things out some other way. Good luck with everything."

I felt like a weight had been lifted off my shoulders when I hung up. I took the receiver off the hook, so some telemarketer wouldn't wake me up, and, I have to admit, so Carmichael couldn't call me back. All alone in the dark, cool bedroom, I slid under the covers and curled up to sleep.

Chapter Twenty-Eight

The sign on the front of the brown house read "Jones' Garage." A hand-painted arrow pointed around back. White rock sparkled in the sun and crackled under my tires as I turned off the Harley ignition and let the bike coast to a stop. A candy-pink late-model stock car, with a silver number 8 painted on the side, was parked under a shade tree. The hood was up and a slender man leaned over the fender; his jeans hugged his hips and the crack of his butt showed. The open garage, beyond the shade tree, was actually larger than the house.

"You Les Jones?" I called to the guy.

He felt on the fender for a shop rag and came out from under the hood cleaning the grease from his hands. He was young, with a mild case of acne and a smear on his chin that might have been a goatee. He said, "Nice bike."

"Thanks." I lowered the kickstand, dismounted and wiped the sweat off my palms onto my jeans. "I'm looking for Les Jones."

The kid pointed. "In the garage."

I crossed the drive. The tinny sound of an AM radio drifted toward me as I approached. Though the area around a tow truck was dark, the bay next to it was lit. A large oscillating fan hummed in the background. A half-empty liter of Diet Pepsi sat on the floor next to a pair of red trouser legs and scuffed tennis shoes that stuck out from under another stock car; this one was silver with a pink number 8 painted on the side. The car was raised and balanced on the front end by a professional-sized hydraulic jack.

I took a deep breath and called out. "I'm looking for Les Jones."

The half-figure under the car jumped, as if startled. Then the dolly rolled out, and it was my turn to be surprised. Her hair was a blonde buzz-cut and her face was tanned. She wore a pair of faded red coveralls. "I'm Leslie Jones," she said, pulling herself up to a sitting position.

I stammered a little. "Harold Tangler told me about you."

"Yes?"

"He said that sometimes you rebuild engines."

She wiped the back of her red sleeve across her forehead, picked up the Diet Pepsi and took a long drink. Her tanned throat moved as she swallowed. She set the bottle down, reached toward me, and said, "Give me a hand."

I took her hand and helped her up. Her movements were light and graceful; had she pulled me up, she'd have needed a crane. She was slightly taller than me, maybe five eight or nine.

"What kind of engine?" she asked.

"Eighty-four Plymouth."

"I mean how many cylinders, cubic inches?"

"Oh. Four cylinders, I think. I don't know the cubic thing."

She picked up her drink. "Can I get you a soda or anything?"

My throat did seem dry. "Yeah," I croaked. "Thanks."

She walked to an old refrigerator in the corner, wedged in the end of the largest work bench I'd ever seen. "I have Diet Pepsi, Strawberry and Orange Crush." She stooped to get a better look. "Let's see, canned Coke and a bottle or two of water."

Sometimes life offers you too many choices. I stood there and looked at her. After an awkward moment, I said, "Whatever is in front is fine."

She pulled out a bottle of Orange Crush and held it toward me, smiling. "Let's go talk turkey."

The office was a small room, about eight-by-ten, on the other side of the towtruck. The walls were covered with pictures of stock cars. A couple of trophies sat on top of a black bookcase; *Popular Mechanic* and *Motor Trend* magazines spilled out of it. She sat behind the desk, and I took one of the two chairs across from her.

"Now," she said when we were both settled and I had my soda open, "tell me about your Plymouth."

"I've been told it needs rings."

"Using oil? Smoking? No power?"

I nodded.

"Could be rings…" She hesitated, "…or worse. How many miles you got on it?"

"I know it's turned over at least once."

"If Harold sent you to me," she said, "I am assuming he couldn't come up with another motor."

I shook my head. "He called several places, even out of town."

Leslie nodded. "Is it running right now?"

"Nope."

"That's not good. We can tow it in, and I can take a look at it. But depending on what I find, you could be talking more than a thousand dollars on a pretty old car. There's no guarantee that something else won't go wrong with it in two weeks. I could put you in a newer used car for less than a thousand."

I sighed and said, "I really want to get this car fixed."

"Sentimental reasons?" she ventured.

"I love the paint job."

She chuckled. "Oh, good. I've never met anyone who was sentimental over an '84 Plymouth. Scared me a little."

I laughed with her, then gave her the bad news. "I don't think I can raise a thousand dollars."

She set a blank invoice on her desk. "Where's it at? I'll have it towed in, and we'll talk about price when I've looked at it. You decide not to fix it, you only have to pay for the tow."

I gave her the address of Red, White and Blue, and she wrote it down as well as my name and phone number. As she reached across the desk to shake my hand, she said, "Have you considered painting a different car to look like the Plymouth?"

I said, "No."

She must have heard the sadness in my voice because her tone got gentler then. "Well, I'll see what we can do to fix you up. But think about that paint job."

I thanked her. Outside I dropped my half empty orange soda in a trash barrel and remounted the Harley. I was feeling pretty good by the time I pulled into work. It was going to be a good day.

I won't say that I didn't think about Anita Alvarez and the drug sting over the course of the evening. I sat out a card game thinking about it. I thought about it at the airport waiting for the St. Louis flight at ten-thirty. But I remembered Pinky and his comment about being an orphan. I had too many responsibilities to be a hero. I thought about calling Toni and telling her about it, but there were still a lot of unanswered questions.

The shift was a slow one, and I decided that after the airport run I'd check in and get some sleep. That way, if they had the nerve to call for me, I wouldn't be there. So when I pulled into the cab station close to midnight and saw Anita Alvarez sitting on the curb near the front door, I considered turning around in the street and leaving. She stood when she saw me, and I slid down the passenger window.

"Get your guys?" I asked, hoping that the sting was over, and she had lived through it.

She opened the door, got in beside me and said, "Let's get out of here."

I hesitated, watching her. "What's going on?"

"I'll tell you while you drive."

I turned on the meter, pulled out of the lot and headed south on Eleventh Street.

Anita's dark hair was slicked back. She wore a pair of faded jeans and a sparkling white shirt. Her face was fixed with a stern expression. After of a couple of blocks in silence, she said, "Head out to the bypass and south."

I tried to sound casual. "Where we going?"

"Cotton Park, near the State Police headquarters."

"You guys got my message, didn't you?"

"Yes," she said. "You're not going to help us."

"Then what's going on?"

She let out her breath slowly. "There's been a hitch."

I raised my voice. "You know, I just can't help you. I have responsibilities."

"Our connection claimed he wanted only one buyer there. We're thinking, okay, we'll send Andrews in an unmarked car, alone. Then the guy said Walters wouldn't have it. He wants you."

I turned the cab east toward the bypass.

"Is it possible that he is a hostage?" Anita asked.

"How the hell should I know? He's been missing since Monday. Does that make him a hostage?" I wanted to believe that he wasn't the bad guy. But why the heck did he want me involved in this mess?

Anita said, "Something is wrong."

We rode in silence for a couple of blocks. The night was turning cool. In the rearview mirror I could see heat lightning.

"Does this Walters seem like a drug dealer to you?"

I shook my head no.

"He could be in danger."

I said, "So you just came to get me? Just like that, you figured I'd help you. Your plan didn't work, so get me involved again!"

"I am sorry about the other times. We will have you covered at all times. Andrews will be in the back seat, armed. You'll have a two-way radio, on our frequency, and a vest. We won't be far from wherever they call you to meet. It's not just me this time, Trudy. It's the best people the state of Illinois has."

Despite my anger, I headed south to where the highway crossed a motionless, colorless lake. Haze filtered the moonlight. I turned the limo left on the dark winding road toward the park. I hadn't really said I would help them, but we both knew I would.

Two unmarked cars sitting under a tree off the main drive were caught in my headlights. At Anita's instruction I stopped. Someone ran toward us. It was Andrews. He carried two leather bags.

Anita swung the door open and we were bathed in the domelight. Andrews opened the back door and threw two bags on the seat. They thudded as if they were as heavy as two blocks of cement. He said, "Call came twenty minutes ago. It's the road over behind the Children's Zoo. We've got to get moving."

Anita leaned down and met my eyes.

I nodded and said to Andrews, "Get in."

Suddenly Eileen was there holding out a vest. "Put this on."

I looked up at her, startled. "How?"

"Under your T-shirt."

"Are you kidding?"

Eileen jerked her chin. "Over there behind the tree. I'll help you."

I hesitated, thankful that the darkness hid my blush.

"Come on, Trudy, this is no time for modesty."

I shut off the ignition and got out of the cab. My aching joints reminded me that I was too old for this kind of thing. I took the vest from Eileen and was surprised by its weight. In the darkness, several feet from the cab and the group of people who had gathered around it, I pulled off my T-shirt and put the vest over my shoulders.

I jumped when I heard Eileen's voice behind me. "You've got it backward."

Her hands reached to help me and after a short struggle I was in the heavy, warm vest and my T-shirt was on. As I got back in the cab, Anita handed me a two-way radio.

"If you are in a situation where you can't use this and you need to contact us, just key your mike. We will monitor the Red, White and Blue frequency too."

For some reason that made me more comfortable. Keying the mike was a common way of letting dispatch know that there is trouble. I'd done it before. We all had.

I don't remember much about the drive around the lake. When we pulled off the main road toward the Children's Zoo, my headlights swept the parking areas. There was nothing. I said over my shoulder, "What now?"

"Pull up over there and shut off the lights. We wait."

Heat lightning flashed again toward the west; seconds later I heard thunder roll in the distance. The dark ground along the road sloped toward the lake, a blue haze drifted along the banks and the nearly motionless water lapped at the rocks below. A breeze had begun to filter through the tops of the large old trees and they whispered to each other languidly. A man came out of the darkness walking as softly as a cat. He had short dark hair and a face like a collapsed lung. For a moment I felt dizzy. He opened the back door and got in next to Ryan Andrews.

I watched his red-eyed scowl in the rearview mirror. His voice was remote and placid. "Drive straight ahead, lady."

I started the cab and put it in gear. My hands shook. The shirt under my arms was wet and sweat rolled down my chest and back. The weight of the vest seemed to cut off my breathing, and I felt nausea rise. I drove straight ahead across the beach house bridge and followed the road around to the left. I slowed as we came to a Y.

"Left," the guy said.

I reached to key the mike, thinking Eileen could at least get our directions, then felt the cold barrel of a gun against the back of my neck. "No funny stuff, lady."

Ryan Andrews seemed to take all this calmly. I could see his eyes in the rearview mirror staring straight ahead. The road was dark and the opulent lake homes grew farther apart as we wound our way along East Lake Drive. I moved the cab slowly, following the reflectors on the center line. What had Anita meant when she'd told me I would be covered at all times? Were they behind me somewhere? I didn't dare touch the two-way radio in the seat beside me, not with Meat Face watching.

"Up here," the guy said. "Take the road to the left."

I almost passed a partially hidden lane that cut a dark path between the brush; I had to cut the limo sharply to make the turn. My headlights illuminated ghostly bushes that reached like gnarly arthritic fingers, brushing the sides of the cab. The tires rattled on the broken pavement as I followed the narrow road father away from civilization. We went from bushes, trees and gravel to a dirt lane that separated some farm fields. Then I saw a light in the distance. A place was cut out of the landscape, a huge transformer. As I approached, I saw the other car and knew before I was told that we had come to the spot.

Bright overhead lights came from the tall poles near the corners of the chain-link fence. As I pulled onto the graveled lot and stopped in front of a black minivan, the doors opened. Two men and Freddy Walters got out and walked toward us. I stopped the cab and at Meat Face's instruction, turned off the motor. Ryan Andrews and Face got out of the cab, each carrying one of the two heavy leather bags. I stayed where I was. Freddy saw me. I couldn't read what was going on, but after a moment he said something to the other four and walked toward the driver's side. He lifted his chin slightly in my direction, being careful to keep his back to the others.

"I see your cab isn't fixed yet."

I opened my mouth but could think of nothing to say.

Freddy turned to the others and gave them a thumbs up, then faced me again. He lowered his voice. "Can you hear me, Trudy?"

To tell the truth I barely could. I nodded and leaned forward.

"Sorry to bring you into this," he said just above a whisper. "When I walk back over there, you need to open the car door quietly and run."

"But—"

He held up his hand to silence me. "I mean it. All hell is about to break loose. It's the only way to save yourself."

"Freddy, what the hell?"

He put his finger to his lips. I could see something in his eyes. Was it fear? Then he turned and started back toward the others. He was still several feet away from the group of men when I saw him pull a gun and aim it at the back of Meat Face's head. That was the last I saw because I quietly grabbed the two-way radio and opened the car door. Behind me I heard the first shot and then it turned into Dodge City.

I almost made it to cover before a bullet got me. I felt the blow, followed by a searing pain in my arm. I went down in the gravel head first, and the radio flew out of my hands. I tried to stand, my head spun, and I found my knees wouldn't hold me. The shooting was over quickly.

I drifted in and out of consciousness for a while. Finally, I felt myself being half-carried and half-dragged back to the cab by someone with blood on his hands—maybe my blood, I didn't know. Whoever had me heaved me up and I landed on top of a spare tire, then rolled sideways. The trunk lid was coming down before I realized where I was. Then darkness.

Chapter Twenty-Nine

The next thing I remembered was rain thumping on the lid of the trunk. That was a relief but I was in the hot and stale dark, unable to see an inch in front of my face. The vest pressed on my chest, and I gasped for air. My shirt was wet and my arm hurt. I tried to relax and quiet my breathing. Several minutes passed. I realized the car wasn't moving. I listened for sounds of the others but heard only the rain. Where the hell was my backup?

I was on my left side, my arthritis-in-the-hip side, not that it mattered—everything hurt. My saliva tasted of metal, and I fought waves of nausea. I might have felt better if I could vomit, but the thought of lying in the contents of my own stomach helped me fight it. I pressed my feet against the back of the trunk, thinking that I might be able to dislodge the back seat. Nothing gave. Unlike a personal car, where the spare tire has a certain place and is hooked in, spare tires at Red, White and Blue usually got tossed in on top of everything. This one was right in the center of the trunk. I was half on it and half wrapped around it. I felt around for the tire iron, and worked to dislodge it from beneath the tire. I had to rest for a while before I felt for the trunk lock. Braced on one arm, I worked with the other. The pain in my right arm was fierce; sweat ran down my face and into my eyes. I wedged the flat end of the tire iron next to the lock and in one motion gave it all the force I could muster. The tool slipped out of position and struck me in the forehead as it fell. Stunned, I lay in agony for several minutes before the crashing pain in my head went away. I positioned the tool again, driving it in as far as I could. This time I managed to get out of the way when the thing slipped.

Where was Anita Alvarez? Had they tried to followed us? I hadn't been able to key the mike or use the two-way radio, which was in the bushes where I had fallen. If they had followed us, had they caught the last turn off the lake road? Of course if they found the cab, they wouldn't know I was in the damn trunk. I took a deep breath and hollered, "Help. Help me," until I was exhausted. Then I lay still, listening to the rain—angry, hurting and scared. Would this be it for me? I moved to take the weight off my aching left hip and realized that something was under it. I braced myself, raised my hip up and pulled a bag out. What the hell? I dragged it up on top of the spare tire and felt inside. My hands closed on a pint bottle of liquor. This had to be the bag of George's stuff. He'd thrown it in the trunk yesterday when I'd taken the cab to work Freddy's shift. The potato chips were crushed flat in the bottom of the bag. Somewhere was a baby-food jar of drug-free urine. Wonderful!

Then, in the loathsome darkness, my hand closed on George's two-way radio. What had George said? "Police Band?" "Battery low?" Definitely, he'd said, "Battery low." I felt for the on and off switch and found it. A weak, wavering light came on with some static. I tried two of the buttons on the top row before I found the send key.

"Help," I said into the mike. "I have an emergency."

I waited. Nothing.

"Break for anybody. I have an emergency."

Considering the strength of the battery, I probably wasn't broadcasting over a block. I took a deep breath and let it out. I said a little prayer— one of those foxhole prayers, please, please please, help me! I tried to relax and, in doing so, cracked my head on the metal inside of the trunk lock. That's when it occurred to me that I needed a stronger antenna to get the maximum distance with the radio. At that point, I was wrapped around the spare tire spoon-fashion. I was going to have to turn over and face the back end of the car. I switched the little radio off, placed it within reach and started struggling. I ended up lying across the spare tire on my stomach, my knees bent and my feet pressed against the trunk lining. In the pitch darkness, I felt for the metal lock mechanism, held the antenna against it and turned the radio on. This time the light only flickered. I swore and shook it. The light came on. I held the antenna against the inside of the trunk lock and tried again.

"Breaker. Anyone, I have an emergency."

I waited. Nothing but weak static.

I raised my voice. "Anyone? Help me. I have an emergency."

I heard her then. She sounded a thousand miles away. "What is the nature of your emergency? Come back."

"I am locked in a car trunk."

"Say again?"

"A car trunk. My cab," I was shouting by then. "Someone put me in the trunk of my cab and left me here." Only later did it occur to me that someone might hear me yelling, open the trunk, drag me out and finish me off.

"Do you know your twenty?"

Tears sprang to my eyes. "Near Jefferson Lake," I shouted. "We turned off East Lake Drive about seven miles north of the beach bridge, then onto a small road for a couple of miles. I am sitting in the middle of a bean field by an electrical transformer."

"Wolf Creek Road?"

"I don't know," I sobbed.

"Big transformer?"

"Yes. Yes!"

"Stay calm," the woman said. "I am near you. I am calling the police. Is it safe for me to...?"

Her last question was cut off as the light on the radio went dead. I shook it again and touched the antenna to the lock. "Hello?" The light wavered and went out. She'd said she knew where I was. I hoped she was right. If she called the police before she came looking for me, I thought, they'd eventually find me. I hoped they found me before I bled to death or, worse, needed to use the bathroom. I was in the county. The woman would have to call the county sheriff's office, and a third arm of the law would be involved in this mess. Well, why not?

I made myself comfortable, my belly across one end of the spare tire and my cheek resting on the other. Cab companies don't keep new tires for spares; I knew it was filthy and didn't care. The blood from my arm had stopped running, though the pain was searing. The rain on the trunk lid had cooled the air around me. In fact, I was chilly.

I heard the car's tires on the gravel far too soon. Had one of the gangsters come back? I lay as quiet as I could. Heavy footsteps passed the limo and the driver's side door was pulled open, then slammed shut. I could hear a man's heavy breathing, then the scratching of keys on the trunk lock. Suddenly the catch gave and light flooded the darkness.

He was the biggest man I'd ever seen with wild, dark hair and a beard, wearing a long black raincoat that looked like a shotgun could appear from under it—at least in a movie, it could. The lights from the transformer cast eerie shadows. He looked at me sort of squinty-eyed, raindrops making rivulets on his huge, grisly face.

I held my breath.

"She's in here, Ma."

Then I saw a woman standing next to the guy, looking down at me. She was half his height, but every bit as round. Her mousy gray hair was pulled back from her forehead, and she wore square-cut, black-rimmed glasses. She reached out a hand to me and said, "I brought my boy here in case there was still trouble around."

I started to move. My feet were asleep and tingling. My knees hurt.

"Let me help." The boy reached for me and bumped his knuckles on the hard vest. "What the heck you got on?"

"Bulletproof vest."

"You police?"

Now that my fear had waned, I could see the wide-eyed kid was quite young. I shook my head no. Better not say too much.

He put both arms around my middle, like a bear hug, lifted me out of the trunk and stood me on my feet. I immediately fell backward, catching myself on the limo's taillight.

"Whoa, lady," said the boy. "You need to sit down."

"Inside the cab," I said. "Will you help me?"

"Sure, lady."

The boy was gentle, but when he put his arm around my shoulders I thought I would faint from the pain. He stepped away from me, confused by my scream.

"Now, what is this?' The woman started fussing at us. She came around the boy and introduced us while she looked at my back. "This is my boy Eddy, and I'm Stella Snodgrass. Have you hurt your arm? Let me see."

I stomped my feet a couple of times to get the circulation going. I felt light-headed and took slow deep breaths. "How did you get here so fast?" I asked.

"Live about a mile away," said Stella. "My husband and older boy are truck drivers. We have a CB set up to keep in touch. I knew when you told me about the transformer right where you were. It's the only big one for quite a ways. County deputy should be here soon. I called 'em before we left home."

My skin felt clammy when she started tugging at the back of my T-shirt.

"Eddy, turn around," Stella commanded, then pulled the thing all the way up over my head.

"Can you see anything?" I asked.

"I do." Stella whistled softly.

"What?"

"This vest caught a bullet. I sure didn't know they'd do that."

My knees buckled. The rainy night disappeared, dark at the edges, then down to a small dot, like a fade-out at the end of a movie.

I came to with rain beating softly on my face. I was under a wool blanket and flashing red lights swirled above me. I rolled my head to one side and saw a county deputy kneeling next to me.

"Got an ambulance on the way, ma'am," the guy said. "Can you tell me what happened? Who did this to you?"

"I don't know," I said slowly. And I didn't—exactly. "Could you call Red, White and Blue and tell them…" My voice trailed off. Tell them what?

"I'll call them." It was Stella Snodgrass, her hair soaked and her huge glasses spotted with rain. "Eddy and I are heading home now. Is there anything else we can do?"

"Now, Stella," the deputy said to her, "I think you should stay around and talk to the Sheriff."

"You know where I'll be, Clarence. I'll even put on a pot of coffee. Ain't no sense in me standing around in the rain." She leaned down close to me. "What's your name, sweetie?"

"Trudy," I croaked.

Stella nodded and called to Eddy, who was in front of the cab. When they walked away together I heard him say, "I don't think I've ever seen so much blood."

I looked up at the deputy; had she called him Clarence? "What is he talking about?"

The deputy jerked his head in the direction Eddy had come. "Three dead men up there. You know who they are?"

"What do they look like?" I asked.

"Hard to say. They got bullets through their heads."

I heard the siren then. The deputy stood and walked toward the road to wave the ambulance in.

Chapter Thirty

Following the ordeal of the trunk, my mother, of all people, called Ralph and told him I would no longer be driving a cab. I spent the night in the hospital and was released the next day. Anita called me at home on the third day.

"We lost you," she said.

"Yeah, well, thanks."

"I'm sorry. We had you on East Lake Drive. One minute you were there, the next you were gone."

"I turned off."

"I know," she said. "Why didn't you key the mike?"

"Fucker put a gun to my head," I shouted. "I thought it best if I didn't."

"I'm sorry," she said softly.

"Andrews is dead?"

"Yes."

"I could be dead." I didn't hear her answer because I hung up. I was angry more than anything. I was angry at Anita for getting me involved and then abandoning me. I didn't want to hear that she had tried. She failed—that was enough for me. I was angry at Freddy for leaving me in the trunk. I now knew it was Freddy because his body had not been among those found by the transformer. I was angry at myself for being a sap one more time.

I borrowed money from my mom and bought a ten-year-old Honda Civic with ninety-five thousand miles on the odometer. I delivered pizza full time until I pulled up in front of a two-story house and a drunk seemingly came out of nowhere and pulled a gun on me. It happened in the middle of my shift, in the nice end of town. I threw the money at him, followed by the heavy red thermal box containing two large pizzas with everything and ran. At the nearest gas station (at that point I was fairly sick of talking to the police) I'd called a cab and barely had enough money at home to pay the meter. Michael took me back the next day for the Honda.

I sat at home with the shades drawn for several days following the armed robbery. Alex gave me worried looks. The pizza place tried to call over and over. They left several messages. I needed to turn in the money, the pizza bag and my hat with the logo if I had resigned. I must have thrown the hat at the guy, too, because I had no idea where it was.

Depression folded over me like a heavy blanket. The only time I left home was to check on Pinky, who was doing better than me. Some days I didn't get dressed. My money was running out, and I couldn't make myself care. I thought about Lotty a lot, especially on days when every meal contained some form of chocolate.

One afternoon I was walking into the living room, a bowl of ice cream in one hand and the TV remote in the other, getting ready to settle in for an afternoon of soap operas, when the phone rang. I let it ring. When the answering machine came on, I heard Betty's voice.

"Trudy, if you're there, pick up."

I grabbed the phone without thinking.

Betty said, "My God, honey, how you been?"

I said the first thing that came into my mind. "I'm depressed."

"That don't sound like you," said Betty. "You still delivering pizza?"

"Nah, I quit last Thursday night."

"What you going to do now?"

"Don't know," I said. "Don't care."

Betty made an effort to sound chipper. "I know you've had a run of bad luck, but you can't let it get you down…"

I wasn't listening. I watched the ice cream melt, the pink running into the brown, the white looking sort of foamy. Alex watched me, his head tilted. I reached for the bowl and set it on the floor. Alex sniffed it, then licked. Within seconds the bowl was empty. A spot of Neopolitan-strawberry-pink on his nose was all that remained.

Betty said something about Number Four.

"What?"

"Which 'what'? I've been talking for five minutes."

"What about Number Four?"

"I told you. Ralph had that Jones woman fix it. Rings or something."

"That must have cost a fortune."

"It did."

"Why bother? No one wants to drive it."

"You want to drive it," said Betty.

I met this revelation with silence.

She rushed on. "I wasn't going to mention that. I just called to see how you were, but when I heard your voice I knew you weren't happy. We miss you, Trudy. The place isn't the same without you. I think you miss us."

I sighed. She was right. If I didn't get out of this living room and away from the TV, I was going to sink deeper and deeper into depression. I asked tentatively, "Would you let me work days?"

"Eight hour shifts if you want."

Driving a cab was all I knew. It went beyond that, really. Driving a cab was who I was. I could feel some weight in my chest lift as I considered her offer. The corners of my eyes were moist. "I could try it, I guess, but—"

"But what?"

"But it needs brakes, too."

Betty laughed. "You got it, honey."

"Weekends off?" I asked.

"Don't push your luck."

So, over my mother's objections, I started driving Number Four again. On the first day of summer my nephew Jonathan, Barb's second-youngest son, had his tenth birthday. I didn't really get an invitation—that would have been easy enough to turn down. A birthday card and a ten-dollar bill would have taken care of the obligation. Instead, Barb called me and asked if I could help her. They'd installed an above-ground swimming pool in the back yard and Jonny was having a birthday swim party with all the members of his softball team, including coaches.

I worked that Saturday until two in the afternoon, then went home, showered and changed. I slipped into my least obnoxious T-shirt and a pair of khaki walking-shorts. I even considered, then rejected, shaving my legs. The temperature was in the mid-nineties, the air heavy with humidity a little warm for early summer.

Cars were parked on the street, the lawn and in the drive. I wove the Harley between them to the carport. When I turned the big machine off, I heard the shouts and laughter of children from the back yard. Jonny came running around the corner of the house toward me, water dripping from his blond hair and fresh cut grass clinging to his wet feet and legs.

"What did you bring me, Aunt Trudy?"

I put the kickstand down, dismounted and turned to the saddlebag. "It isn't wrapped," I told him. "I think I should wrap it."

Jonny jumped up and down. "No, no, it's all right. I don't want it wrapped."

I handed him a blue plastic bag that was clearly marked "WalMart."

He held the bag open and his face disappeared. It was a kid's size snorkel outfit, with water wings, mask, and flippers.

Jonny squealed with delight and started running toward the back yard.

"Jonathan Lawrence Merrick," my sister said, "What do you say?"

Jonny turned and waved. "Thanks, Aunt Trudy!"

Barb had her hair swept back and up. She had on a matching yellow swimsuit and sleeveless big-shirt.

I said, "Don't you look nice."

"Are you kidding?" she said. "Every time I go into the sunlight, I see another spot on my legs that the razor didn't get. Look at these stretch marks and varicose veins." She twisted so I could see her thighs.

I bent to get a closer look, then pointed. "You know, if you joined these two spiders it'd make a grotesque tattoo."

Barb yelped and gave me a shove. "Come on in the house. There's a ton of stuff to do."

I followed her toward the front door, trying not to look at Eileen's house across the street. And when I could resist no longer, I did my best not to be too obvious.

"She said she couldn't come."

"Who?"

"Eileen," said Barb. "That's what you were wondering, wasn't it?"

I shrugged.

Inside we were busy with the food. Boys of all sizes ran in and out, tracking water and grass across the kitchen floor and down the hall into the bathroom. My brother-in-law, John, was out back cooking hot dogs on the gas grill. Most of the adults in the back yard were men, softball coaches, I guessed, settled in with bottles of beer, listening to a game on the radio. Once in a while they'd cheer or groan in unison.

Time seemed to go fast. First it was five o'clock and we made all the boys sit around the picnic table and eat hot dogs, potato salad and chips. Then Jonny blew out ten candles on a green and chocolate frosted race-car-shaped cake. By dusk Barb and I were walking around the yard gathering empty paper cups and plates that were sticky from melted ice cream.

I was busy with a net dipping grass out of the pool when I felt someone behind me.

"You look like you know what you're doing," came a woman's voice.

I turned. She was *The Ice Storm* Sigourney Weaver this time, soft, feminine, with eye makeup, her hair curled softly around her shoulders. "How are you, Trudy?" Eileen asked.

I stared at her, unable to think of a damn thing to say.

"You're angry."

I turned back to my work. "I don't have anything to say to you."

"I understand," she said. "I thought you might have questions is all."

"I have a question, all right." The net slipped out of my hands and I watched it sink slowly to the bottom. "Why aren't you and your whole damn Valkyrie force in jail?"

She met my sarcasm with silence.

The yard was empty. For the moment, at least, everyone was inside. Determined to end the conversation, I left her standing by the pool and walked toward the house.

"Wait," Eileen hurried after me. "Please don't go in."

My mistake was stopping. Once I had, I knew I would hear her out. Lawn chairs were scattered around the gas grill on the patio. I stood among them as she strode toward me.

"Come on," she urged. "Sit down for a minute."

Irritated but silent, I selected a webbed chair and sat.

Eileen said, "Thanks," and sat on a chair next to me. She didn't say anything more for a while. The sides of the long lot were lined with an overgrown hedge. Fireflies twinkled in the purple shadows.

Finally she asked, "Have you heard from Freddy Walters?"

"You mean since he left me in the trunk of the limo to die?"

"Yes." She tried to meet my eyes. "I'm sorry."

I looked away. I wasn't having it. Of course I hadn't heard from Freddy. No one had. It was as if he'd disappeared from the face of the earth—along with a lot of money and cocaine. I'd always counted myself a good judge of character, but Freddy had me fooled. He'd had me wondering if I ever really knew anyone or anything. To Eileen I said, "Wouldn't tell you if I did know where he was."

"How much did Anita tell you?"

"Why don't you ask her?"

"Help me, Trudy." She touched my arm. Her fingers were hot.

"Help you what?" I said through my teeth. "What do you and your lunatic girlfriend want now? Can't you see that I don't want to talk to you? Can't you see that my involvement in her schemes hs ravaged my life? Good Lord, Eileen, go home. Leave me alone."

I heard the sliding glass door behind me and my sister said, "Oh, hi, Eileen. Glad you could make it for a little while, anyway."

Eileen craned her neck around. "Thanks, just wanted to talk to your sister for a few minutes."

"You want some iced tea or soda? We have plenty left."

"No, I can't stay long."

"Well," Barb said, "I'll leave you two alone to talk then."

The door slid closed behind us.

Eileen said, "Did Anita tell you about her family?"

I didn't try to control the anger in my voice. "The one in Central America, or the one in North America?"

Eileen watched me, waiting.

"Oh, yes." I counted on my fingers. "Her mother in El Salvador, her dead sister Theresa, her murdered brother Ricardo, her sister the nun and her brother who grows cocaine. Then we have Aunt Rosalyn. And, oh wait, I forgot the most important of all—her father, the governor of Illinois."

"You told me once," said Eileen, "that your father was very important to you."

"If I did, I told you too much."

"Seeking approval from her father was how she got into this mess."

I'd never had to seek approval from my dad. That had been there, no matter what. Of course, there were things we hadn't discussed. But I thought that was normal for young adults. I sure as hell wished he were here to talk to now. I felt myself being drawn into the conversation with Eileen despite myself. Why the hell had she brought up my father? I watched in silence as the fireflies floated in the sultry air.

"Trudy?" Eileen said softly.

"Well, I'm sorry about her father," I said. "But every time I try to help Anita, I end up worse off than before. Right now, I don't care if I ever see her again."

Eileen nodded. "Have you realized by now that she and I are lovers?"

"I may be naive, but I'm not stupid. I saw her picture on your bedroom night stand. I wasn't sure at first, but the night you walked into the Alamo, I knew. Anita told me the story about having a lover in Chicago."

"Working on the same case is difficult. It's like being on duty twenty-four seven. Anyway, Anita and I have been trying to find Freddy Walters. He doesn't appear to have any close family in this area."

"Lotty," I said, "his dead wife, was from Jefferson. Freddy is from somewhere up north. Maybe Chicago. That's probably where he is now."

"The police have checked. His family hasn't heard from him, nor has Lotty's family."

"Well that's very interesting. But even if I could help you, which I can't, I wouldn't lead you to Freddy."

Eileen leaned forward, her elbows on her knees, and stared down at the patio. "You were friends with Walters, right?"

"We worked together—played hearts when we were between trips. I don't think I knew him very well at all."

Eileen stood and stretched, raising her hands toward the darkening sky. And just like I'd been extremely friendly, she said, "If you hear from him, will you let me know?"

I crossed my legs and folded my arms over my chest. "I will not be calling you for any reason."

She knelt beside me then, her face close to mine. "We don't think Walters knows how much trouble he's in. These drug dealers eat their young. And when Freddy Walters has served his purpose, they'll kill him if they haven't already."

I pulled away from her a little and tried to meet her eyes.

The lines in her face softened. "I think Freddy got involved in this to try to find his wife's killer. I think he got swept up in it. He may have murdered a police officer. That's a capital offense. Death penalty. But right now, if he's alive, he may be in a position to lead us right to the top. We could put all those scumbags out of business if we could find Freddy. If he helped us, we could give him leniency."

"Tell me, how did you get next to my sister? Did you and Anita arrange our meeting? Was that whole business at the LESA dinner just a set up?"

Eileen smiled wryly. "Not exactly. I mean, it was an accident, the house across from your sister's. Anita discovered it. She ran a check on you after the business at Jimmy's Bait Shop. Anita wanted us to meet. Evidently, so did your sister."

"I don't believe you."

She shrugged. "I was as surprised as you were that night at the Alamo. Anita and I had a terrible argument about your involvement. I thought, and still think, it's too dangerous. She trusts you. She told me you saved her life more than once. Anita is always willing to take shortcuts. We come from different cultures, you know."

"I know," I said. "If you don't think I should be involved, why are you talking to me now?"

"Freddy asked for you," she reminded me. "That night Andrews was killed."

"The night I was left for dead!"

"Freddy Walters insisted you drive our man out there. We can't get close to him. I think you can. The question is, do you think he's too dangerous? Are you willing to help him?"

I pressed two fingers to the bridge of my nose and shook my head. I said, "I'm through being involved. I've done too many impulsive things for a woman my age who wants to live another thirty or forty years."

Eileen nodded. "Just think about it."

The patio door slid open behind me. I heard my sister's voice. "I've wrapped up some birthday cake for both of you to take home."

Eileen stood, reached for a foil wrapped paper plate and said, "Thank you."

I watched her walk around the side of Barb's house.

"You all right?" My sister was behind me.

"I'm fine," I said. "Just give me a minute."

She left me alone.

I propped my elbow on the arm of the chair and rested my chin in my hand. I was tired and could feel the pizza-robbery depression setting in again. What I had to think about was whether I'd tell Eileen anything if I could find Freddy. Of course, there was the little fact that Freddy, my friend and coworker, had left me in the goddamn trunk of a taxicab. If he was in trouble, why should I care? How long would it take for me to end up with a bullet in the center of my forehead?

Moonlight reflected on the rippling surface of the swimming pool. The rest of the yard had grown dark. Eventually Barb came back out and sat in the lawn chair where Eileen had been earlier. She passed me a can of diet soda.

"Kitchen's done," she said. "John is taking the birthday boy to rent a movie. Want to stay and watch it with us?"

I shook my head no, popped open the can and tipped it back.

Barb didn't argue.

"I let go of that net-scooper thing in the pool and it sank," I said at last.

"The wand?"

"Maybe."

My sister said, "Good. Now I have an excuse to get in the pool tomorrow." She crossed her legs, lighted a cigarette and sat next to me staring out across the back yard.

Chapter Thirty-One

I overslept the next day and woke to the ringing phone.

"I hope you have a broken leg and are lying there waiting for the ambulance."

It was Ralph; Betty had sent in the big guns.

"I don't feel good," I croaked.

"And just who in the hell is going to take this purple cab out on the street?"

"Okay," I said. "I'm getting out of bed right now."

I tossed the phone on the floor, not bothering to hang it up and rolled over to meet Alex's stare. He was beside the bed, his snout resting near my chin. "I'm moving," I said. "Go on, I'm right behind you."

Alex waited until I had feet both planted on the floor. I hobbled into the kitchen behind him, still favoring my gunshot-wounded foot. Though the bones had long since knitted, it still hurt like the dickens first thing in the morning. I opened the front door and hot air rushed in as the dog rushed out. On the kitchen table, a paper plate covered with foil contained a large piece of race-car birthday cake. I poured cold coffee from the pot, stuck the mug in the microwave, and punched the two minute button.

By the time I had let Alex in, washed up, pulled on a pair of shorts and a T-shirt, and run my fingers through my hair, the coffee was about the right temperature. I sat down at the messy table and pulled the foil off the cake plate. The green and chocolate slab was about six inches square, with a thick border of icing. I'd read somewhere that dogs weren't supposed to eat chocolate, so I poured come dry Cheerios in Alex's bowl. We ate in semi-silence, Alex crunching, me slurping and yawning.

I didn't have time to make a new pot of coffee. I wouldn't have tasted it anyway; my taste buds were totally anesthetized by the time I'd finished the cake. I could feel the energy from the sugar and chocolate course through my veins.

Hot wind whipped against my face as the Harley moved toward town. The roots of my hair were damp and my T-shirt was sticking to my sides by the time I'd gone a couple of blocks. Normally I don't ride the motorcycle in shorts, but the air conditioner in the Civic makes the engine stall and I was running too late to change out of jeans when I got to work, so I risked it. With the extra sugar, the waves of heat raising from the pavement and the white sunlight pounding from above, my head was throbbing by the time I pulled into the Red, White and Blue parking lot.

Number Four was parked in front, gassed up and ready. I checked in and drove downtown to the Amtrak station. I was third in the cab lane and sat there with the motor and air conditioner running—thinking.

Everything had gone on as usual after my last brush with death. The Alamo, for instance, opened for business the next day. Rosa and Antonio's partnership continued. Business went on at the governor's mansion with somewhat stepped up security after the shootout at the gates. Besides me, Toni Matulis was the only one doing anything different. She'd taken a leave of absence. There were two females, a sergeant and a rookie, on her beat now. I had checked because I had wanted to talk to her following the trunk incident. Now I really wanted to talk to her. I thought about trying to reach her at home. She'd said she lived in a trailer park. How many people with the name Matulis would be in the phonebook? I knew most of the street names in the larger parks. I could probably find her. But should I?

And then there was Freddy. His cab had been found in an alley behind an abandoned house during the period I was delivering pizzas. It had been stripped of everything but the engine block. Ralph sold it for salvage and came back from an auction up near Peoria with two nice-looking, mid-sized Fords that he got with the salvage money.

I considered the conversation with Eileen the night before. Sure, I was curious about what had happened to my Freddy, maybe even concerned. What could a couple of phone calls hurt? I tried to remember Lotty's maiden name. Had I ever known it? I could feel the pinpoint of a headache stating to throb.

A sound startled me. Someone had tapped on my window. I turned. George stood there. I checked the rearview mirror. My nemesis, the limo, was behind me. I cracked the window, not wanting to let the cool air out.

"What?"

"Pull up!"

The lane in front of me was empty. The porter at the curb was signaling. I dropped Number Four in gear and rolled forward. As the porter helped an elderly couple into the back, George tapped on the window again.

"What?"

"You seen Henderson?"

"I ain't been looking for him," I answered. "Why?"

"Son of a bitch lost thirty-four dollars in poker, then didn't come in last night when he told me he'd pay. He owes me."

"He was off last night," I said, a little annoyed. "How come you need money?" Then I smelled it, and he didn't have to answer. He was drunk.

I waited until I'd let the old couple out at the Ramada and then radioed Betty. "George is three sheets to the wind."

"It's not even noon. Are you sure?"

"Positive."

Over the static I heard the weariness in her voice. "Thanks, Trudy. I'll call him in."

"Ten-four." I was about to set the mike down when something occurred to me. I keyed it again. "You seen Henderson?"

"He's here now putting a new water pump in his cab."

"Ask him to stick around, will you? I need to talk to him."

The bay doors were all open. Johnny sat, shirtless, on the floor in front of a large box fan that even on high did little more than move the hot air around. He watched me approach and smiled.

"You come to help?" He jerked his head toward the cab with the hood raised behind him.

"Sorry," I said. "I'm driving."

He pushed himself up off the floor, picked up a bottle of water and tilted it back. His light brown body was lean, with a hairless chest and fairly good muscle definition. A pair of cutoff jeans hung loosely on his hips.

"I'm gonna get a soda," I said. "Can I bring you anything?"

He handed me the water bottle. "Refill this while you're in there, from the tap please. Can't take cold water in this heat."

I dug in my pocket for change as I made my way to the office. When I pulled the door open, the cold air almost knocked me backward. The room was thick with cigarette smoke. Betty was on the phone. I bought a Coke from the machine and filled Johnny's water bottle in the bathroom. I still couldn't go in there without thinking of Lotty.

Bracing myself, I opened the door to the garage and walked back into the heat. Johnny had a boom box going. His taste in music ran mostly toward necrophilia—the Doors, Jimi Hendrix, Nirvana and a couple of dead rap artists. His head was under the hood and I stood between him and the light to get his attention. He took the water from me; his long thin fingers were grease-stained, some of it permanent, like my dad's.

"I have a question for you."

"What?"

"Remember last fall when we talked after Lotty's funeral?"

Johnny shrugged. "I guess so, why?"

"You said you went to high school with Lotty's sister."

"Right, Anna."

"And dated her, right?"

He smiled, as if remembering. "Sure."

"What was Anna's last name?"

Johnny considered this. "Bart. Barker, something like that."

"So, Lotty's name would have been the same?"

He shook his head. "I don't think so. Some of those girls had a different father."

I sighed, moved a tool box off the bench and sat down. Though I was getting a little air from the noisy fan, sweat ran down my sides and my back.

Johnny picked up a used-to-be-white T-shirt off the fender and wiped his face. "Why do you ask?"

I looked at the moist red Coke can in my hands and said, "I want to find Freddy."

Johnny whistled.

"Something in me feels that if I can find Freddy Walters, everything that's happened will make sense."

Johnny turned his back to me and leaned over the fender again. White Fruit-of-the-Looms peeked over the top of his cut-offs. He worked for a moment, then held out his hand. "Reach me that box-end nine-sixteenths."

I looked down. The tools were laid out on the floor. I picked up the wrench and slapped it into his palm like a surgical nurse. "How about who she married, can you remember that?" I asked.

"Anna? What makes you think she's still with the same guy?"

I shrugged. "It's all I've got."

Johnny stood again; this time the old water pump was in his hand. "She got pregnant in her junior year and married one of the jocks. Pettit, Cochran, Beechler, one of those guys."

"Pettit was a year ahead of you. Went to state. Turned pro."

"Wasn't him, then."

Fatigue washed over me. This was a dead end. I didn't know Beechler. But Tom Cochran was the son of a well-to-do family. If his girlfriend got in trouble, they'd have taken care of it. Betty might have some information on Lotty in the personnel files. Of course, I couldn't ask her about it—in addition to employee confidentiality, there was my very public and disastrous track record.

"You know," Johnny said. "I think the youngest girl runs Cloud Nine out on the south end."

I knew the place. Most of us had taken fares there at one time or another. I asked, "What's her name?"

"Don't remember," said Johnny turning back to his work. "But you'll know her, if she's there."

Back inside Number Four, I could barely breathe. The vinyl seat-covers burned the backs of my thighs. I started the engine and hot air shot out of the vents. I went three blocks before the cab started to cool. Two short trips later, there was a lull. I told Betty I was taking a break and headed south on Sixth Street.

Cloud Nine was a nightclub that had an adult bookstore just inside and to the left. The store sold hardcore pornography, magazines, books, sexual aids, flavored hygiene spray and an assortment of whips and chains. I'd heard there was a back room where for a quarter you could view twenty seconds of a dirty movie. In the nightclub there were live performers who sold couch dances along with an assortment of acts—singers, strippers, and comedians. One night a week was amateur night. The neon-painted building used to be a theater on the edge of a residential neighborhood. The folks in that subdivision had been trying to get rid of Cloud Nine since the three X's went up on the marquee.

I stopped at the Taco Bell on the corner and ordered a couple of burritos and a Diet Coke, then took a seat facing the nightclub across the street. At three in the afternoon there were only a couple of cars in the fenced-in lot. I tried to remember the family that sat in the front row at Lotty's funeral. They'd been big women, mostly blonde. As I watched, a gold Lexus roll into the Cloud Nine lot. I asked myself what was the point. I didn't know the woman's name, or even if she still worked there. And if I found her and if she had information on Freddy Walters, what was I going to do with that? The thirty-five thousand dollar car rolled into a space near the building marked "manager." The car door swung open and a woman got out. She wore powder-blue jeans and a tight gold-lame tank top. Her blonde hair was in a thousand shoulder-length, corkscrew curls. At about five and a half feet tall and three hundred pounds, she was a beautiful woman. From this distance, except for the hair style, it could have been Lotty herself.

I tossed the remnants of my late lunch in the trash, grabbed the drink and walked out into the heat. By the time I stood outside the dark double doors of the Cloud Nine, the waxed paper cup had turned to wet mush. I sat it down under a fake palm tree and pulled a door open. Inside, the lobby was dark and cool. I blinked and let my eyes adjust. Crimson carpet led to a roped-off door that must have been the nightclub. To my left, as I'd heard, was the store. At least the lights were on in there.

Patchouli incense and cold air rushed at me when I opened the door. The place looked innocent enough. Magazines with covers of full-front nude men and women were in individual sealed plastic covers and arranged alphabetically by subject matter from anal to whipping. In the back of the store was a dildo display in what seemed to be a random order. Most of them were too large for any woman's practical use—that is, the women I knew.

A man appeared behind a glass counter filled with videos. "May I help you?"

He was probably in his thirties: blond hair, two-day growth on his face, and a white jacket that screamed early Don Johnson.

"Was there something specific?" he asked. "Or are you just browsing?"

"I want to see the manager."

He raised an eyebrow, looking me over. "Do you have an appointment?" I suppose he was used to screening potential performers.

"No."

As if that settled it, he said, "Well then, is there something I can help you with?"

"I'm a friend of her sister's. I thought she might have a minute to see me."

He shook his head doubtfully. "I'll check, but no promises."

I thanked him, and he left me alone. I continued to look around, and I have to admit there was some interesting stuff on the shelves. But the people who made the flavored panties could have been more imaginative. The flavors were strawberry, chocolate, bubble-gum, and banana. What about blueberry cheesecake, Snickers bar or barbecue chicken? Those outfits need someone in their flavor department who likes to eat.

"It's Trudy Thomas, isn't it?" came a woman's voice from behind me.

As I turned, she grabbed me and gave me a hug. My damp T-shirt disappeared into her soft powdery chest.

I was stunned. "You remember me?"

"From Lotty's funeral."

"But were we introduced?"

"Freddy talked about you after you left. You're a driver, right?"

"Yes."

"Come on back to my office." I followed her through a pair of crimson curtains and down a hallway lined with more of the same. Finally, we came to a rich wood door, and through it was an office bigger than a bank president's. A huge lighted aquarium full of exotic plants and fish lined one wall.

Tinted glass behind her desk looked out into the empty nightclub. Probably from the other side it was a mirror. A gold nameplate on the cherrywood desk read "Charlene Smith."

Charlene didn't sit at the desk, but took me to a group of easy chairs arranged around a glass coffee table and motioned for me to sit. "Can I offer you a drink—beer, wine, soda, water?"

"No, thanks." I sat and the soft chair practically swallowed me up.

Charlene sat across from me, her bulk settling in sensuous layers. "Now, Trudy. To what do I owe the pleasure?"

"Well, Lotty and Freddy were friends of mine. We'd worked together a long time."

Charlene nodded.

"Now Lotty is dead and Freddy has disappeared. I wondered if he'd been in touch with your family?"

"So do the police."

"They've talked to you?" I tried to sound surprised. Charlene's long fingernails were the color of white pearls, and a blue rhinestone sparkled from the tip of each chubby pinky.

"Not me," she said. "My mother. They asked if we'd heard from him, if we knew his family, that sort of thing. There have been other inquiries, also."

"I'm sure this has all been awful."

Charlene looked me over. Her pale blue eyes traveled from my worn-out leather tennis shoes to my damp messed-up hair. It was time to get tough and her voice was flat. "Why do you want to find Freddy?"

"We're friends."

"No, really—"

I swear, I mark this moment as my first hot flash. Although the temperature of the room was probably about sixty-eight degrees, I felt a small explosion inside me and suddenly sweat was pouring out of my hair and running down the side of my face. My arms and legs were covered by a wet film.

"Good Lord," said Charlene. "Are you all right?"

"I don't know," I stammered a little shocked and confused. "This heat."

Then she was beside me, thrusting a cold bottle of water into my hands. "You're not going to faint, are you? Here, put your head between your knees."

She gave my head a push, but my legs were too close together and my seat too low for me to get my head down there.

"I'm fine," I protested. "Just give me a minute." I could feel the sudden heat dissipating.

Charlene returned to her seat, watching me with careful concern.

The room seemed to be getting cooler. I opened the water and sipped. An idea was taking shape in my mind. It involved a lie, but what the hell, everyone I'd met lately had lied to me. I touched my forehead and said, "I'm sorry. I haven't been well."

"Oh, dear." Charlene wrung her hands. "I thought you were going to faint. Do you want to lie down for a few minutes?"

"The treatments take so much out of me. And there's no telling how much time it buys."

Her blue eyes grew wide. "Cancer?"

I nodded, as if the word were too hard to say.

"Are you ?"

I held up a hand. "Please, let's not talk about it."

"Oh, you poor thing."

"Freddy and I were friends," I said. "If I could just talk to him, just know he's safe…"

I felt bad when I saw her eyes glaze with tears. But the feeling was brief. A buzz of excitement sounded in my brain as she got up and went to her desk. A moment later she returned with a blue Post-it note. The address and phone number were written in pencil. "I know he'll want to talk to you. He told us that you were the one who found Lotty that night. He seemed to think a great deal of you. I'm sorry about your, uh, hard luck."

"Oh, thank you so much." I pushed myself up out of the soft chair, no small task.

"Do you need to rest a minute?"

I waved her off, staggering somewhat. "I'm fine. I've taken enough of your time."

I added my morning limp as I crossed to the door.

Chapter Thirty-Two

At home I took a shower and threw a load of laundry into the machine. The air conditioning and the shower made me tired, and my plan was to stay in. Alex was restless, but when I let him outside, he was soon back at the door barking. The temperatures were still in the mid-nineties in the late evening as the sun began a slow descent. I didn't even turn on the stove for supper. Sitting at the table in a pair of boxer shorts and a T-shirt, I poured a glass of milk and made a couple of peanut butter and jelly sandwiches.

The blue Post-it note with Freddy's phone number and address sat next to the telephone. I stared at it while I ate. What could I say to him that would make sense? Or better, what could he say to me? Had Freddy wanted me dead, I would have been. I knew that much. But what the hell was he up to? Had he been the one who'd shot Ryan Andrews? What about the other guy, my old friend Meat Face? His real name had turned out to be Sylvester Nullis. The newspapers had said he was a Chicago man who'd served time in Pontiac for delivery of stolen goods and racketeering. What the hell was Freddy Walters doing with a man like that? The police were after Freddy, but why should I lead them to him? Of course, according to Anita, Freddy had asked for me. He'd made sure I was there. So, on the other hand, why should I protect him?

As I looked at the innocent slip of paper, I remembered lying across the tire thinking I would die in the trunk of the limo. No wonder I'd had the hot flash earlier. My body was telling me to get the hell out of Cloud Nine and forget about anything connected to Lotty and Freddy Walters.

After my cold supper, I started digging through the stack of mail next to the phone. There were two Matulis' in the phone book. The first was Mike, who had a rural route address west of town. The second was A. M. Matulis. I took a shot. A child answered.

"Is your mom there?"

The kid dropped the phone and hollered, "Mommy!"

A short time later a woman's voice said, "Hello?"

"Toni?"

"Yes, who is this?"

"Trudy Thomas."

She hesitated, and then said, "What can I do for you, Trudy?"

"Can you talk?"

"Yes. Wait a minute, I have something on the stove."

I sat down on a kitchen chair and stared at the stack of magazines and newspapers on the counter.

Finally Toni returned. "What's up, Trudy?"

"Anita Alvarez works for the state police."

"Really?"

"The night those men were killed, the night I was locked in the trunk of the cab…"

"Yes?"

"I was supposed to be helping them with a drug sting."

"Oh, Trudy…" Her voice trailed off.

After an awkward silence I said, "I saw their badges. I know some of the others involved. You'd be surprised how high this goes."

"You know, honey," she said softly. "Illinois tends to put ex-governors in jail."

"Does one police department work with another?" I asked.

"What do you mean?"

"Well, if the state police had a program, would city and county police necessarily know about it?"

"Usually," she said. "We wouldn't know every single thing. But the big deals, we'd know about them. At least our drug enforcement division would."

"Didn't you tell me once that you were pulled off the break-in at the mansion even though it was on your beat?"

"Yes," Toni admitted. "So, what's your point?"

"Have you heard of Valkyrie?"

"Sure. It was an offshoot of COBRA."

"COBRA?"

"That was several law enforcement agencies all involved in getting drugs and gangs out of Springfield. They made some high profile arrests back in the '90s. Anyway, Valkyrie was set up to train state police in drug enforcement."

"That's exactly what I was told."

"By whom?"

"The head of Valkyrie is the lover of Anita Alvarez."

There was a long silence. I could hear her breathing. I waited, giving her a chance to let it sink in. Finally she said, "What's his name?"

"Her name is Eileen Sheridan."

"I'll be damned," said Toni.

"Last night Eileen asked me to—"

"You know her too?"

"She lives across the street from my sister," I said. "Anyway, she asked me to help her find Freddy Walters."

"And?"

"Today I found out where he is."

"And you're wondering if this is all legit, if you should give them the information."

"Yeah, kind of."

At length she said, "I am on medical leave. I am more out of the loop than usual. Let me make some phone calls and get back to you. Don't do anything until I call you. Just sit tight."

I thanked her and hung up.

I pulled a ripe banana from a dwindling bunch on top of the refrigerator and went into the living room. I'd intended on watching a network made-for-television movie, but the tension was too much for me—a married couple argued while their baby screamed, a heart patient died on the table because of a resident's error, blood gushed, paramedics wheeled in another victim every couple of minutes, shouting vitals. I flipped the channels. Drew Carey and his office staff were doing some kind of choreographed dance to disco music, Mimi in a go-go cage, Drew doing some amazing moves despite his size. Alex curled up in front of the sofa and we were both asleep before the ten o'clock news.

The heat held the next day. By noon the temperature was over one hundred. Red, White and Blue was busy. No one wanted to walk anywhere. I picked up my lunch at a drive-through and spread it out in the break area. I had a regular at one-fifteen; Greta Hobson worked in the hospital kitchen five in the morning 'til one in the afternoon, and there was no point in sending me out before I picked her up. The table was empty and I shoved the ashtrays as far from my food as possible. Betty was at the dispatcher's desk with a cigarette going, working on a new crossword puzzle book. I heard the phone ring and figured Betty would add another trip to my list.

Betty called out. "Hey, telephone."

I assumed she was talking to Ralph. Drivers aren't allowed to take calls on the dispatcher's phone.

"Trudy."

I looked up. She motioned for me to come over there.

"What?" I asked as I approached her.

"You got a call." She held out the black receiver. "She says it's an emergency."

I took the phone from Betty and said, "This is Trudy."

"It's Charlene Smith."

"Oh, hi," I said, suddenly very nervous.

"Sorry to bother you at work," she said. "But Freddy's in town. I told him about your visit and your problems, and how you wanted to see him."

"Gee, thanks…"

"Actually, he wants to see you, too."

Oh boy.

"He's staying at the Yukon Motel. Room number seven. He wants to know if you can come out there tonight around nine or ten."

Betty gave me a questioning look. I turned away from her and said, "Yes, I think I can."

"You know the place?"

"Peoria Road, right?" I knew the place all right. Anybody who'd ever cheated on anybody did. The cabins were off the main road and each had a carport that hid your vehicle.

"Good. I'll tell him you'll be there," she said. "And, by the way, I'm sorry."

"Sorry?"

"About your illness. The cancer."

"Oh, thanks."

"Is it colon?"

Betty had stood, rounded the desk and was trying to meet my eyes.

I ducked my head a little and said, "Did I tell you that?"

"No. But I know that's one of the worst kinds. Usual treatments don't work on colon cancer."

"You know, I've got to go," I said. "I'm tying up the dispatcher's phone."

"Oh," said Charlene. "Sure. I'm glad you two are going to get to hook up. Let me know if there's anything else I can do."

"Sure, thanks again." I handed Betty the receiver.

"Who was that?" she demanded.

"No one."

"Is it a new girlfriend?"

"No." I walked back to my cold greasy lunch.

Betty followed me. "'Cause if it's a new woman, you got to tell her that she can't reach you on that phone."

"I will."

"Where'd you meet her?"

I looked at Betty. She meant well. I wondered if I was going to have to lie to her, too. Then I felt that burst of heat and my forehead broke out in a sweat. I started fanning myself and dabbing sweat off my forehead with a napkin.

"What's wrong?" Betty asked. "Don't you feel good? You're all red in the face."

"Hot flash, I think."

"Good Lord, you ain't that old."

"I'm forty-fucking-seven! I had one yesterday, too."

The dispatcher's phone started ringing. Betty glanced that direction, then back at me. "Well, you better be nice to this woman. You're getting too old for the chase."

I murmured, "Thanks for the advice," to her back. She'd gone to answer the phone.

That evening I tried to reach Toni Matulis. I left two messages for her to call me, one at six and the second at seven, then waited. At nine I left a message about where I was going and why, then put my shoes on again and went out to start the Harley.

I didn't know what to say to Freddy. I kept thinking that we had been friends for years and whatever had happened he'd have a good explanation. But why would he insist that I drive the cab that night and then warn me to run? Was he really one of the bad guys? Was I riding into another trap?

The sign for the Yukon Motel was weathered and chipped. Neither of the neon O's worked, the M hummed and flickered. I shut off the bike and let it coast past the office building and back between the rows of cabins, where I dismounted. Number seven was on the right, the fourth one down. If this was a trap, I didn't want to be too far from transportation. I could see there wasn't a vehicle in the carport. I poked my head around the corner and was startled by a figure sitting on the steps in the darkness.

Freddy Walters was there smoking a cigarette and smiling.

"Uh, hi," was all I could manage.

Freddy stood, walked toward me, and held out his arms. His embrace was strong and reassuring. He smelled of stale cigarette smoke and after-shave. "Where's the bike?"

"Around the corner," I said, happily returning the hug.

"Come inside, Trudy," he said, "where it's cooler."

"Do you believe this heat?"

He shook his head. "I do not."

Inside was knotty-pine paneled with a brown tile floor and Goodwill-type furniture. The bed was made; a threadbare chenille cover thrown over a thin mattress. A small TV was bolted to the wall. A rickety round table had two unmatched chairs pushed up to it. Freddy indicated the more comfortable looking one for me and sat in the other.

I had a hard time meeting his eyes. Because of the lie I told to get his phone number, I felt as if I were the one who'd caused all the trouble.

Freddy smiled and said, "I didn't know how much I missed you and cab driving until you pulled up on that Harley tonight."

I remembered the night Lotty died—Freddy coming into the office with a gun drawn scaring the hell out of me. Had I misread that? "Everyone misses you," I said. "What the hell is going on?"

Freddy shrugged. "The less you know, the better off you'll be."

That made me mad. "You know, I have been shot in the foot, on crutches for months, thrown in jail and left to die in a car trunk. Not to mention the near-death experience of sinking my ex-lover's new SUV in the fucking Sangamon River! So give me a break, will you?"

His smile sort of froze. After a moment he said, "You want a Coke or something?" His eyes traveled to the bedside where a small cooler, beaded with condensation, sat on a braided area rug.

"Yeah," I said. "I'm thirsty."

Freddy went to the cooler and pulled out two cans of Coke. He sat one in front of me and popped open his own. "So," he said. "I hear you're sick."

"Let's talk about you first."

He'd made up his mind to tell me. I could see that much. He took a swallow from his can and set it on the table. "I got in some financial trouble about a year ago. Gambling debts. Instead of telling Lotty and figuring a way to pay them off, I decided to borrow some money and try to win everything back."

My eyes widened.

He held up his hand. "Not the smartest thing in the world, I admit. I lost that money, too. So somebody told me about how to work my way out from under, and at that point I didn't see any other choice."

"How much money you talking about?"

"Ninety-four thousand."

I let the number sink in, took a swallow of Coke and said, "And this method to earn the money was criminal?"

"Selling cocaine."

"If that had worked, we wouldn't be sitting here, would we?"

"And my wife would be alive. These guys in the drug trade make the loan sharks look like ballerinas and teddy bears."

"What happened?"

"I got robbed," he said. "I was making a delivery over on South Wert and a couple of guys held me up. I should have let them kill me, all things considered. Add to what I already owed another ten thousand in cocaine."

"Jesus." The story was making me sick to my stomach.

He nodded. "That's when I told my wife."

"Lotty knew?"

"Yes, finally," he said, studying the brown-tiled floor. "She sent me to Charlene, thinking that her sister, who worked in the porn trade, might know someone with influence. As it turned out, Charlene did know somebody. But the assholes came after Lotty before I could act." A single tear escaped the corner of his eye. He wiped it away quickly with the back of his hand. "As soon as I saw her body, I knew what had happened. I had been warned."

I stared at him with my mouth hanging open. I couldn't think of a damn thing to say. Lotty was dead because her husband owed the wrong people money. All this time I'd thought it was me and that damn key. "But" I asked, "why did they break into my cab?"

He met my eyes. "They didn't. Why would they?"

"My cab," I insisted. "Remember?"

Finally he nodded. "It had to be a separate thing. What was missing?"

"Nothing."

"Kids," he said.

Or Anita Alvarez, I thought. "These drug dealers," I said. "Are they from out of town?"

His head bobbed up and down slowly. "Out of the country is more like it."

"Tell me what happened the night of the shoot-out."

"I am so sorry about that."

"What was going on, Freddy?"

He crushed his empty soda can and tossed it toward a plastic waste-basket across the room. "Two points," he said, as the can dropped in.

I wanted to reach across the table and shake him, but I made myself wait for him to go on. Finally he said, "These local guys, these dealers I owed money to, had a big shipment from Central America. They wanted me to do the talking, be the front man. Hell, Trudy, I was trying to pay them off a hundred a week. I had to do it."

"Go on," I urged.

"Then they found out one of their own guys was an informant."

"Ramie Malone," I said flatly, remembering the chunks of blood and brains on the carpet, the refrigerator pushed back from the door.

He met my eyes, frowning. "How do you know that?"

"Newspaper," I said. "Go on."

"I figured I was next. I mean, what did they need with me after this sale? So, I made this stupid plan," said Freddy, looking off toward the other side of the room.

"You called me into this?"

"I said it was stupid." Freddy put his elbow on the table and held his head, his small fingers disappearing his black hair. "I planned to take the money myself. I didn't care if they killed me, really. Someone on my side decided that the buyer should come in a cab. He figured that if these guys were cops, they wouldn't do it, wouldn't risk getting someone else involved."

"Well, he underestimated the police, didn't he?"

"We had to ask for a specific driver. Someone that I would recognize, so they wouldn't just put a second cop in a cab."

"And you thought of me."

"The dealers thought of you, Trudy. They knew who you were. I didn't know what to make of that." Freddy sighed and went on. "So we're sitting out there in this van and here comes you in Number Twenty-one with our guy Sylvester and the buyer. I tried to warn you. I was hoping you would get away before the shooting started. But it was like an explosion went off, and all of a sudden all hell broke loose."

"You left me in the damn trunk."

"I'm sorry," he said. "What else could I do? I did come back as soon as I could. I drove by in my own car. The county police and an ambulance were there by then."

I leaned back in the chair, stretched out my legs and folded my arms across my chest. I wanted to get out of there. I wanted to feel the night wind in my hair as I rode along Peoria Road going faster than I ought to.

"So you got twelve million dollars?"

Freddy nodded. "And a shitload of cocaine."

"Then why are you in the Yukon Motel instead of the Cayman Islands, for Christ's sake?"

"I'll be leaving the country soon. Brazil, I think." Freddy smiled. "I have a few loose ends to tie up. I'm glad I got a chance to see you again."

A knock on the door startled us.

"Did you tell anybody you were coming here?" Freddy asked quickly.

I shook my head no.

"Probably Charlene," he said. He stood, crossed the room and hollered through the door. "That you, Charlene?"

A man's voice called. "Police. Open up."

Freddy looked at me and half-smiled. He pointed a finger my direction and shook it. Then he opened the door and raised his hands, becoming a dark silhouette against the red flashing lights.

Chapter Thirty-Three

Since the Yukon was outside the Springfield city limits, the Sangamon County Sheriff's Office had sent two cars, the Illinois State Police made up the other three. I thought I was going to simply get on my Harley after they took Freddy away and ride home, but they took me in, too. I gave a statement to some red-faced County Mounty who was young enough to be my nephew, and then sat in an interrogation room and waited. An older officer came in and out once in a while to clarify something I'd said. I asked him if they were going to keep me. He couldn't give me an answer. At about four in the morning Eileen Sheridan came into the room with two cups of coffee. She sat a cup in front of me and pulled out a chair. Before I could ask any questions, she said, "Thanks for your help."

I looked at her then. There were dark circles under her eyes. Her hair was swept up in back and secured with a plastic clip. Quite a bit had fallen out on the sides and in the back. She wore jeans and a blue T-shirt with lettering that read State Police.

"I didn't help you," I finally said.

"Toni Matulis called me," said Eileen. "You talked to her. She talked to the drug enforcement guys for the city. They gave her my name and phone number. You called her with the information about Freddy Walters, and she called me. So you did help me." She stirred a packet of sugar into her coffee. When I didn't respond, she added, "I was telling you the truth about the Valkyrie sting. I've always told you the truth."

I was tired. I just wanted to get on my bike and go home and go to bed. Right then I didn't care about the truth. And I sure didn't care about her. "I am still angry with you and Anita."

"I imagine you are," she conceded. "Look, there's a diner a few blocks up Ninth Street. How about I buy you a big breakfast and we can talk. Afterward I'll run you home."

"My Harley is still at the Yukon."

"I'll run you out there to get it, then. Come on. I'm starving."

"You mean I can go?"

"Sure you can. They don't need you here anymore."

"What will happen to Freddy?"

"We'll talk about that over breakfast."

Since she was the only one to mention that I could leave, and since without a ride I'd have to call a cab or my mother, I stood and followed Eileen out of the County Building.

The place used to be called the Sunrise. The new owners, Wanda and Floyd, had turned it into twenty-four hour, seven day a week diner. If it couldn't be cooked on a grill, the place didn't serve it. This early in the morning the diner was full of people who had closed the taverns. When we made our way to the only open booth things got quiet. I realized that the drunks could see the word Police in big letters across the back of Eileen's shirt.

The special was pancakes, eggs and bacon. We ordered two from a waitress in a baseball cap and a pair of shorts. She brought a tall, sweating glass of iced tea for Eileen and coffee for me.

"Thanks for coming with me," Eileen started.

The air conditioner in the place was working overtime, and I warmed my fingers around my coffee cup. I studied Eileen and wondered what she wanted now.

I asked, "Is Freddy going to be all right?"

"If we can convince him to give us some names, he'll get off easy. He's not the guy we really want."

"Well, for his sake, I hope you get who you want," I said. "Freddy may have a few flaws—okay, maybe some big flaws—but people do worse than he's done all the time and they walk around free."

Eileen nodded.

"Would he be safe if he talked?" I asked. "Wouldn't the mob or whatever come after him?"

"There are programs…"

"You mean witness protection?"

"Something like that."

That didn't sound good to me. "All Freddy knows is driving a cab."

"And selling drugs," she added. "And murder. I think Freddy will manage."

"Are you going to get the money back?" I asked.

Eileen nodded. "Short about a million-five. That'll help him, too."

The waitress set our breakfast specials in front of us. I picked up my fork, suddenly hungry. We ate in silence for a while.

Finally I asked, "Have you seen Anita?"

"She's in Chicago." Eileen set her fork down and reached for the syrup.

I lowered my voice and leaned toward Eileen. "You said you hadn't lied to me, although there are a lot of things you left out. Anyway, let me ask this is—she really the daughter of the governor?"

"It would appear that way, but…" She hesitated and looked toward an older couple sitting near us.

I was impatient. "But what?"

"He's an asshole."

"Politically? Or, as a father?"

As Eileen considered my question, the melancholy creases around her eyes deepened. Her complexion appeared ashen in the fluorescent light. I guess I was feeling kinder toward her, though I wasn't ready to forget about being shut in the trunk and left for dead. But Freddy had a part in that too.

Eileen picked up her fork and pushed eggs around on her plate. Finally she said, "Anita has a lot of problems. She feels responsible for her sister's death."

"Theresa?"

Eileen nodded. "She was a child when that happened, for Christ's sake. Someone should have been taking care of her. Before that she saw her brother killed. Did she tell you that?"

I shook my head no. "She told me he was killed. She didn't say she'd witnessed it."

"Several men came for the boy. Anita, who had been alone at the house with him, followed them on foot. She had hoped to tell her mother and stepfather where they'd taken him. In short order, Ricardo was lined up with three other men and shot. They threw his body in the back of a truck with the others. Anita wandered around in shock for hours. She turned up at home that evening and the decision was made to hide her and Theresa. Eventually her mother convinced her real father that the girls should come north. Everyone was positive that Ricardo's killing had something to do with him being the son William Wright."

I met Eileen's eyes.

"Yes," she said. "The governor of Illinois. Although he wasn't that then."

"You haven't answered my question," I reminded her.

"He's been a good father financially to all his children. But that's the extent of it. As far as politically, I think he was a good man once. But he had his fingers in a lot of things in El Salvador, and I think he still does. It takes money to run for office. It takes money to have the power he has. He doesn't seem to care anymore where the money comes from. Maybe that happens to a lot of politicians. Anita thinks she will please him by breaking up this cocaine ring. I'm not convinced."

"Why?"

"Well, for one thing, she's never been able to please him. She spent her first year in North America in a mental hospital. She learned to speak English on a children's psych ward. When she was released, he put her in a Catholic boarding school. While her father paid for it all, he didn't give her a minute of his time. She stayed there holidays and everything, led a life right out of a Dickens novel. Finally, her Aunt Rosalyn stepped in."

"But" I protested, "she's close to her father. She comes and goes at the mansion all the time."

"Who told you that?"

The waitress was suddenly beside us refilling my coffee cup. I shoved a bite of pancake in my mouth and had almost forgotten about Eileen's question when she repeated it.

"Who told you that Anita spent a lot of time at the mansion?"

"She did," I lied. I wasn't sure what the problem was. Why shouldn't Anita spend time at the mansion?

"When was this?"

"Well," I said, "the first time I saw Anita, I took her from a bank downtown to the Manor View across from the mansion. As I was leaving, I saw her cross the street. It was pouring down rain, but I'm sure it was her." Toni Matulis had been the one who'd told me that Anita came and went at the mansion fairly often.

Eileen stared at a spot somewhere over my shoulder, thinking.

I changed the subject, asking, "Were Ricardo's killers ever dealt with?"

Eileen shook her head. "Not that I'm aware of. Every once in a while the old man claims he has a lead. I never believe him. Anita does."

I suppose I should have left it alone, but my curiosity got the better of me. "So she's not really close to her father?"

Eileen shrugged. "If he calls her, he probably wants something. When he can use her or her families' connections, he contacts her. She always comes running. She wants his approval desperately."

I felt sorry for Anita then. I thought of the night I took her to the Cardinal Apartments and all she'd gone through last winter at Jimmy's Bait Shop, how she'd been beaten and barely escaped with her life. Anita had told me she was doing her father's bidding. She'd killed two Salvadorans and almost gotten killed herself. Now Eileen, someone who should know, had said that Anita's precious father had been using her.

"Who are the bad guys here?" I asked. "They seem to be this shadowy group of foreigners."

Eileen said, "The drug trade has a lot of levels. From the farmers to the guys who stand on street corners, the drug has passes through hundreds of hands. We have been dealing with folks on a pretty high level. They call the guy in El Salvador Escobar, after the head of the Colombian cartel. That isn't his name. We don't know his real name. Anita's brother Michael sold to this guy, this Salvadoran they call Escobar, at one time. Then her brother tried to go a more direct route for a larger profit, and Escobar's men came after him. The men at the Cardinal Apartments were salesmen for Escobar. We've also dealt with some of the local guys, Freddy's friends. In a way, the local guys are more dangerous. This area may be a big piece of the pie to Escobar, but it's the whole pie to the local drug trade. We do the best we can, as does the DEA and local police departments. Getting Freddy to roll over on these guys will shake things up for a while."

"It's overwhelming."

"Isn't it?" said Eileen.

We finished our breakfast quietly, and then Eileen paid the bill and drove me north to the Yukon. My bike was parked where I'd left it. She stopped the car, got out, came around and shook my hand, repeating her thanks. "If you need anything, if I can help you in any way, please let me know," she added. "I do want us to be friends."

"If it's all the same to you," I said, "I'll just go back to my boring life, the one I had before I met you and Anita."

She smiled and got back in her car. She waited until I had the Harley started before she pulled out of the lot and onto the highway heading back toward town.

Chapter Thirty-Four

On a Saturday night a couple of weeks later a guy hailed me outside the Hilton. I was back to my old routine of twelve hour shifts and nights on weekends. As I pulled to the curb, all I could see was an average sized man, well-dressed, with thick salt and pepper hair. But when the dome light came on and I got a good look at him, I flinched.

This guy was Hispanic, and he looked like someone I'd seen before—in a freezer.

His smile didn't quite win me over, but I could see he was making an effort. I told myself he was probably a business man in town for a conference, or somebody's grandpa.

"Where to?" I asked.

"The Old Luxemburg."

"Are you just going for dinner?" I asked. "That restaurant is pretty far out."

The man smiled indulgently. "A wedding reception. My granddaughter."

I said, "Right," then radioed in and reached to put the flag down. The guy was dressed for a wedding reception, even though he didn't have a present. Maybe he was the type to give an envelope of money. Maybe he'd bought the couple a Caribbean cruise. He looked like he could afford it.

I turned Number Four south on Fifth Street and said over my shoulder, "I guess it's pretty nice out there since the remodeling."

His voice was soft. "Pardon?"

"The new owners remodeled," I said. "Place was closed all winter."

"Oh, yes," the man said. "My son tells me it is very nice."

You know how you feel that something isn't right, but can't figure out what? I had that feeling all the way out of town, a free-floating anxiety. I crossed the lake bridge and passed the last of the streetlights. The guy was quiet. When I checked the rearview mirror, I could see him watching me.

I turned off the main road by the billboard that read "Two Miles to the Old Lux" with a picture of the twelve-ninety-five prime rib special. At first there were a few houses and a gas station. Very shortly the road ran between two soybean fields and the only light came from the half moon.

The old guy's cell phone rang. He fumbled and answered it in Spanish. I half-listened to him as I approached the restaurant. Then I realized what had been nagging at me. The new owners had had a problem getting their three o'clock liquor license. The grand opening had been delayed. The parking lot was lighted but the restaurant was dark.

The guy seemed to be arguing with whoever was on the phone. I pulled into the empty parking lot and stopped. I brushed my clipboard onto the floor and bent to get it, reaching under the driver's seat and grabbing my Glock.

"What are you doing?" the guy asked in English.

"That's fifteen dollars and forty-five cents," I said turning toward him. "This place is closed."

"Mister, pay me and get out of my cab."

He was quiet for a second, then he said, "Maybe I have the place wrong. I will call my son."

"This trip is over. Get out."

"*Por que?* Ah, what, for what?"

I lifted the Glock and pointed it over the back of my seat. "Out."

"Madam," he said. "Please, madam." His hands were shaking a little as he held them up in protest.

I waved the nose of the Glock toward the door.

The old guy got out, mumbling and walked toward the side of the building, punching numbers on his cell phone.

I pulled away wondering if I'd made a mistake—if Betty would be on my ass in the morning for losing the fifteen bucks. I picked up the mike to radio in, then stopped. I could take a couple of minutes to see who he called to come for him. But if someone were looking for me, I was a sitting duck in a lavender Plymouth with a big number four painted on the side. Past the soy beans, I swung into a circular driveway, rolled around until I could see the restaurant, cut my lights and waited. Next to the cab was a large, white, two-story house. I could hear a dog barking, but no one turned on lights or hollered for the dog to be quiet. I was taking a chance that no one was home.

I watched the old man pace in the lighted parking lot. Twenty or thirty minutes later I saw the headlights, then the black Lincoln Town Car passed me and glided into the lot.

The feeling I had when the old guy got in my cab downtown returned—I'd seen that car before. Lots of times. I remembered the night that the car pulled out of the Cardinal Apartments, the night I was shot—

the same car that followed Anita and me as we escaped from Jimmy's Bait Shop?

I didn't want to confront them. I considered abandoning everything and heading back to town. Maybe I'd call Eileen Sheridan when I got to a phone and turn them in. The more I thought about it, the more I was convinced that these were the mobsters who'd been after Anita.

But if the old guy had friends with a nice car, why was he riding in an old Plymouth cab? Freddy had told me they knew who I was. He hadn't wanted me driving as much as the drug dealers had. As a cabdriver, I was literally accessible to anyone. I was glad the guy was out of my cab. I decided to wait until they left and head back to town myself. Maybe I'd work days for a while until things cooled down.

I watched as the old man opened the driver's side door. The driver, a very big guy, got out and using a remote, he popped the trunk.

Two men bent over together and pulled someone out. I picked up the mike and keyed it. "Four."

"Four go," came Minnie Ballinger's quick reply.

"I think there's going to be some trouble."

"What's up? You want me to call the law?"

"I'm on Dell Road, near the Old Lux. Two men just pulled a woman out of the trunk of a black Lincoln Town Car."

"I'm calling the law," said Minnie. "You stay away from the trouble. Stay in your cab."

"Ten four."

"I mean it, Trudy. Stay where you're at. I'm calling it in."

"Right."

As the two men dragged the small woman into a lighted area, I saw Anita Alvarez. They had her hands tied, and the three of them staggered, like they were in a sack race, around to the side of the building into the shadows.

I reached above me and loosened the dome light, grabbed my Glock and shoved it into my pants pocket. I rolled the cab out of the driveway and past the house, stopping walking distance away, but out of the light of the parking lot. I then opened the door and slid out, staying low along the side of the road and behind shrubbery as I neared the front of the building.

The stone-facade building loomed before me like a Medieval fortress in the night. I moved around the side and saw light falling through an opened side door. I heard their voices as I approached. The door must have gone to the kitchen as there were two good-sized dumpsters enclosed behind a fenced area that blocked the sight of the trash from anyone in the parking lot. The fence made good cover, so I slipped behind it and checked the ammunition on the Glock. I was hoping that the police would arrive before I was forced to use the gun, but I'd use it if I had to.

I knelt in the shadows. Though the dumpsters were empty they smelled bad and the sweet rotten scent of garbage assaulted my nostrils. I wished I could understand Spanish. But even if they had been talking about tacos, I wouldn't have known because they were speaking so fast. I couldn't see Anita. From the way she had been tied up, and the fact that they'd brought her out here in the trunk, I figured it wasn't good. But did I have time to wait for help, or did I need to move now? The only way to be sure would be to wait too long and then slap my forehead.

There are a lot of things about being a hero that nobody tells you. For instance, when Clint Eastwood kneels behind a dumpster getting ready to attack, he doesn't mention his arthritic knees. My heart raced as I stood and my knees were stiff as I quietly walked to the open doorway. The men had their backs to me. The big guy was holding a revolver to Anita's head. The old guy spoke to her in low tones. Her eyes grew round and I knew she'd seen me, though she sat perfectly still.

I carefully got into position, my feet apart, both hands out in front of me, holding the Glock. I took a deep breath and shouted, "´¡Hola!"

The old man turned, saw me, and said something. The big guy raised the gun he held and came down with a sickening thud on Anita's forehead. She made a soft "oof," and her head rocked back at an odd angle. The big guy then spun around and was taking aim when I fired. The first shot missed him entirely, the second brought him to his knees, and the third hit his thick trunk. He went over backward like a falling redwood tree.

The old man ran at me, and though I was planted pretty solid, he managed to knock me backward against a counter and run out. He moved pretty fast for an old guy. I got my balance and chased him, but by the time I was at the corner of the parking lot, he was putting the Lincoln in reverse. I took aim, then noticed the flashing lights coming toward the restaurant on Dell Road. The Lincoln screeched backward spitting gravel and headed out, away from the police cars.

I was leaning against the cool stone building when I heard a thunderous crash. Moments later flames were leaping into the air. That's when I realized that the Lincoln Town Car had crashed into my cab. Number Four was on fire.

A mixture of sweat and blood, though I couldn't say whose, ran down the sides of my face as I headed back toward the kitchen. Taking several shots with the Glock was messy business. My hands felt gritty from gunpowder, my nostrils stung with the scent of sulfur, like I'd been at a fireworks display.

Anita was still slumped in the chair. Her breathing seemed shallow. I said her name several times, and she didn't respond. I dropped to my knees beside her and tried to loosen the ropes that bound her hands and feet. The knees of my jeans felt sticky and damp. I looked down to see myself in a pool of the big man's blood that was expanding from his thick body toward us. The room started to spin.

Outside I heard footsteps pounding in the gravel, then a dark shadow filled up the open doorway. "Police. Drop your weapon!"

My lips trembled and the lump in my throat nearly choked me. Then I recognized the brown uniform of the county deputy standing next to me.

"Drop your weapon, Miss," he said, almost kindly.

I looked down at the Glock still clutched in my hand, then laid it on the blood-splattered tile floor.

I spent the night at the hospital. My only injury was to the shoulder that I'd hurt when the old guy knocked me against the counter as he escaped. I hadn't even known I was hurt until Anita was loaded into the ambulance. Then the pain hit me. A county deputy had been standing with me, taking a statement. He'd asked a question and I hadn't answered. He looked directly at me and said, "Are you sure you're all right?" And I said, "My shoulder hurts."

"You look pale. Why don't you sit down in my car?"

I did and he drove me to the hospital. We got there shortly after the ambulance. X-rays revealed that nothing was broken. Another detective, city this time, interviewed me. He asked me to tell the story over and over. Why did I follow the Lincoln? How did I know Anita Alvarez? Why did I feel I needed to use the gun? In the end he told me to come into the station as soon as I was well enough to answer more questions. I didn't like the sound of that and wondered if I needed a lawyer.

I was glad when about four in the morning Anita's Aunt Rosalyn came to the hospital and talked to me. The police had found her phone number on Anita and she'd flown in from Chicago. She took me aside and told me that if I needed her help with the police, she'd be available. She thought I'd be arrested at some point, but said that self-defense was a legitimate defense and I needn't worry. I think the hospital staff was more concerned that I didn't have adaquate health insurance than with the fact that I'd killed a man. Too frustrated for words, Rosalyn Richards finally dug into her purse, pulled out her wallet, and slapped a Platinum Visa card down so hard that everyone was startled, including me.

Before she left me, I caught her hand and gave it a squeeze. "Let me know about Anita," I said, "as soon as you know anything."

"I'll do that, Trudy."

"Who are those guys anyway?" I asked. "What the hell is going on?"

She sat down across from me on an uncomfortable looking stool. Her eyes were puffy from lack of sleep, her white, cottony hair was tousled. "You've earned an explanation," she said with a measure of gravity. "I don't know who the man you shot is, but the older man is Eduardo Pantone. He is from Chicago by way of Central America, a big man in the drug trade. I think he had an idea to kidnap my niece and recover some of the money he lost recently."

"So," I said. "He's local, but works for the guys down south ?"

Her eyes widened a little, but she didn't answer.

"He thought the governor would pay to get Anita back from him?"

Rosalyn looked at me dubiously and shook her head. "My brother wouldn't pay to get his only living daughter away from those criminals, and they knew it."

I remembered the conversation I'd had not so long ago with Eileen Sheridan. I sighed and said, "Anita is lucky to have you. Did they think you would pay them?"

She said, "They would have contacted her younger brother, who grows cocaine in the hills of El Salvador. He is her richest family member. But even if he paid, they would have killed her. You saved her life last night. She and I owe you a great debt."

I suppose I was still in shock because I couldn't think of a thing to say. I was glad Rosalyn was there, though, and managed to tell her that much.

She said, "Thank you for helping Anita. I know she will thank you herself when she is better."

"How is she?"

"I don't know. They took her to X-ray and I came to find you. I need to get back."

We talked for a few more minutes and she left me.

All I knew at that point was that the big man was dead. One officer had asked to see my FOID card, but no one had given me trouble about the shooting. It certainly helped that the old guy who crashed into Number Four was a drug king who was in custody on a charge that looked like it might stick. I heard later he had a broken leg, a concussion and second degree burns on his hands. He would be well enough for jail shortly. That was a good outcome for everyone.

My own mother pushed her way past security and the police at five. She embraced me and I could smell stale cigarette smoke and Chanel Number 5. My arms went around her automatically. "What am I going to do with you?" she said into my messed up hair. "When are you going to learn?"

I reached for a box of tissues and we both took a couple.

"I'm all right," I assured her.

Her voice shook. "You've got to stop driving that cab."

"I love driving, Mom. I'm all right. Just a couple of bruises."

"You're just like your father. So, so stubborn."

A nurse in purple scrubs and a white sweater opened the door, saw us embrace, let the door close, and left us undisturbed. I was pretty sure they were nearly done with me, and I was about to be released. For once my mother's timing couldn't have been better. I really wanted her with me. I wanted her to drive me home.

"I just can't keep getting these phone calls in the middle of the night," Mom said, stepping back and looking me over. "You don't know what it does to me."

"You want me to put Barb's name down as next of kin?"

My mother considered this and then said, "No, she's got five kids of her own." Then we both kind of chuckled.

"I'm sorry," I said. "I know it's hard." And then I realized that at least she came when she got a call, at least I didn't have to rely on my aunt or something.

The sun was coming up when Mom pulled her car next to my trailer. "Look," she said, "the leaves are starting to turn already. You'll have to be raking soon."

"I leave that to Pinky. He likes to burn 'em."

"Still in the grill?" She smiled.

I nodded.

"You want me to get that prescription filled for you?"

"I'm not in pain anymore," I said. "Just shaken up."

"It might hurt later."

"It probably will. But I'll be all right."

She touched my arm. "You don't look all right. Want me to tuck you in?"

I let my breath out slowly. I remembered her bringing me home on crutches and me just wanting her gone. I remembered trying to reach her from the county jail. I thought about the times she'd tried to help me, and all the times I'd pushed her away. My eyes were burning and I almost choked on, "Would you?"

I slept most of Sunday and skipped work on Monday. Sometime in the afternoon I called Les Jones and asked her how long it would take to put a lavender paint job on one of Ralph's new mid-sized Fords. She didn't sound surprised to hear from me.

"The Plymouth give out again?" she asked.

"Naw. It got wrecked."

"Sorry. But I'm sure we can paint the Ford to your liking."

"Can we talk about the price?"

"For you, eight hundred, trim, numbering and all. I have a beautiful metallic shade that I think you'll like."

"The thing is, I have to pay for it, and I don't exactly have eight hundred dollars."

Her voice sounded cheerful. "How much do you have?"

"About forty-five or fifty." I rushed on, "I wondered if I could make monthly payments, or weekly payments if you prefer?"

"You know," she said, "I've been needing some help around here. Do you think you could give me a hand in your spare time and work off the debt? I'll pay you to work and you pay me fifty dollars a week cash. You'll have it paid off in no time."

I quickly agreed and phoned Ralph. He didn't want one of the new Fords painted lavender, but Betty took my side. So he insisted I pay for it. Believe it or not, the driver of the Lincoln Town Car had good insurance, and though my Plymouth was totaled, they'd arranged a settlement already. Ralph really came out ahead.

Les and I actually had a lot in common. I could imagine her on the back of my Harley. I could imagine shooting pool with her at the Crone's Nest and belly rubbing to a slow dance. We were the same kind of lesbian, she and I. Maybe my old boyfriend, Harold Tangler, had had an agenda when he sent me to her. I could imagine us all at the stock car track, Harold with his wife and redheaded granddaughters and me and Les in matching red coveralls and buzz-cuts.

Of course, I would wait to make my move until I had paid her in full. Owing a woman money put a romance out of balance.

Later that afternoon I got a call from Rosalyn. She told me Anita was awake and doing better. The doctors wanted to keep her for a few days and watch her. I was relieved and anxious. I suddenly wanted to get out and go somewhere. I almost felt as though something were calling me. I got on my

Harley, and rode across town to the little house on Pickett Street—the house my father willed to me, the house I lost.

The neighborhood was quiet, with children in school and most parents at work. The old man down the street, the one who led the campaign to get rid of Georgia and me, had died two years ago. The new owners of my father's house had torn down the old garage and put up a new one. The leaves on the full-grown Chinese elm tree in the front yard were starting to turn gold. I had played with green plastic army men and held wars in the dust around the roots of that tree. The neighbor kids and I, including the daughter of the asshole down the street, had stolen ice from the milk truck in the summertime and crunched on it there in the shade while rivers of cold water made streaks in the dirt on our arms. This had been a good neighborhood. It probably still was as long as you followed the rules, as long as you didn't do anything that was too different.

I stood there for a long time staring at the old house, feeling grateful for my family, for my father who came to my rescue all those years ago, for my mother, whose kiss from when she tucked me into my own bed I could still feel on my cheek, for my sister who managed to love me and even tried to fix me up, despite our differences. I never counted myself rich. I mean, I stay ahead of the bill collectors most of the time by an inch or two. But when I thought about Anita risking her life for her father's approval, seeing her sister and brother die and feeling responsible, well, her family may have had lots of money, but of the two of us, I was the rich one.

Anita Alvarez taught me that.

Also by Martha Miller

Nine Nights on the Windy Tree, A Bertha Brannon Mystery

Bertha Brannon is a struggling black lawyer looking after her grand-mother. Life takes an odd twist when a woman seeks legal counsel for a murder not yet committed. Then the intended victim shows up dead in Bertha's office. She's even more confused when the young cop on the beat seems to be smitten by her. Is she ready for romance with this single, white mom? But first Bertha has to figure out what danger threatens her grandmother. Who is the real Sally Morescki? And what family secrets are converging to give Bertha a serious headache?

$10.95   ISBN 1-892281-11-2

"Martha Miller graces us with a splendid cast of characters—people so real you feel you know them or want to know them or are glad you don't know them. The relationship between the protagonist, Bertha Brannon, and her grand-mother is worth the price alone!"   —Joan Drury

"Bertha Brannon…is very real, interesting and complex. Her first adven-ture…set amidst a myriad of increasingly amazing, yet believable plot twists and turns."   —Therese Szymanski

Skin to Skin: Erotic Lesbian Love Stories

Frank stories about the doubts and delights of sexual intimacy between women.Warm, generous, sexy stories about women you will recognize.

$12.95   ISBN 0-934678-86-3

"Martha Miller is one of my favorite erotic writers."   —Susie Bright

"If you've given up hope of finding imperfect, realistic characters with sexual exploits you can relate to, try reading Skin to Skin.   —On Our Backs

Order from New Victoria Publishers, PO Box 27, Norwich, VT 05055
Or from our website at: www.Newvictoria.com
Email: newvic@aol.com